A TIME TRAVEL THRILLER

BOOK 2 OF THE RECKONING

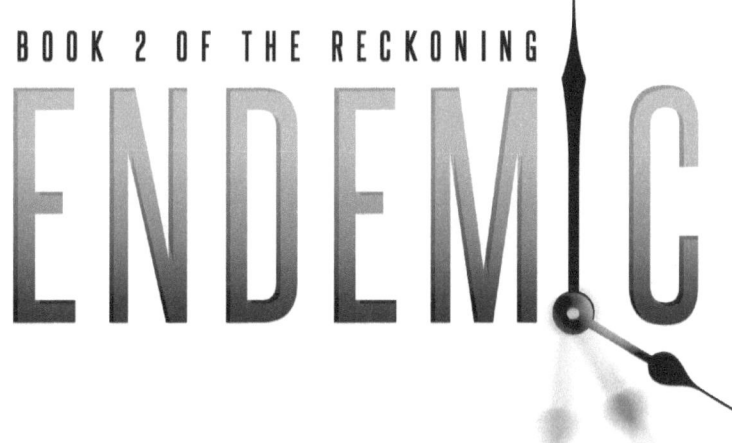

ENDEMIC

D.M. TAYLOR

ISBN: 978-1-7345442-2-0 (EBOOK)
ISBN: 978-1-7345442-3-7 (PAPERBACK)

Cover Design by 100Covers.com
Interior Design by FormattedBooks.com

Quantum
Entanglement
Publishing

For those who choose love

CHAPTER 1

Danika Farkas, director of The Patriot Party—the secret government organization I worked for as lead scientist of time travel technology—as always, was an incredible presence in any room. Hers was an effortlessly harnessed strength which oozed from her voice, took hold in her posture, and was demanded with her eyes. Intrinsically motivated to be like Danika Farkas, I rose to her every challenge.

As usual, she was accompanied by her entourage—Joseph Warren and Bernard Richardson. Upon their presence a formal tone spread through the offices of my sterile laboratory, indicating the seriousness of our expected meeting.

What I further liked about Ms. Farkas was that she did not mince words and was exact with her intentions. There was no notion of deceit or a hidden agenda. With her in the lead, I had chosen the right side in this fight for equality and reconciliation of our democracy.

She and her male counterparts had already settled in their seats within the glass-walled conference room, waiting for us at the industrial oval table.

I stopped crunching the numbers I'd been recalculating from our DNA sequencing. "Abel," I whispered to get his attention.

Abel Mihal was the kind of person who focused all of his energy on the task at hand. His ability to tune out extraneous surroundings was a phenomenal skill, except when I was attempting to distract him.

He didn't hear me. I tried again a little louder. "Abel, they're here." I tapped him on the shoulder to get his full attention and nodded my head toward the conference room.

"Dammit. I wanted to get in there first this time." He looked at his watch, visibly annoyed. "They're thirty minutes early."

We scurried from our work stations and stopped by Dakotah's office to alert her. My best friend, Dakotah Hughs, also liked to be the early bird and was walking toward the door—already on her way to get situated before Abel and I showed up.

"The meeting already started."

"Are you serious? They drive me nuts." Clenching her jaw, she glanced at the oversized clock hanging above her. "You'd think being a half-hour early would be plenty of time to set up before they arrived."

"It's a dominance thing," Abel said as we followed The Patriots' hasty entrance as quickly as we could.

"It has to be. No matter how often we meet with them, or how organized we are in preparation, it always feels like we are unprepared." Nodding my head, I agreed with Dakotah. Scattered was a feeling that didn't bode well with me. I stepped into the glass room breathlessly, greeting them upon my entrance.

The start of our meeting reminded me of the morning over a year ago, when The Patriots had shocked me with news of The Reckoning. I didn't want to believe them all those months ago when they told me our country was under terrorist attack.

"Los Angeles and New York have been taken and no one knows. They jammed all of our communication systems," Ms. Farkas had said.

I reeled from her news, fear-stricken that my sister, Ruth who lived in L.A., was in danger. While I was still grappling to understand what she'd relayed, Ms. Farkas continued to explain why she had shared classified information with *me*, one of her scientists.

"We need your time travel to stop The Reckoning before it ever starts."

So many innocent people were murdered in cold blood for the sake of The Reckoning. It was truly a horrifying attack. One which was thankfully undone through time travel, but not so thankfully still remembered by those of us who'd time traveled to undo it.

The new timeline developed as a result of our first time travel mission. We returned from the past, expecting a hero's welcome. But no one knew what we had done, what we had sacrificed.

I realized this quite quickly after we returned to the present.

"Abel," I said, grabbing his arm. "I don't think they remember we left."

"No way. You were dead." He pointed to a corner in the back of the lab. "They placed your body on that table. Ruth, tell her."

"She was dead?" My sister balked.

Abel's countenance revealed his obvious skepticism. I think for the briefest moment he actually considered we were joking. Even if The Reckoning had not been wiped from everyone's memory, New York and Los Angeles experienced the terrorist attacks first-hand.

"You don't remember your sister was dead?"

Ruth frowned, steadily dragging her eyes to me, hoping I would not confirm Abel's lunacy.

"No. He's making this up, right?" Her question almost felt like a plea.

I thought it best to set my death aside and inquire about other Reckoning-related events.

"You were in New York. Do you remember that? You told me you were holed up in a motel for weeks, hiding with the kid who worked there."

"Yeah. Trey. Of course I remember, that just happened. You guys, what is going on?" Ruth spiraled into a panic.

Until then Dakotah remained silent, analytically observing the conversation.

"I think I understand what's happening here." Each of us fell silent. "Besides Abel's soldiers only the two of you were on the last time travel, correct?" Abel and I nodded in confirmation. She turned to Ruth. "But you were on the time travel mission before that, weren't you?"

"I was," Ruth said, folding her arms.

"So you remember this supposed 'Reckoning', and you were part of the time travel that ended it, but you don't remember that Taden was, evidently, dead, *and*…you weren't a part of *that* time travel." Her eyes bulged. "Do you see the connection?"

"Oh!" I exclaimed. "I see where you're going with this."

"I don't know anything about The Reckoning, and I don't remember Taden dying…but I didn't time travel at all. It seems like the only people here who experienced these hard-to-believe episodes from yesterday are *you* guys." She pointed to me, Abel, and Ruth. "You're the only ones who time traveled."

We all stared at each other, unmoving. There was a mix of emotions swirling among us. Ms. Farkas and her comrades were excitedly bewildered. The Patriots had been desperately waiting for a breakthrough with time travel in order to fix our democracy. Abel's soldiers stood at attention, revealing nothing. Dakotah seemed deep in thought, her wheels spinning about how to access all the different memories held in the same room. Ruth was clearly distraught, unable to move past the concept that I had died. Abel and I remembered everything. How would we relay the trauma that had been done to our country? To me?

 So much had happened among the people gathered within this conference room in the year since the events of The Reckoning, but meeting with The Patriots was still as intimidating as ever.

"Good morning," Ms. Farkas greeted as we took our seats. "Nice to see you." Her professionalism allowed no room for warmth. She rested her gaze upon me. "Dr. Barrett, tell us what you've got for us today."

"We have a lot to update on the advancements we've made since the start of the week," I said, looking over to Dakotah with an extended arm to indicate the spotlight was hers.

Dakotah smiled pleasantly and then blinked three times to warn me I'd get an earful from her later for putting her on the spot.

"Thank you, Dr. Barrett." She pushed back her chair and walked over to the glass wall near the front of the room. Swiping her hand in the air toward the direction of the glass, she powered on the presentation viewing. The lights in the room automatically dimmed as we waited for her to log into her files. I took the moment of reprieve to settle my nerves and clear my mind before it was my turn again.

"This DNA sequence belongs to one of our time travel agents," she said, swiping in the direction of the glass again, cueing the next image. "This one is its genetic match. As you can see in the view on my next slide, we've successfully attached the donor match to the tail of our agent's strand of DNA." She pointed her handheld laser onto the image. Dakotah led the Patriots to follow along as she finished her presentation with reference to our sequencing data. I practiced steadying my breath until she said my name. "Dr. Barrett?"

"As Dr. Hughs inferred, by extracting the DNA from a genetic match we can create a serum specific to each time traveler that will, in essence, trick the timeline to extend beyond their birthdate and into the past." I was consciously making an effort to engage each person with eye contact as I spoke. "What has been most interesting in our study is the inability to create this same phenomena with an extra injection of the subject's own DNA. The timeline cannot recognize it as an extension. Instead of attaching at the ends to lengthen age, the subject's own DNA replicates into the preexisting DNA with no extension to the timeline. Dr. Hughs, can you share the microscopic views of each?"

While Dakotah reviewed the magnified DNA slides my eyes fell on Abel's, and he instinctively smiled at me. In return, without my permission, a genuine smile took its place on my own face. My breathing finally steadied and my nerves started to settle. He nodded his head in approval, letting me know I was doing a great job. I didn't even know why I was nervous to begin with. Surrounding me were people who believed in me and had gone through extraordinary measures to save my life. If it wasn't for these people I would still be trapped in the past, dead. This included Danika Farkas. She believed in me, too. In seconds I calmed, and I could feel the internal powerhouse of my mind come to life for the remainder of our presentation.

"Do you have any questions?" I looked to Ms. Farkas for inquiries.

"Just one, Dr. Barrett, and I'm sure you won't be surprised by it."

I nodded, knowing exactly what she was going to ask. It was really the only information Ms. Farkas ever wanted.

We both spoke in unison: "When will it be ready?"

The two of us were momentarily amused with ourselves. It was short lived, though, as all eyes soon settled upon me.

"The only stumbling block we have is finding old enough DNA matches for each member of our time travel team. Requesting the DNA without a disclosed reason has proved difficult. Once I have access for each traveler the alterations can be made to mix our compounds, and we can begin testing time jumps beyond their lifetime."

Mr. Warren, seated to the left of Ms. Farkas, spoke up in response to my request. "We have unlimited access to the family genealogy of every team member. My department will handle the DNA extraction and be sure you have access to whatever you need."

I didn't expect the ease with which The Patriots could access this genetic material, and tried to hide the surprise on my face.

"I would say that if we have the DNA matches in our possession, we can be ready to launch within the month."

Ms. Farkas looked pleased with my tentative timeline. "Have you found your new team member yet? I assume this projected deadline includes a fourth person's workload." She raised her brow with judgement. "The lack of a fourth member has already taken a toll on the rest of you." Dakotah and Abel winced. Ms. Farkas was referring to Marius' absence. While we had benefitted from a sense of peace and wellbeing without him, she was right. Being down a person (even such a terrible person) had increased our workload.

With each new day Marius' betrayal, terror, and murder moved further into my past. It had already been over a year since Marius was the man I loved more deeply than I loved myself. He was an important member of the team, of course—his intelligence, in some aspects, was unparalleled—but an even more important person in my life.

Before I was confronted with his double life, I hadn't even noticed how much of myself had eroded away through the process of loving him. I had never loved so passionately. I had never hated so passionately, either. With Marius, and my heart, it seemed to be all or nothing—and as a result I had to live with the memory of pushing a blade into his chest. It was self-defense, yes, but I had killed him, and I had to live with that.

That is, I had to live with it *unless* Abel went on a time travel mission and somehow wiped away my memory of killing him. He would. If I asked him to, Abel would travel back and take my role. He'd kill Marius. It was tempting, but of course I would never ask him to do such a thing. Everything I have done since then has been a result of that night. I didn't want to change the past anymore or undo what I had learned.

"Dr. Barrett, I'm advising you fill the open position on your team by the start of the week."

Accepting her orders, I nodded. "We've already combed through the candidates you suggested and have narrowed it down to two people who I am scheduled to interview on Monday."

"You were right about the Navy Seal," Abel said to Mr. Richardson. "I'm looking forward to interviewing him."

"Perfect," Danika said with a quick smile. "As always, I'm pleased with the progress this team is making." She glanced at the man to her right. "Mr. Warren will contact you about scheduling a meeting next week to update us on memory tracking." He tilted his head to confirm her statement. "I look forward to meeting your new team member by then." She turned to her other side. "Mr. Richardson will get you the genetic samples." Without looking up, he tapped the screen of his phone and nodded his head in agreement. She lowered her chin in my direction. "Let us know if you need anything further, Dr. Barrett."

With the same hasty energy as they had entered, Danika and her entourage rose from their seats.

I groaned internally. I didn't want to fill the open position. I didn't want to fill the void Marius left behind. I had settled on leaving that space empty, as a reminder to never again lose myself in another person. But what Danika wanted, Danika got.

I politely walked The Patriots to the door and then joined Abel and Dakotah at the table. Resting my chin on my fist as I sat down, all three of us exhaled a sigh of relief.

"How do you think it went?"

"It was great, except when you passed the microphone to me with no warning," Dakotah said with playful narrowed eyes.

I smiled at her sheepishly. She looked pleased that I felt some distress for throwing her in front of the wolves first.

"Seriously though, we nailed it," she added, then paused. "Do you really think a month is enough time? It feels a bit rushed."

"I do. But what do you think, Abel? Will a month be enough time for you to get *your* team ready, if we're ready with the memory tracking?"

"No problem. We'd be ready to go tomorrow."

Eyebrows raised, I looked back to Dakotah. "Of course you would be." We both smiled. Abel was always prepared. "Dakotah and I *will* catch up to you."

"You can try, ladies."

7

"So, how do you think Mr. Richardson is going to access the DNA we need?" The question had been nagging me.

Abel shrugged. "Not sure, but I don't doubt for a minute they *do* have access."

Unsurprisingly, the resident biologist, Dakotah, had an opinion. "If you want to know my theory—" She didn't wait for approval. Flipping her hand in the air, she launched into her speculation. "—all those genetic testing companies, you know, the ones that collect DNA samples to link you up with unknown relatives or ancestors?" She lowered her chin, slanting her right eyebrow upward. "Lots of people say those companies are controlled by the government to keep records on everyone."

"You think we're getting our DNA from genealogy businesses?"

She assertively shook her head, "If there is enough DNA collected in any given family, the DNA of those who have not participated in the process can still have assumptions made about theirs."

"That's kind of creepy," I said.

"I'm positive the conspiracy theorists win this one. Clearly, the government must have access to everyone's DNA. How else would they have gotten it on such a wide scale? She put her hands up and shrugged her shoulders. "We probably have the same access the government does."

"So you're saying we can find the DNA match to any person ever, through the databases of these genealogy companies?" I still didn't buy it.

"Yep." She paused and pressed her finger to her top lip. After a moment, she opened her palm. "I'm just not sure how they will go about getting the extractions we need once they find a match."

"With the way our economy is struggling as a result of our *wonderful* president, I'm sure money will get most people to hand over some DNA," I said, feeling queasy about the alternative means of acquiring the genetic material.

"Money does talk," Dakotah agreed. "Especially when everyone is really struggling. Today, on the way to work, I drove by no fewer than a dozen people begging for food or money. Berthold's militia was pushing them around to get off the streets. I saw one guy woken from his sleep as they kicked him in the ribs."

"It's a shame to say this, but I bet a lot of the DNA will be easily obtained without any offer of payment. Just brute force."

Abel wasn't wrong. We lived in a country that no longer valued the rights of its people. But to fix that, we needed the genetic material. I had no intention of our time travel discoveries stopping. I would not stop until I was able to figure out how to travel forward in time—once we fixed the presidential debacle.

"Have I said how much I hate that man?" Dakotah asked in reference to our dictator of a president.

"You know we all do. As soon as we take care of Berthold in the deep past, we can stop going back altogether."

If we could visit the outcomes of our choices in the future, then we could work on altering them in the present rather than rewriting our past and erasing our memories.

And to do any of that, we needed DNA.

CHAPTER 2

Since I wasn't time traveling anymore, I was only lucky enough to work with Abel when we were cross planning a mission or practicing self-defense. Abel was mostly consumed with training the soldiers he led into time travel missions and his post-time travel memory uploads. He wasn't keen on my new inactive time travel role, made official at a previous meeting with Ms. Farkas and The Patriots.

"Dr. Barrett will no longer be active as a time traveler," Ms. Farkas stated as she rose from her chair. She placed her hands on the oval table and gave me a polite smile before returning to her command posture to finish relaying the news. "Her focus will instead be centered on integral work here in the lab. Priority number one being the study of how much farther back we can send our units, closely followed by perfecting a stable database of original memories."

Ms. Farkas' "order" was mostly for show. The whole meeting was simply a formality. I had already made this decision on my own, but as the head of The Patriots she liked to be the one who delivered the orders. She walked from the head of the table, passing Mr. Richardson before standing next to me. I became conscious of my body language, and responded quickly to align with her directive. I sat taller in my chair and returned her smile, leading the rest of my team—sitting beside me at the table—to follow suit. However, there in the pragmatism of the conference room, the smallest part of me felt a grieving process begin for my obsession with the past.

She rested her hand on the back of my chair. "It is imperative we make our next military move to rectify our democratic process as soon as possible. Dr. Barrett, we are waiting on you."

Abel eyed me while Ms. Farkas formalized the new assignments within our team. I had already had this conversation with him over a dozen times, ensuring him it was the right move.

"I just want to say I agree with Ms. Farkas' decision." I looked to Abel first. He still seemed to be struggling with the concept. "Obviously, I am a supporter of time travel." I smirked at the irony. "The problem I see with going back in time to prevent something awful from happening in our world is that no one remembers the negative event. It never happened for them."

"That's why I think you should continue time traveling, though," Abel suggested. "Dr. Barrett, shouldn't you know all of the memories we change?"

"I suppose it can seem confusing, why I believe this is a problem, but the fact of the matter is that history as a study of human civilization is important. We study history so we don't find ourselves repeating the same terrible mistakes. Each mission we take back into time to correct our mistakes—like the selection of the first President Berthold—means humanity will unlearn the error we made as a nation in selecting him in the first place. We become void of memory about what it is like as a country to have basic civil rights slowly stripped away."

"I feel like you are saying the same thing as I am," Abel pressed on. "And I don't see how you being inactive in time travel addresses the issue."

A nervous laugh escaped my lips. Clearly, Abel was not thrilled about the proverbial fork in the road this might mean for the two of us. Danika smiled tightly. She'd already told me how her patience for Abel's struggle to accept my adjusted job description was wearing thin.

"While I appreciate your respect for Dr. Barrett as a leader, Dr. Mihal, it is time for you to assume this role. She has other just as important—if not *more* important—accomplishments to make in order for us to successfully serve our mission."

Ms. Farkas took her time returning to her chair at the head of the table. Standing before us, staring Abel harshly in the eye, she continued, "We are living in the era of our demise. President Berthold is more poisonous than his father ever was. We need now, more than ever, to be one hundred percent focused. Dr. Barrett's attention is right to be focused on something other than you, Dr. Mihal."

My face reddened. I hated that our personal feelings were even a part of this discussion.

"My energy needs to be spent on our future," I said. "I can't do that if I'm constantly changing the past. In fact, the more we change the past the less prepared we are for the future. The less we know."

Mr. Richardson, Ms. Farkas' military commander who usually stayed quiet at these meetings, chimed in, startling us. "We set ourselves up, doomed to keep repeating the same damn history we already lived through, fixed, and repeated."

Abel averted his eyes to the floor, like a scolded schoolboy, at this reminder that his long-standing interest in me shouldn't be more important than his mission to make our world a better place to live. My stomach still flipped whenever Abel said my name, but I agreed with The Patriots. He needed to get his head on straight and stop putting me as his focus. We had important work to do. Abel conceded.

Abel was my sanctuary of reprieve. He kissed me for the first time the very night I killed Marius. Marius was dead at my feet, and I couldn't get a hold on reality until I looked into Abel's eyes and he convinced me I was safe. He pulled me out of my fog with his steady presence. The kiss he then placed on my lips was unexpected, as was each time I felt a deep connection to him. When his mouth pressed against mine, I didn't feel a power shift occur or a passion consume my brain as I had with Marius. What I felt instead was love. It was pure, safe, gentle, and reminded me that *I* was the force of love within.

Since that night, there hadn't been another kiss or moment alone with Abel outside of work. After the unfavorable outcome of my relationship with Marius, The Patriots advised against work relationships. The only non-work time I spent with him in the last year was during my self-defense sessions.

"I don't really see the necessity in continuing with these sessions," I told him during a recent training. "It's not like I'm going on missions with you anymore."

"You've been too busy working on perfecting the execution. Once you've got it fine-tuned, of course you'll be back in the missions and out there with us. Besides, you have to be ready to defend yourself regardless, even today. There's plenty of danger here in the present."

"You have a point there." Doing the work we were, it only took one leak of information and all hell could be released. I winked and added, "Plus, I like beating you each time."

He laughed, just as aware as I was that he let me win every sparring match we had.

The unspoken, actual reason for continuing our training, was that it bought us time together we otherwise wouldn't have.

"Oh, you think you can beat me, eh?"

Abel wrapped his arms around me in a bear hug to simulate being held against my will. He expected me to use the side-step move he had recently taught me.

"I don't think it. I know it."

Raising our hands, I felt the heat move between us. He laughed again as I pulled my right foot up and placed it behind his opposing foot while I simultaneously grabbed his pants with my right hand.

"Nice work, Ta—"

With my head momentarily rested next to his chest, I breathed in his musk. It was a slightly complicated maneuver, made difficult mostly because being released from his hold went against every urge in my body. On my exhale, I bent my knee into his and pulled him to the floor.

"Whoa. You got me down perfect. Now what?" he asked.

"Now, I finish you off." All I had to do was roll over to face him. I was already on top of him, and all I had to do was dig my elbow into his stomach until he released me, but I was dizzy with the scent of desire. Not giving in to my loss of control, I dramatically enacted an elbow blow to him and jumped to my feet.

Standing over his body still on the floor, I said, "Looks like it's one to nothing."

He reached up and grabbed my hands. "Oh, yeah?" In one swift move, he'd pulled me back down on top of him. This time our eyes met, and our breathing danced in the shallow space between us.

His mouth moved toward mine. "Pinned ya." In an instant, he'd rolled over top of me and I was on my stomach with my hand pulled behind my back. He leaned down to my ear and whispered, "It's a tied game."

I wanted so badly to breach our friendship and give us a chance to be together, but neither of us seemed to know how to get there. It didn't help that we would be breaking the advisement of our bosses. Plus, once we returned from The Reckoning, our work lives were in a frenzy. The line between Abel and me had become difficult to keep from blurring.

Figuring out the new hire meant more time with Abel, which made it even more difficult to remain distant. Plus, for every trip he took back that I didn't, I lost memories he held on to. This blurred the lines on an even grander scale.

CHAPTER 3

ABEL

My team called me the Keeper of Memories. Taden invented the title for me as a joke, but then everyone else joined in and soon I found myself stuck under the weight of the moniker. Nevertheless, it described who and what I had become.

It was daunting to consider, but often situations would arise where only I had the truest insight, based on my first-hand knowledge of memories that had changed for everyone else. Holding memories, paired with my job as a military head for The Patriots, meant it was difficult to stay grounded in the present.

"Four solid days," she said as I entered the lab.

"Huh?"

"If you smell something ripe. It's me. I've been here four solid days now. I haven't gone home at all. I showered at the gym after our session yesterday but it wasn't enough to remove the air mattress, dirty hair, letting myself go funk I'm emitting. You might want to keep your distance."

"Good to know. I can stop searching for the dead lab rat." For the record, she still smelled like something I wanted as close to me as possible.

"I've gotten the first few to attach to their DNA already." She backed away from her microscope and pointed for me to take a look.

Peering through the lenses, I could see the strand in her sample had been extended. It was only something I could observe after many attempts to perform the task with DNA of our own relatives.

"I'm impressed. Though, I typically am with you."

Her coy smile demonstrated she was pleased with my compliment.

"I wasn't given the specifics of how far back in the past The Patriots want to send you guys. It's not on my clearance level anymore, but based on the ages of these samples Mr. Richardson sent us I have my theories."

She looked at me with her arms crossed and eyebrows raised. I already knew Ms. Farkas' goal. There was some discussion we might need to go much farther back than the handover of power to President Berthold to eliminate the threat he brought to the country.

"You know I can't confirm or deny your theories. It's classified information, Dr. Barrett."

She huffed and returned to her microscope.

"According to my estimated math I'm guessing approximately before the president was born, and I've made my guess at their target. You're going after Berthold Senior before Junior was conceived, aren't you?" She looked over her shoulder from the lens, and when I didn't respond to her guess she returned her focus back to the specimen on her scope's stage. "Okay, Memory Keeper. It's fine. Keep your secrets."

It was hard not telling her every thought in my mind. But it remained that she had to stay on target, and I couldn't impede her progress with the information I was required to keep.

Even harder was when I'd mention a memory Taden and I shared, and she'd look at me with misty, unrecognizing eyes. I'd find myself caught between the pride I felt for what she'd accomplished, the weight of what I must carry for the world, and the lonely disconnection being the only one who still had memories meant for two. I didn't bother any longer to try to fill in the missing gaps between us in her memory. Actually, I no longer knew what memories I had that she didn't.

I could see my intense need to keep our history the same was wedging a different kind of distance between us. It had been months since the last time I pressed the issue. I'd detected a new memory formed for Taden while we were talking about the first year President Berthold succeeded his father.

"After six collective years sitting as a corrupt president, his father, Berthold Senior, handed the power over to his son. Do you remember? It was midterm and he didn't give his seat up to the vice president."

"Of course I remember. It was a disgrace to our government. There were no elections either."

"You were furious. You wanted to organize a freedom march."

"I remember that. Dakotah and I talked about it a few times, but we never did it."

"But you did. You organized a protest against human rights violations." She absently blinked at me. "Your passion for the safety of immigrants was your driving force. So many had been killed coming here. Hunted down like wild animals. You'd had enough."

"Abel. We never actually held the protest."

"I'm telling you, you *did*. It had a huge turnout. But President Berthold's militia came and gunned down at least five people." I looked at Taden pensively, waiting for her response. I could clearly remember that day. She and Dakotah were ready to die for this cause. Her face burned with the injustice—stained with blood and tears—of the proceedings. But now, here, her absent reply left me alone in the memory.

"No way. That did not happen. Be serious." Watching my reaction, she understood she was missing something, something I knew which she no longer did. That was the moment she understood a new timeline had formed from a time travel I was a part of that she wasn't. "Wait. Are you telling me those things really *did* happen? How could I not know? I mean, I get it. I know how it happened, it was like this after The Reckoning when no one else remembered. It's just bizarre being on the other side…without you."

I didn't know what to say to her. It felt like she needed to be consoled about the loss, but I also felt a loss. She reached out to me and I grasped onto her like it was the only way I could keep us from slipping apart.

It didn't take long for Taden and Dakotah to establish a sophisticated system for collecting and recording each time traveler's memories of the rewritten timeline. It had been a challenge to document them, but even more challenging was keeping the documented memories from rewriting as a result of recent time travels.

Following the protocol used to retrace the events after The Reckoning, Taden and Dakotah extensively interviewed each member of the traveling unit upon every return. The concept evolved—over many working dinners—to embed memory data collection as a part of all time travel events.

"If we record within time travel, it would be retained similarly to the memory of the time traveler." Taden swirled her pasta noodles around her fork before shoving them into her mouth, rushing to finish dinner and get back to work. "The key is to have the data linked to our Timed Release Bands," she mumbled in between chewing.

"Like our brain's memory, the band—while on a time travel with us—could retain any data stored."

"Exactly." She pointed her fork at me and then to her head. "Do you want some of this pasta salad?"

My face cringed before I could tame my response. "Did you make it or buy it?"

She pushed her chin down, peering at me. "Not everything I cook turns out bad."

I scoffed while redirecting our discussion back to the safer topic of memory collection. "So, when do you think you'll have a prototype ready for my unit to test out?"

"Dakotah is uploading them as we speak. I think you'll be able to take them for a trial run your next trip back."

"It'll be a welcome change," I told her. "I love Dakotah and all, but those Q and A sessions after each mission are mentally exhausting."

Our test trips proved their theory. As long as the source of the data came from our bands, and our bands were with us in the time travel, the data collected in the past wasn't undone by a time travel event.

Eventually, we added the perfected elements to our newly-branded TRBs (Timed Release Bands) which included an audio-visual recording mechanism. Now we had proof of what we experienced and could share our insights about the reconnaissance mission we were on.

"I feel foolish," I said into the microphone on my TRB. "It's like I'm recording a diary."

I wasn't a huge fan of the videos in particular, but I valued the important piece it lent to recording the past and any changes we made to the timeline that I no longer would be expected to remember alone.

"It's day one of mission thirteen. I've arrived two years into the past. This is a test of our memory collection storage." I didn't know what else to say, so I ended the transmission.

Since our data was uploaded into Dakotah's system back in the lab in real time in the present, I also saw it as a way to get messages to Taden while I was gone.

"Still day one. I've stopped at the Top Hat burger joint. Look what I got, Taden." I waved the burger she loved in front of the screen. "Can't get these anymore." I took a huge bite of the burger. "Mmm, that is good. Bet you wish you were here with me." When I returned home at the end of the week, I fully expected a disgruntled response from Taden about taunting her with the burger.

I often wished Dakotah would figure out a way to transmit messages to me from the present. I never asked her to; I felt childish even wanting the ability, but it got lonely on long trips back into the past. I often thought about what Taden was doing. I would've given anything to correspond with her through the TRB.

"It's been decided, after an overwhelming vote," Ms. Farkas announced, "that in an attempt to retain as much of the present as possible, our official protocol for returning from a time travel will require the team to return in present time."

"How do you mean, ma'am? We already return to the present from each of our time travel jumps." I was confused by her statement. One I hadn't been asked to participate in the voting for.

"Rather than return to the time departed from, your team would arrive at *our* present time," she said.

Mr. Richardson sipped his coffee and set the mug on the table. "The concern with your time travelers returning to the moment they left from is about the loss we here in the present experience of each day your time travel trip took place."

"I understand," I told him. "If we were on a time travel for two weeks, the present timeline continues forward fourteen days without us. When we return to the moment we left, those fourteen days are lost to the non-time travelers."

"It is a far better option for the few who've time traveled to be simply absent from the span of time they were gone versus everyone else re-writing the present timeline upon your return."

As a result of this policy, I'd be missing out on days lived while I was gone on each time travel mission. On one hand, it'd give Taden and me endless topics of conversation once I returned. But in another way, Taden would be adapting to life with a lot less of me in it.

CHAPTER 4

TADEN

Ruth was the only person I was comfortable freely talking to about Marius. He was not an easy topic with Abel, given the fact that he'd killed me once. Honestly, Abel *never* liked Marius, even before he hurt me, but my murder at the hands of Marius in a time travel was the metaphoric nail in the coffin.

Unraveling all of the events tangled within The Reckoning was a complicated process. Even more so in the first week. Ruth stayed in Maryland with me at my apartment until the dust settled and we'd gotten a better grasp on all the fuzzy details.

"I still can't wrap my head around the idea that you were dead."

Ruth sat above me on my couch, her legs folded into a pretzel. I sat below her on the floor, feet stretched out in front of me as she brushed my hair. I didn't respond. Her brushing had lulled me into a relaxed state and I didn't want to revisit that night *again*.

"I know you've had to endlessly relive all of these details at work so The Patriots can start to put the pieces of The Reckoning together. I can see how you might not want to talk about it with me, but I think you should. It will be good for you. I'm pretty sure there are things you need to get out that you aren't going to include for them."

She continued to brush my hair and let her suggestion linger. I gulped down my glass of water, hoping she would let it go.

"I remember everything but the part where Marius hurt you." Damn. She wasn't going to let it go. "Just tell me how that part happened."

I sighed heavily. "Okay. Fine. But you have to keep brushing."

"Yeah, yeah, yeah. I said I would. Go on, then."

"So after Abel returned here with my body, you were with the team figuring out how to bypass my death."

"I do *not* remember that."

"I know. Abel filled me in on this part. You had a note Dr. Pasterski had written from the past. She gave it to you right before you time jumped back here."

"Holy crap. I do remember that part. I was worried about you. Abel had been crying and I was freaking out about what had happened to you. Dr. P sent me here with that note."

"Yes. That's correct. Once they devised a plan he jumped back into the time loop again, arriving just before Marius choked me. That time around, instead of me dying I…"

She finished my thought, "Killed him in self-defense. You had no choice, Taden."

"I know." I swallowed the surge of anguish trying to break through. "I just can't believe it. I watched him die. He looked scared. I didn't know what to do or say."

"No one would in your situation. But Abel said you didn't leave his side. Until he…"

"I held his hand. Promised him I would make sure his sister was safe in the new timeline. It was all I could think of to reconcile taking his life."

I could no longer hold in the onslaught effect of having killed a man. Ruth continued to brush my hair in silence as I hemorrhaged the feelings inside me. Once my breathing returned to a more regular rhythm, she cut into the heaviness.

"I'm going to braid it now."

"Okay," I mumbled.

She separated my hair into three sections with her comb. The gentle tingle of the comb dragging down my scalp eased me back into a calm.

"My memory of what happened picks up there. You returned with him and none of us remembered you were... you know."

"Dead," I said.

"Yeah. Anyway, once we convinced your secret agency people this thing really had happened you, Abel, his G.I. Joe men, and I went back to that dilapidated house where The Reckoners operated."

I nodded in confirmation.

"The Patriots were going to destroy every last Reckoner so there was no way of a resurgence. You went because you knew the child version of Marius was there, just initiated into The Reckoning."

"There was no way I would let Abel's men harm his younger version. The Reckoners had hidden him inside their shady headquarters, grooming him to become something awful." I felt the need to justify my actions on behalf of child-Marius—even to Ruth.

"I went because I wasn't letting my sister risk her life again. I remember all of that part correctly, right? Nothing has happened all timey-wimey to that part of my memory?"

"That's how it happened." I hesitated. "I know you don't want to hear this—"

She had already weaved my hair together at the crown of my head and was pulling the sections tautly down the nape of my neck.

"Tell me anyway."

"I caught glimpses of good in him. It's hard for me to accept he was really evil at his core. It's easier for me to accept he simply had bad circumstances in his life than for me to admit to myself that I had been a fool. Bad people took advantage of his situation, and brainwashed him into believing he was doing the right thing."

"I get that."

"I convinced myself if the boy version of him could be freed from those men, he would live a better life and turn out to be a good man. You think it's possible, don't you? That's why you came with me."

"It's possible. He was just a boy, and he deserved a second chance. You made the right decision."

"There's more you don't know."

"Taden Barrett, what is wrong with you? What did you do?"

"Don't freak out. It wasn't dangerous…*really*. I kept my promise about Marius' younger sister. I found her and made sure she didn't die either. In the original timeline, under the orders of our twisted government, she was detained upon entry to the country and died shortly after."

"Oh my God."

"Yeah. I know. Instead, I intervened and made sure she was placed into a safe haven I found—which facilitated her adoption into a caring family. I had to do it. I needed to ensure Marius would not go down a path toward darkness. I made a promise to him, as he drifted into his death, that I would save her if I could."

Ruth wrapped the rubber band around the end of my braid and then rested her chin on my head.

"I want to be like you when I grow up."

"Shut up."

"No, really. Who holds the hand of a dying man who terrorized her, promises to change history and save his dead sister, and then also saves the boy version of him?"

"I might be science smart but the way you spelled that out, I'm most likely lacking in the common sense department."

"I'll say it again. I think you made the right decisions."

"Ruth?" I turned around on my knees, looking directly at her.

"Hmm?"

"The idea of him turning out to be a good man is really the only thought to override this replaying memory of pushing a blade into his heart. Be honest. Do you think he could be a good man this time around? Wherever he is?"

"I think he could. You've made it a possibility."

I lay my head in her lap and she glided her hand along the silky braid she had just finished.

Ruth was my only non-judgmental outlet for this topic. These conversations were a give and take with Ruth, because I was the only person with whom she could reminisce about Maria. Ruth was grieving the loss of her best friend. In the previous timeline, Maria was instrumental in helping Ruth climb out of the despair of our mother's death. In the new timeline, she didn't leave a trace in Ruth's world.

Marius and Maria, two important people from our past, who no longer played a part in our present, became a bond between us beyond our sister relationship into a new kind of friendship.

Our relationship was also made easier having not lost our dad in the new timeline. Ruth didn't have to raise me alone at eighteen like before. She didn't have to carry the duty of caregiver for our dying mother since our dad was alive in this branch of time. I didn't live with the regret of abandoning her in the throes of turmoil, leading her to become drug addicted. With so many stressors removed from our lives, but with the memories of what life down the other path felt like, we deeply appreciated each other and our present.

Our phone conversation the morning before reminded me of how much closer we had become since her other life in L.A.

"How did you sleep last night?" she asked.

"Ha-ha. Right. Like I slept," I scoffed.

I sat at my desk—heaping with data to analyze—and eyed the floppy air mattress I kept attempting to sleep on.

"You really should leave the lab and go home to sleep. It's not healthy for you to work as much as you do."

"Honestly, you should talk." I sipped my coffee. "I know I'm overworking lately, but we're under pretty tight deadlines. Not to mention the whole, 'saving the world' thing."

Ruth scoffed. "Look, you can save the world tomorrow. You need to sleep."

Just like the older sister I grew up with, she couldn't help mothering me. I looked at my office couch, thinking maybe that might be more comfortable than the glorified airbag I had been sleeping on. Not wanting to be lectured about my sleeping habits, I flipped the focus of our conversation to her.

"Are you still having those dreams?"

Her breath hitched. "Mmm-hmm."

"Want to tell me about it?"

Maria frequently haunted her dreams. Often, she would replace Maria with Trey, a teenager she met while being held hostage in New York by terrorists. In her dreams, she would watch Maria be gunned down by a radical soldier the way Trey had actually been killed. In the new timeline he wasn't killed but, like Maria, he didn't cross paths with Ruth. Plus, Ruth couldn't forget the sound of the gunshot causing Trey to die at the hand of a Reckoner. The loss of both people entangled within her nightmares.

25

"Not really. It was just another nightmare. It always comes down to watching her die. I wish I could figure out how to make it stop." Her desperate tone was not lost on me.

"Well, you're coming into town this weekend, right?" I opened the planner on my computer to see the red font flagging her visit.

"That was the plan."

"We should try acupuncture. I heard it helps with sleeping and dreams. It's worth a try, don't you think?" With a soft murmur, Ruth agreed to try it out. "I've loaded up on ice cream and cookie dough, so if the acupuncture doesn't do the trick we can drown our memories in junk food." This time Ruth giggled.

"Actually, I was hoping to come in tomorrow so I don't miss Sunday dinner with Dad and Dr. P. But it's looking like I won't be able to leave until Monday."

"You're going to make me tell him tomorrow, aren't you?" She didn't respond. "Are you listening?"

"Huh? Oh, sorry. You don't have to tell him anything. He's a smart man. When I'm not there, I'm sure he'll figure it out." She paused again. The volume turned up in the background. It sounded like a news report.

"Ruth?"

"Yeah, I'm here. What were we talking about?"

"Dinner at Dad's."

"Right. Besides, we can stop by after—"

She was clearly distracted by whatever she was watching.

"Are you busy? Do you want to call me back?"

"Hmm? No. Hey, Taden, have you heard about this woman, Mary Moore?"

"Isn't she the one challenging the president's office?" I asked.

"Get online. Whatever news source. She's broadcasting live right now."

I clicked open the internet and searched her name to find a live stream of what Ruth was referring to. We both watched, keeping the line quiet.

"She reminds me of someone, but I can't quite place it. How about you?"

"Umm, I don't know. She just has that trustworthy, 'I've known you for years', aura. Listen to what she's saying about healthcare." I turned the volume up on my computer.

"For decades, two out of every three citizens in this country haven't had access to medical care. We have suffered long enough. No longer should we hold our breath for fear that our family could be one health crisis away from devastation. No longer should the wealthy top thirty-three percent be the only people to be cared for. It's often said that when you hit rock bottom you have nowhere to go but up. I'm telling you it's time. It's time to rise up. We are living at rock bottom no more."

"I have goosebumps. Isn't she amazing?" Ruth asked.

"She seems untouchable. Even if the government wanted to take her down, I don't think they could. I've never seen anything like it."

"She's a breath of fresh air like we haven't known since we were kids. She seems to be getting traction with the people, too."

"I'm pulling for her. If she succeeds here, it will make my life a whole lot easier. I can go back to solving time travel at my own pace, not at a breakneck, save-the-country-again, pace."

"The most interesting part of this to me is how everyone is usually too afraid to speak out and fight against the president, but she's hit a nerve. I'm shocked with how much visual support she's gained in just a few weeks."

Ruth made a good point about the brazen support Ms. Moore received. Citizens had learned to keep their voices low on topics like politics and government structure. It was custom only to share disapproval in secret, and only with those who you knew would keep your insights to themselves. Only in the anonymous online forums were truths freely shared, and over time even the online forums had become a dangerous place. Resentment was carried within the repressed people of the Berthold empire. But thanks to Ms. Moore, that empire was—just maybe—going to crack.

"Taden, I gotta let you go; my client just arrived."

As I hung up the phone, I looked at the framed picture of my dad. My mind drifted to my mentor, Dr. Pasterski. She had recently retired from The Patriot Party and mostly used her at-home lab to tinker around. I had missed the last two Sunday dinners with all the craziness at work. My dad was starting to take it personally. Right then, I put a reminder in my planner for the next day so there would be no way I'd miss it again.

 Knocking on Dr. Pasterki's front door, I felt like a foreigner in my own land. Countless years I had spent inside her home building the foundations of my path into time travel, and here I stood waiting for my dad to answer the door. This was his place now.

"Sweetheart," he said, opening the door, his eyes glowing with delight that I hadn't skipped another week.

"Hi, Dad." I planted a kiss on his cheek and he squeezed me like he hadn't seen me in months. "I know, I've been busy."

"Is your sister coming?"

"I just talked to her yesterday and she really wanted to, but work…"

He huffed, pouting. "Will I ever get both my girls together for dinner again?"

"Don't be so dramatic. She'll be here tomorrow and you know we'll be over to see you."

"Are you going to come in, or shall I pull out a chair?"

"Oh boy, it sounds like you're in a mood."

Dad and I could go back and forth bantering like this on an endless loop. It often annoyed the people around us. He laughed and shuffled into the kitchen to get Dr. Pasterski.

Her voice rose an octave higher than normal—I suspected he had just told her I was here—and was quickly followed by her gliding down the hallway, arms open wide.

"My girl," she said.

I loved that she still called me that. She'd been calling me her girl since I was really just a girl, coming here to work alongside her in her lab. In that instant, it struck me as strange that I still called her Dr. Pasterksi. After all this time, I couldn't possibly call her anything else. Certainly not 'Mom'. That name was only reserved for one person—regardless of how important to me Dr. Pasterski had become.

"I've missed you both. It's been so hectic at work."

"As always." She beamed. "Come on, let me show you what I've got cooking up in the lab."

I still spent a fair amount of time discussing and testing time travel theories with her behind those doors. Inside that laboratory, nostalgia of a childhood that I wouldn't trade a day of felt like warmth and sunshine.

Eventually, Dad knocked on the door. "Dinner's ready. Come and get it while it's hot."

"We'll be right there," she answered back. We finished our discussion about the memory tracking process with the Timed Release Bands and headed outside to the patio for Dad's meal.

I followed her through the living room. I unintentionally scanned the room, identifying Dad's belongings that had made their way within as if they'd always been a part of the furnishings.

"You go ahead. I'm going to wash my hands and I'll be right out."

She smiled and left me inside. I reached out for the little blue-glass elephant figurine sitting next to an array of books on the bookshelf. They were among a half dozen of Mom's knick-knacks that had also been implanted about the shelf.

A sting splintered my heart, seeing mementos of the past. I didn't know if I felt bothered because they didn't belong there or because of the visual reminder my mom was gone. I considered how my mom might feel about Dad and Dr. Pasterski if she were still alive. But she wasn't alive, so I let that thought go. It wasn't as painful as it used to be when I was reminded of her.

Either way, alongside the dull ache of healing grief, a joy prevailed over having all of 'my people' together.

I pulled open the sliding door to join them on the patio and beheld the sight of them sitting across from each other, so engaged in conversation they didn't even notice my entrance.

"Hey, you two lovebirds, the kid is in the room so change the topic of conversation to be more suitable for my ears." They both laughed and turned their attention to me. For I was a shining star in their eyes.

"My girl, tell your dad what you told me about the DNA test responses."

She smiled so brightly, her face could've beaconed a lost ship at sea. He scooped up an oversized serving of mashed potatoes and plopped it onto my plate.

"I'm all ears. It sounds like good news, eh?"

It was freeing to carry discourse over family dinner regarding time travel. It wasn't too long ago this part of my world was off limits to conversation. I had felt isolated, unable to talk about the most important parts of my day—which was likely the reason I fell so hard into Marius. On this beautiful evening I sat across from my family, sipping tea, relaying the successful results of my work, looking beyond them at the old apartment building I grew up in across the street. I spotted the window I used to sit and watch Dr. Pasterksi from, wishing I would one day know a life like hers. Here I was, in that very yard.

Life was good.

CHAPTER 5

Monday morning continued with the same headlong dive into work that had become my norm. In the few days after our last meeting with The Patriots, I'd been working around the clock with Dakotah to enhance the Timed Release Bands to be more specific to the needs of military operations and memory collections. Up until that point, the Timed Release Bands were pretty basic. Besides basic health monitoring, they could only automatically release an injection of the serum which sent us back in time, and then release another preset injection to return us to the present.

"I've got the coding established. Take a look," I told her, handing the tablet to Dakotah.

She scrolled through, tapping on each line of numbers and letters. "Girl! I think you got it. All right, I'm going to run this to my office and upload it into Abel's band so I can start executing tests." She was brimming with excitement.

"You want me to come with?"

"You've got enough going on here. I've got this. How are the genetic extensions coming along?"

"Almost done. I only have three of Abel's team left. Then I can start making their compounds. Hopefully they attach as quickly as the first seven did."

"No kidding. We need to get their serum mixtures ready like yesterday if we plan to meet the crazy timetable you gave to Danika."

She served me a wry look before leaving my side at the industrial counter space in our laboratory.

I called out to her as she walked away, "You're gonna miss the interviewees."

She turned around, still walking backward, shrugging her shoulders. "You don't need me to sit in on interviews with you." Her dramatic fake yawn conveyed her interest level. "Besides, you can fill me in tonight. We're still on with Ruth, right?"

I frowned with disapproval. "You should help me pick the new person. I don't always make the best judgement call in people."

"Don't I know it," she said, mocking me.

"We're still on with Ruth. Dinner at my place?"

"Let's stick with take-out." She winked, conveying her cheeky dig.

"Why does everyone hate my cooking? All right," I huffed. "Let's just eat out."

She shot me a thumbs up and quickened her pace. Nothing would impede her drive to finalize the Timed Release Bands.

She'd been exceptionally motivated to embed the memory recording into them since her own memory had been fully altered from time travel events. Dakotah had never been on a trip to the past so she held on to none of the memories of The Reckoning or any manipulated events since. We needed her work in the lab while travelers were out there.

As a result, most of her memories of Marius at the end were either gone or jumbled. She knew the basics as retold to her, from my intact memories, but Marius really wasn't a part of our lives or a topic of discussion anymore.

Dakotah and Ruth had both already been an important part of my world before, but it amazed me how the absence of a controlling relationship in my life opened the possibility for even closer and healthier ones in only a year's time.

 The first interview was Abel's pick: the Naval Academy officer. Lieutenant Jaxson Duncan had been responsible for operating nuclear reactors at sea. Mr. Richardson saw the opportunity to pluck him from the Navy before he re-enlisted.

While his disciplined demeanor was definitely something to take note of, he also had immaculate manners.

"Good morning, ma'am." He reached his hand out to shake mine and gripped it so tight, I couldn't hide the surprise on my face. "My apology, I didn't intend to squeeze so hard."

"No, it's all right. I'm not a wimp." My face reddened from the awkwardness of our initial exchange.

He saluted Abel, who returned the gesture. The three of us sat down at the conference room table—Lieutenant Duncan careful to be the last seated.

"We're honored you would consider joining us here at the National Institute of Science and Technology. Your résumé is astounding."

He sat erect in his chair, not a hint of pride reflected in his face.

"Thank you ma'am."

"What about this position caught your interest?"

"Off the record?" he asked.

"You want me to keep your answer to that question private?"

"Ma'am." He nodded his head to indicate his appreciation that I understood.

"Sure. We won't say anything about why you want to work with us."

I looked to Abel in an attempt to assess if he thought Lt. Duncan's request was weird as well. Abel not only didn't acknowledge the oddness, but he mirrored Lt. Duncan's formal body language as well.

"Mr. Richardson shared with me the classified nature of the work you do here," Lt. Duncan revealed.

"He did? I have to tell you, I'm surprised to hear that."

"Ma'am, I am in receipt of a vast array of confidential information. It is the nature of my Naval experience."

His intelligence was impressive, and no one would tire of listening to his experiences. I just didn't feel a spark with him. I needed to find someone I felt a connection to, who could work in a groove with me. He wasn't who I was searching for to fill the void Marius left in our team.

Abel and Lt. Duncan exchanged military stories for what felt like an eternity. I was sure I would have a heck of a time trying to side-step Abel's push for me to hire him.

The other candidate scheduled to interview arrived while Abel was still deep in conversation with Lt. Duncan, so I excused myself. It wasn't fair to leave her waiting outside while I sat listening to these two become best buddies.

The moment I laid eyes on Quinn Jones, I was struck by a strange sense of familiarity. If I was to discover she was in my previous timeline but had been wiped from my memory due to time travel, I would not have been the least bit surprised. I'd learned not to brush off this kind of déjà vu anymore. It must've meant a lost memory was in play. I mentally noted to have Abel check her background.

"So Quinn, one of the first things that popped out to me when I was looking through your résumé was that you went to UPenn. You might already know this, but it's my alma mater, too."

She blushed, admitting, "I know. You graduated my freshman year. I've kind of been following in your footsteps ever since."

Consciously aware my ego was being fluffed, I steered the conversation away from my accolades.

"Don't be silly. Look at this C.V.! You're an incredible candidate. No need to be in my shoes. They can be quite uncomfortable."

I understood my time travel discovery was a big deal, and that it would be my legacy, but Quinn Jones didn't know I had solved this puzzle. She had no other reason to hold me in such esteem, and I found it humbling.

"Enough of that," I said, closing her file and sliding it to the side. "Tell me who your favorite professors were. I loved Dr. Patel's lectures. Did you take any of her classes?"

We bantered back and forth about UPenn for a while before delving into the most impressive aspect of her working on my team: she was brilliant.

"I was a part of The High Energy Physics Experimental group. We worked on a wide variety of experiments aimed at understanding the fundamental structures of subatomic phenomena."

"What major projects were you involved with?"

"I worked on neutrino-less double beta decay. Probing the nature of neutrinos in search of whether the neutrino is a Majorana fermion."

With each word she spoke, I was decidedly choosing her.

"I love the interdisciplinary research that happens on projects like that," I said.

She vigorously nodded. "Exactly. Within the double beta decay experiments, the work we did—between our math department and physics and astronomy department—crossed the typical interdisciplinary boundaries in place."

I listened to her passionately recount the rapport established among her peers. It reminded me of working alongside my team.

"Crossing those boundaries is essential in answering the complex scientific questions still in need of answers."

Quinn had no idea how accurate her statement was. There was no doubt that she'd fill the role I needed. Pending Abel's inquiry into her, I had every intention of hiring Quinn. I was looking forward to meeting up with Dakotah and Ruth later on to tell them all about the new team member.

CHAPTER 6

RUTH

"Are we going to order an appetizer?" I looked between Dakotah and Taden. "I just got into town and haven't eaten a thing. I'm starving."

Taden replied, "Well, seeing that it's a Monday night, and we have an incredible amount of work waiting for us tomorrow, I think it's probably best if we take it easy on the beverages and fill up on pizza." Dakotah and I both cracked up at her constant attempts to force us into splitting a pizza.

"Is it cool if I stay at your place tonight instead of Dad's? I'm still not comfortable enough to sleep at Dr. P's house. Dinners are one thing. Overnight stays are just a little weird," I asked, still scanning the menu.

"No problem. Speaking of, Dad missed you at dinner last night."

"Oh yeah, you were supposed to get here yesterday," Dakotah chimed in. "What'd you have a hot date?"

"I wish. No, I've been promoted at work and so I've been getting first pick at some of our bigger clients."

They both congratulated me, holding up their glasses of wine.

"Bigger clients equals less personal time, though," I said, clinking my glass with theirs.

"She's preaching to the choir," Taden simpered to Dakotah.

"Right?" Dakotah said with animation as she placed her menu down and turned her full attention to Taden. "Oh hey, how'd the interviews go today?"

"I found *the one*," she said, theatrically lifting her hands to signify the divination she felt about her new hire. We were both entertained by my sister's absurdity.

I leaned in. "Is he hot?"

"Umm. No. He's a she."

"Is *she* hot?" I asked, raising my brow unblinkingly.

"Not the point. She is amazing, though. Her name is Quinn Jones. She's from UPenn, too." Then she slapped both hands on the table. "You know the females in physics club I started there? Guess who took it over after I left."

"Oh, so another mega geek," I jabbed.

"You didn't want the Navy guy?" Dakotah asked. "Because *he* was hot." She leaned toward me, smacking her lips.

"You may want to temper that heat," Taden said. "I've submitted a formal request to add Lieutenant Duncan to the team, too."

"Two new people? It's going to be fun having all that fresh blood around the place." Dakotah looked to me. "You'll get to meet the newbies. Don't you have a meeting with The Patriots this week?"

"I do, tomorrow morning. There's some underground talk of this political movement of Ms. Moore's building in the city," I said as the waitress delivered our steaming appetizers.

"News on Moore? That's sounds interesting," Taden said, fanning the hot mozzarella stick in her mouth.

"It is, but I'm more interested in checking out *The Chosen One* and *The Naval Officer*." I was having an internal debate over whether or not I should finally come clean with Taden about who Mary Moore really was.

It was *her*. I watched her unblinkingly, unaware that I was beaming at my television until my cheeks began to twinge.

I had let go of Maria. It was the best way I knew to move on with my life. I had no idea our new timeline somehow brought her here to New York, but there she was, challenging the president.

Maria saved my life. At least, it was her intention anyhow to save my life. She got me out of Los Angeles to avoid the terrorist plot, but unbeknownst to her I landed in New York right in the heart of it. In her mind, though, I was safe in Maryland, visiting Taden.

I missed her face more than I had let myself realize, and the relief I felt watching her on the television, trying to save our country, could not be ignored.

I had known Maria to be active politically. The fact that she was involved in The Reckoning did tweak at my thoughts, but I knew her better than I knew anyone else in my life. And whatever her reasons were, I believed she was doing what she thought was right. As I listened to her bravely confront the president, I did not doubt she would lead with high moral fiber.

"We are living in a country where our democracy has been replaced by an authoritarian government. Four years ago, President Finn Berthold was halfway through his second elected term when he altered the foundation of our country, handing his office over to his son. We doubted this corruption could ever happen in this great nation, but nothing could be done to remove him and his corrupt cabinet."

The camera panned to a small crowd in an alleyway to whom she was speaking. Their faces were hungry for the truth she boldly spoke. They were risking their safety, allowing their identities to be revealed on screen, even if this *was* local broadcasting.

"As the next generation of Berthold's years in power progressed, freedoms that had always been taken for granted were slowly stripped away. Under his authority a new caste system developed, tying each family's existing economic status to their children's education. His system first showed up in our elementary schools, where those whose families produced below the means—determined by our dictator in command— were only educated in skills of physical labor. The greater the child's potential (as decided by Berthold, according to wealth), the higher his educational opportunities."

Murmurs of agreement rose from the crowd. A man's voice shouted something inaudible.

"You're one hundred percent right, Mr. Flores," Mary said, pointing to the man. "It has to stop. It will stop. Everyone deserves an equal education."

A dull warning went off in the back of my mind, but I ignored it. The Reckoning wasn't even an agenda in this timeline. Besides, I was sure The Patriot Party had been monitoring her closely and wouldn't have allowed her to move into this role if it was going to endanger us in any way. I certainly wasn't going to alert anyone of this potential red flag.

While she spoke of education and challenged the corruption of our government, I remembered her dancing around our loft in her fuzzy pajamas, laughing at her choice in music. *Who knew if she even liked boy bands in this timeline?* Either way, it didn't matter. I wasn't going to put her in danger. Besides, our country needed this.

The fact that Maria changed her name wasn't much of a concern to me either. In order to live in this country and work in the political climate we were suffering under, it was necessary to be ethnically ambiguous. Maria's name change was a simple first name variation to Mary, but she adopted an entirely new last name to avoid flagging her culture. Mary's debut onto the political scene was fascinating to watch from the get-go. She came virtually out of nowhere and managed to unravel the two-year dictatorship of President Berthold with seemingly zero effort.

She had been mostly grassroots with her strategies of gaining traction, starting her movement by knocking on people's doors and talking to them face-to-face. Her momentum was building as she began attending unsanctioned government gatherings hosted by rebel citizens, where she was sure to share her voice. Eventually, she was hosting her own town-hall-style meetings, like speakeasies of the Prohibition Era.

Every speech she made was recorded and then broadcasted to get to as many people as possible. Her network was highly skilled at using methods of broadcasting that were almost impenetrable by government interference. By the time a broadcast was targeted and removed, it had been viewed by many people and passed on to so many more. It had become like a badge of honor to be a part of her campaign, or even simply to share her messages of hope. I felt I might burst with pride each time I listened to her speak, knowing at one point in time we had established our roots side by side.

As soon as she started appearing in nationwide news, I felt less responsible to share her presence with Taden. After all, she knew Maria, and it was an important attribute of Taden's career to be attentive to details. But as time went on and her appearances became regular, it stunned me that Taden apparently didn't recognize Mary as Maria. To top it off, we had even watched one of Mary's live addresses together over the phone.

To be fair, she didn't look much like the Maria we knew. Her hair wasn't long and flowing as it had been; instead, it was cut into a smart bob. She wore glasses instead of her contacts. Her clothing was drastically more modest than the fashionable outfits she wore in the old timeline. Really, Mary's overall appearance seemed years older and more intelligent than Maria's. Regardless, Taden's ignorance seemed uncanny.

I'd kept my knowledge of Maria from Taden for so long that it was to the point that I couldn't bring myself to tell her—solely based on how awful I felt for having not told her.

CHAPTER 7

TADEN

"I did a thorough check on Quinn."

Abel rested against the doorframe of my office. His hair was damp from his morning shower. The sandalwood scent of his soap had a distinct rugged smell that I came to associate with him. Every urge suggested for me to get up from behind my desk, leaving the stacks of notebooks, and wrap my arms around him.

It would've surprised the heck out of him. I wasn't ever that forward, though. He probably would've laughed being caught off guard, but I was full of such anticipation about Quinn, the surprise I had for him about Lt. Duncan, and just overall pleasure to see him.

Instead I stopped working, folded my hands, and offered Abel a toothy grin.

"All I found of any interest was a sealed adoption record. So I looked into her adoptive parents. Nice people. Good family. Nothing to worry about there." He'd given me the green light on Quinn. "Are you sure, though? *Another* female around here?"

"You're hilarious," I said with sarcasm. "I have a surprise for you!"

"You do?" he asked, dropping his arms to his sides, as he approached me. When he was right in front of me he rested his hands on my desk, leaning forward until we were looking directly into each other's eyes. I breathed him in. "Do I have to guess what it is?"

"That might be entertaining," I said, pausing to consider what he might guess. "But I can't sit on this any longer. I put in a formal request for a fifth team member to include Lt. Duncan."

"Did you?" he asked, hinting a smile.

My eyes widened. "The Patriots are sold on the idea, especially once I implied that it could move up our timetable."

The corner of his eyes crinkled and he finally showed off his dazzling smile. He remained still, only slightly tilting his head toward me. I, on the other hand, was charged with adrenaline and needed a distraction before my mouth landed on Abel's. Absentmindedly I lifted random objects spread throughout my office, in search of my phone.

"Are you looking for this?"

Teasing me, he held up my cellphone. I accepted it, allowing our hands to brush past one another. The smallest touch made me want more. Digging deep for remnants of self-control, I dialed Quinn's number. Listening to the phone ring on the other end I gave Abel my brightest eyes, eager to make the new hire official.

"Hello, is Quinn Jones there?"

"This is she," she answered. Already her voice was shaking.

"Hi Quinn, this is Dr. Barrett from the National Institute of Science." Silence on the other end. "I'm thrilled to ask you to be a part of our team." Again, silence on the other end. "Are you there?"

A shriek filled my ear. Chuckling, I pulled the phone away.

"So, I'll take that as a yes?"

"Yes! A thousand times yes. When do I start?"

I was relieved she brought it up. In all honesty we needed her *last* week, and I was debating how to get her started as soon as possible without coming across as a tyrant.

"Well, officially, you can wait until next week, but if you're ready I already have plenty for you to jump in and start doing. It's completely your call, and I don't want you to—"

"I'll be there in half an hour. Is that okay?"

"That's actually perfect."

"I only have to get dressed and I'm on my way."

Just from our brief conversation I already knew, without a doubt in my mind, that she was going to fit right in.

As if Quinn wasn't already a potential rookie sensation, Dakotah loved her from the get-go, too. She synced right up with the two of us, and then we were three. I loved the idea of being a trio of badass female scientists, sending people throughout time to save the world.

Lieutenant Jaxson Duncan and Dr. Quinn Jones were easy additions to the crew and, as two new kids on the block usually do, they buddied up nicely with each other.

CHAPTER 8

ABEL

As soon as Ms. Mary Moore stepped onto the political stage, she was on my radar. Taden was smitten with Mary almost right away. Ruth had actually gotten wind of Ms. Moore's movement before it started to catch fire across the country. In a meeting with Mr. Richardson, she reported rumors that Ms. Moore's activism to stand against the corruption of Berthold may be turning into a campaign to replace him.

"The word is that she's holding her first rally at a speakeasy in Brooklyn next weekend."

"Does it seem like it's going to have a good turnout?"

"It seems like not a lot of people would risk the danger to go."

"Her campaign designated tickets to ensure who attends." She held up her phone, showing the screen. "I got two. One for me—and one for you if you're interested."

"Why do you want to go?"

"Besides the fact that she is about to take down our evil dictator? I just can't believe he is still operating as our president—if we should even call him that," Ruth said, crossing her arms. "He freaking *bypassed* the sitting vice president and just *took* office because his daddy gave it to him."

Listening to her spell out our recent history like that still made me dumb-founded. It didn't make any sense how we had gotten to this point in our society.

"I don't know how we let it happen," I commiserated.

Ruth continued, "I mean, he didn't even hold an election."

She threw her hands in the air, shrugging her bewilderment.

"Even with the shifty reelection of his dad's second term, none of us saw this absurdity coming," I stated.

"How did any of this happen? How have we still not united to demand his removal? He will be stopped," added Mr. Richardson.

"It's looking like Ms. Moore has a chance to lead us there," Ruth said.

"Are you worried about any blow-back if you go to the rally?"

"Like how? With our government?" Ruth furrowed her brow. She tapped the screen on her phone a few times before sliding it across the table to me. "Look at her."

I picked up her phone to see an enlarged image of Mary Moore. "Okay. Am I missing something?"

"That woman is my best friend from L.A. Maria Hernandez."

"I see it now. She's changed a lot more than her name."

"That she has. I'm going to her rally. You can come with me or not."

"Dr. Mihal, I want you there. We need eyes on this," Mr. Richardson directed.

 Entrance to Moore's rally was more secure than going through customs at an airport.

"I need to see your tickets and identification," the security officer told us.

Ruth presented our tickets on her phone and we both handed over our licenses. The officer scanned each and then snapped what felt like a mug shot of both of us. Once we passed the first stage of entry, we were funneled through a series of metal detectors and then patted down.

We arrived early because Ruth desperately wanted to see Ms. Moore at the meet and greet. I left her in an already extensive line of people who were looking forward to the same, and took the opportunity to do some snooping around Moore's people.

I was intent on collecting some facial scans of my own. Any member of her staff I found—easily identified by the lanyards hung from their necks—I snapped a quick photo to run through our scanning. That's when I first spotted him in the back of a crowded hall, standing with her supporters. That *face*. His were the hands that had strangled the breath from Taden's lungs.

I was looking at Marius Touma.

The moment I saw him standing behind her, it became certain to me that presidential candidate Mary Moore was dirty. Marius' presence was all the proof I needed. Taden might have methodically set up the timeline so that he wouldn't go down the same route to darkness as he had when I knew him, but some people are just rotten to the core. It's the argument of nature versus nurture. In regards to Marius, there were no redeeming qualities that I felt a nurturing environment could impact.

I kept it quiet from Ruth so I could spend some time investigating both of them without interference.

My first action once back in my office was to contact Bernard Richardson. He was the military official in The Patriot Party and my direct commander.

"We knew he was out there," Mr. Richardson said.

"Somehow he moved into this hotbed of political activity right under our noses, sir."

"Dispatch a task force to monitor him. It might be nothing to worry about, but keep me updated."

"Understood, sir."

His resurgence was more personal for me, so I tapped into every outlet regarding Marius. My team was watching him closely. After a few weeks, I had nothing of relevance to offer to my commander.

"On first impressions, it appears his record is spotless."

"I'd suspected," he responded.

"He hasn't done so much as harm a hair on anyone's head."

"Seems suspicious."

"More than suspicious, though—his record is *too* clean. Not so much as a parking violation over his whole life."

"Gives the impression it might have been wiped," Mr. Richardson suggested.

"I was thinking the same."

"What have you found on Moore?"

"Despite her connection with Marius, she's flawless. She was an immigrant fleeing the dangers of Honduras. She arrived with her family through the Mexican border, along with a large number of other immigrants. Unlike the masses, her family had political connections in our government who helped them gain legal citizenship and safely transition into our country."

"Anything else?"

"No sir, that's all I have at this time."

"Okay. Keep on them. Report to me directly."

 Mary used her immigrant background to appeal to the people and to break down the old requirement of being a natural-born citizen as a rule, qualifying her to be eligible to become president.

"Our current dictator in command is a natural-born citizen of this country. That outdated requirement didn't protect us from his influence. I am here to change that," Mary shouted during another rally. "I may not have been born here, but this is my home. I will protect it and the citizens who live here with my life."

Her background painted a picture of a woman who had worked tirelessly for human rights. She began developing her pathway into politics as early as high school, working part-time for local politicians. By the time she graduated from college, her experience was varied and many of her humanitarian efforts were gaining traction. Mary was on track to become the first president not born in the country.

She seemed squeaky clean, but with the knowledge I had of the past this wasn't immediately a free pass. Marius had been able to disguise himself as a leader in our country for most of his life, in both timelines.

In our previous timeline, I learned in the days before his death he had been an operative assigned with dismantling our country from the inside. And even though I had never trusted him, it was still jarring to learn the truth about him. *How did he get so far into our government?* I would not ever make the same mistake again.

From then on, every person I was tasked to investigate was held in suspicion until I could prove them otherwise. Mary, though, had a solid reputation of being well respected. *So why didn't I trust her?* I found no evidence of a partner or even a love interest in her life, and other than her activism her personal life was surprisingly lacking. Besides this working association with Marius, she gave me no other reason for suspicion. I considered she might have just been as innocent as Taden was in her unfortunate mix up with Marius.

But I just couldn't shake the feeling something was wrong. So I kept watching.

All of her work stood still a few weeks back when our country woke to the shocking news of President Berthold's assassination. I was watching the morning news before I left for work.

"We've just received word that President Berthold is dead," the news anchor reported. "He was traveling to New York, where several protests had been staged to remove him from office." The screen cut to the protestors standing in shock. "His goal was to squash the movement in its core location."

The story panned to a bystander. "As he was entering his apartment here in the city, someone approached from the street and shot his gun into the group of Secret Service agents accompanying Berthold," recounted the eyewitness.

"Then what did you see?" she asked the witness before pointing the microphone in her direction for a response.

"When the agents responded to the gunfire, another person appeared from the alley next to the building." The woman pointed in the opposite direction of the first gunman. "Then a bodyguard or something escorted him into the building to flee from the attack."

The broadcast cut to the news anchor, briefing us of the outcome. "Once inside, gunfire was exchanged and both President F. Berthold and his bodyguard were killed. In the confusion, the group responsible for the assassination fled the scene and disappeared into the night. After his autopsy confirms cause of death, there will be a closed-casket funeral this weekend. Suspicions are looming around the details of this case. If you have any information, contact local authorities."

For days, our country was frozen with shock—but the ice cracked when a movement to place Mary in office swept the nation. Berthold did not have a vice president. His power move refused to acknowledge an alternate plan. He was intentionally the only man for the job.

It made sense to everyone: put Mary in office and let her get our country back on track toward democracy. This accelerated her movement and impressed the intensity of our investigation into both her and Marius.

Our country was like an orphan left on Mary's doorstep. Because of the massive movement she had thrust herself into by trying to remove Berthold, eyes were on her to fill the opening. Essentially, a spontaneous demand for a vote to name her as interim president began to spread throughout the country.

Communities united to collect votes in an outcry for her to lead us through this stage. For the first time since my childhood, people felt unafraid to take political action. They got away from their screens and took to the streets. Their voices were being heard.

CHAPTER 9

RUTH

Over lunch, my client and I were discussing her upcoming event my company was hosting. In my view, directly behind her, hung a television broadcasting the swearing in of our new president. I had been following all the news I could on Mary since the first night I became aware of her, and this was no exception—despite the client meeting.

I stopped listening to Gayle (my client, who was going on about the downlighting of the room and color scheme of her party) to focus on President Mary's speech. That's when I spotted the devil himself. Marius Toumas was standing behind her, in support of my Maria. *What the hell was he doing on stage with her?* I had been following her every move for months now, and I had never noticed him mixed in.

A litany of thoughts ran through my brain. None of the ruminating led me to an option that felt good. I needed to end the meeting with Gayle immediately and tell Abel. He was the only one with any good sense about this creep. He was the only one who would take him down with no questions asked. I would not sit back and let Marius wriggle his way into Mary's life.

I made an excuse to Gayle, tossed money onto the table and bolted, my mind unable to shake the image of Taden's drugged up body strapped to a bed in a mental institution at the hands of Marius. I couldn't unsee her death at his hands. I was halfway home when a different sinking feeling struck me. It wasn't just Marius who was trouble. *Maria* was part of The Reckoning in our old timeline. She worked for the same people as Marius did. Marius standing behind Mary, our newly sworn-in president, didn't bode well.

Despite my newly-born, conspiracy-theorist self, I loved Maria. She had a good soul. But somewhere, somehow, she was a part of a fight I couldn't defend with any decency or goodness. If she chose to be a part of them then, when I knew her inside and out, what could I possibly know about this version of her?

I touched Abel's preset on my car's console and burned through traffic to get home and pack for my upcoming weekend in Maryland.

"Thanks for letting me know. We're aware of Marius and have been keeping a close watch."

"Wait, you knew? For how long?"

"I saw him the night of the rally we attended."

"And you didn't tell me?"

"I didn't want to raise alarm unless it was necessary."

"Is it?" I asked, pressing more firmly on the acceleration.

"I don't believe so."

"Does Taden know?" He didn't answer the question. "Does she know, Abel?"

"No." His pause communicated he shared the same guilt about keeping this from my sister. "I don't know how to bring it up."

"One of us is going to have to summon the courage and fill her in here," I said, hoping he would be the one.

CHAPTER 10

ABEL

Quinn transitioned into our rhythm so smoothly and so quickly it was remarkable. It felt like she'd been around for years, when it had only been a few weeks. She was a detail-oriented person, just like Taden. She observed with keen interest and could pick up routines with high efficiency.

She asked an incalculable number of questions—enough to make my head spin—but in Taden's mind it was a clear sign Quinn was interested and learning. Dakotah chimed in and fielded many of Quinn's inquiries while pulling her into some of the biotechnology facets of our work. Her probationary stage was ending, and I was the point person to explain to her the nondisclosure aspect of her position.

"Should I be nervous?" she asked me as we walked into my office.

"Nothing to be nervous about." I gestured toward a chair at my small round table.

I sat across from her, purposely not crossing my arms or legs in order to keep a relaxed message. She was already anxious, and I wanted to try to diffuse it before I got to the time travel part of her new job.

"I know you've got a long day ahead of you, so I'm going to try to make this quick."

She tried to smile politely, but she was so nervous her attempt seemed painful. I had to stifle a laugh.

"First of all, we're extremely pleased with the work you've done so far. So really, truly, you have nothing to be nervous about. Taden hasn't stopped singing your praises."

She beamed from ear to ear at receiving accolades from Taden. It was obvious to everyone that Taden was something of a legend to this one.

"So we've officially decided to keep you."

She giggled with a nervous edge, maybe not realizing we were watching her to determine if she would be permanent.

"That's a relief. I'm thrilled to be working here, and it would've been devastating to find out it was only a trial," she told me through a series of flustered chortles.

"The reason I'm meeting with you is to be certain you are committed to your work here, and to review some important classified features of your position in order for you to move forward with us."

Her giggling stopped quite abruptly. She sat taller in her chair, replacing the nervous disposition she held before with a formal and serious demeanor.

"What do you mean?"

I pushed the tablet in front of her. She glanced at it and then back to me. I nodded for her to accept. Without apprehension, she read through the non-disclosure agreement. I watched her facial expressions display the beginning of her understanding that she had only scratched the surface of her work here.

"I'm fully on board," she said, with no detection of hesitancy.

"Did you read the part about how you cannot speak a word of your NIST work with anyone outside of the program?" I asked her, making sure she understood the gravity of the situation.

"I read that. I also read the part about working for an unnamed organization. I read in between the lines, too." She traced her finger across the screen, signing her name on every line of commitment. "I've stumbled upon something big. Something once-in-a-lifetime big. Haven't I?"

She looked back to me with anticipation, and an eagerness reminding me of Taden.

"Quinn, you have no idea." I double-checked every signature and swiped the tablet off. She wasn't the first person I had explained our work to—I led an entire squad of time traveling soldiers I had brought on board—but the excitement in this person was bubbling over, and I stumbled a bit trying to reveal the intricacies without getting her even more worked up.

"I'm just gonna put it out there," I said finally. "Your job description is to assist Dr. Barrett in molecular activity for the purposes of time travel."

Her response was akin to someone who won the lottery. Her eyes bugged out and strange squealing sounds pushed through her mouth. It was clear Taden had found her person.

"While your main role will be to assist Dr. Barrett in the lab, you will also play an important part in the execution of our memory collection process. Dr. Hughs is the lead on that task." She was waiting with bated breath for me to continue. "When time has been altered the memory of what has been undone is no longer retained, with the exception of those who've traveled in time during the alteration." I paused. "Does that make sense to you?"

"It does. What you're saying is, you know things that have happened that I don't remember ever existed."

"Correct. One of the many issues involved is that the time travelers are unaware of which memories are from their previous timeline—'new memories'—or from their old timeline—'old memories'. We have developed a line of questioning that stimulates body responses. We can record these responses and detect old memories that flow in the same structure as the new memories surrounding it. In essence, our interview process releases the original memories that have become entangled with the new ones."

"You might have lost me a bit there. Are you saying that after a time travel event you remember both memories, but you're not aware which memories are the new ones?"

"I am. For example, Taden remembers life without her dad, growing up orphaned after her mother died. But she also didn't live that life in this timeline because her dad wasn't killed. She prevented it in a timeline. She carries the memories of both lives. It can be difficult to sift the memories from her traumatic orphaned life and the life she got to have from the new timeline. On a personal note it can be a struggle, but when the memories that entwine affect our government and national history the issue is amplified."

"I imagine so," she said, fully engrossed in the idea.

"So, you'll be—" Hearing a soft knock on the door, we both looked over to see who it was. Taden popped her head in.

"I hope I'm not interrupting."

"No. Certainly not. Come in. I've just gotten Dr. Jones to sign on the dotted line and have been filling her in." Quinn bugged her eyes at Taden and mouthed the words 'oh my gosh', sharing her thrill to be working with us.

"That's wonderful. I'm elated," Taden said, glowing at Quinn.

"Does Lt. Duncan know already?" Quinn asked. "Or did I get accepted first? We're kind of in competition."

All of us had a good laugh, neither Taden nor I clarifying that Lt. Duncan knew before we even interviewed him.

"Abel, you asked me to stop by your office before lunch; is now a good time or should I come by later?" Taden asked me, glancing at the clock.

"I think right now is best. I don't want you to miss it." I left the table to retrieve my remote and powered on the television.

Quinn interjected, "Oh! You're showing her the swearing in of President Moore, aren't you? That's today right? Can I stay?" She looked back and forth between us with excitement in her eyes, until she concluded she had been too forthcoming inviting herself. "I don't have to, though. I'm sorry! It was a little pushy of me."

Both Taden and I were amused.

"Is that today? How did I forget? You can most certainly join us. Right, Abel?" Still chuckling at Quinn's awkward interaction, she looked back at me expectantly.

Quickly weighing my options, it occurred to me Quinn's presence might actually help Taden stay centered and better held together when she spotted Marius.

"Yeah, sure, you can join us. But Taden, I want to warn you—what you're about to see could be a little shocking. Are you all right with managing your feelings in front of Quinn here?" I side-smiled at her to make the warning feel humorous, but still offering her a warning nonetheless. Taden lowered her chin and looked up at me as if I were poking fun at her. She had no idea what was about to be revealed.

"Quinn, if I freak out watching Mary Moore becoming the first woman president of our country, I'm sorry ahead of time." She returned her eyes back to me. "We good?"

I was not looking forward to the loss of her humor after she watched the swearing in. It caught her off guard when I placed my hand on hers and gave it a little squeeze before pressing play. Quinn smiled in a way that revealed she was uncomfortable and shuffled in her chair, possibly feeling like a third wheel.

As I cued up the broadcast, I hoped Taden didn't notice my nerves engage. A serious level of doubt surged within me; I probably should have just told her instead of showing her the recording. Sat her down. Had a drink ready. Then just said it, like an adult. Rather than be forced to utter the words, here I was—creating a much-larger-than-necessary drama. I supposed it was too late to alter my plan at this point, so I carried on with my idiotic idea.

Pressing play, I tried not to gawk at her while we watched the ceremony begin. She smiled wide as the first female president took an oath to rescue our country from the power-hungry grips of President Berthold. I noticed her eyes flit around the screen, paying acute attention to every detail. I didn't need to see her reaction once she spotted him. I felt the tension in the room pull tight across my chest. Her eyes landed on his face and I watched them cloud into darkness. With a grimace, I held her in my view. She crossed her arms, shooting me a widened stare. She didn't like to be coddled, and so my desire to swoop in and fix this for her was not an option.

Quinn was still chattering on about what President Mary was wearing and the poise with which she spoke. We both ignored her. I held Taden's dark stare until she looked to the floor and subconsciously rocked from one foot to another.

That's when Quinn picked up on the energy shift. She stopped talking mid-sentence, looking to me for confirmation that something was wrong. I winced in response and hoped to convey a suggestion that she might want to leave. Relief settled that she was perceptive enough to receive my nonverbal suggestion. With a knowing nod, she slipped out of the office. Taden was not cognizant of her exit.

"You okay?" I took a step toward her, offering my arms as solace. She gravitated to my offer, and we embraced. Charged with the privilege of holding her like this, not wasting the closeness she was affording me, my hands wrapped tightly around her waist. She settled her head onto my chest and I, in turn, buried my face in her hair. She smelled of chocolate and marshmallows. Her soft auburn hair brushed my cheek, and without conscious thought my hand began stroking her silky locks. Making a concerted effort to give her silence, I didn't speak first. I knew Taden liked to collect her thoughts and process ideas before she engaged in a conversation. When her contemplation was over, her eyes were clear.

"It's him. Isn't it?" she asked. I nodded. "Do you think my plan could've worked? Could he be different this time around?"

"I hope so. I hope he made the right choices this time. Now that we know where he is and who he's working with, we're going to find out exactly what sort of person he turned out to be."

I pulled my face back so she could see me clearly. My hand stilled on her hair before moving to her face, where my thumb skimmed along her cheekbone.

"It can't be too bad, Taden. He's been on our watch list and hasn't sounded any alarms up until now. I don't know how he's managed to work with such a high-profile political party and not trigger some kind of alert, which is a red flag, but there's a very real possibility that you saved him. You might've made it so Marius turned out to be on the good side this time."

I had to force myself to spit the last part out in the same breath as his name. He was always going to be nothing but a monster to me. I'd never see him as anything close to heroic.

She rested her face back against my chest.

"I don't think I should be involved with this investigation of him. I don't want to make any contact with Marius, just in case…" Her voice trailed off.

I heard notes of despondence, the emotion I'd predicted from her. However, I didn't know exactly what filled her with despair. Naturally she would be fearing he would finish what he started, but did her worries run deeper? Did seeing his face unearth levels of grief she hadn't dealt with yet? Did she still love a version of him? Was she struck with the memory of killing him? I knew, firsthand, that killing a person was a difficult act to process. The questions looming in my head were not released to Taden. She had enough to come to terms with.

I wasn't there to force her to quell my own fears about Marius. I was there to help her get through the revelation that he was back in our lives. Upon learning this fact, she found comfort in my arms. For as long as she would let me hold her, I would. I was hoping for forever.

It had *felt* like forever since Taden and I kissed. I ached for her, but I wanted to be certain she was ready. I didn't give a damn what The Patriots thought about inter-office relationships. To make a move toward an us, all I needed was to know she loved me. And I knew it. I could feel it. It was in her eyes when she looked at me—she definitely looked at me differently than before. As if she was seeing me for the first time, or suddenly catching on to my affection for her.

These days, her voice would change when she talked to me. We were often much closer to each other while we worked together, and the occasions for our skin to touch had greatly increased. Our constant sexual tension had built a charge within my body. Whenever she entered the room every nerve ending triggered messages of her presence, and my body's senses heightened. Blood pumped at an accelerated rate and focus could only be given to her.

We had been in and out of meetings with The Patriots at least twice a week in the aftermath of The Reckoning. Our initial time travel protocols had been analyzed and were in the process of being perfected. We were getting closer to the launch of my next major assignment (technically, our original mission), and everything was starting to fall into place.

The smallest windows of opportunity for Taden and me to have some alone time presented themselves. This was time we deserved with each other, and this was especially true before I launched this mission.

I was coming to terms with the fact that each time I went back into the past, I might not return. It felt even more dire with all that had come to light regarding the presidency and Marius. I didn't want to waste any more time without her.

In the midst of all we had going on in our professional lives, so much time had already slipped away from us. It was past the right time to ask her out on a date—a legitimate, romantic date.

The weekend was approaching, and I saw my chance to finally change our momentum.

After I held on to her for some time, she pulled herself together and suggested we get back to work.

"Are you sure?" I asked her. "You could take the rest of the day to go easy, if you need to."

"Not a chance. I'm not letting him dictate my life again. I have so much to do. Plus, I'm sure my nerves will settle once I get back into the rhythm of work. You know what I mean?"

"I do, but if you need me, or you change your mind, I'm here for you."

I hoped she wouldn't need me, that she would be affected by him as little as possible—yet a part of me wanted her to need me. To signal the end of our embrace, she rolled up onto her tiptoes and kissed my cheek.

"I really needed that hug. Thanks for cluing me in that he's back in the picture. More importantly, thanks for letting me wallow with you after."

She turned on the balls of her feet and headed to the lab. Almost through the doorway, she stopped and turned back around. A faint smile pushed through her worry.

"You coming?"

"I'll be out there soon. I've got few loose ends here first." I paced the floor of my office with my hands folded behind my head. I really wanted to be wrong about Marius.

All of us would know the truth soon enough.

CHAPTER 11

TADEN

Back to work in the lab with Quinn, still shaken from the footage of Marius, I could see she was waiting with anticipation for me to open the conversation. I sensed her watching me as I moved around the room. She was chomping at the bit to find out what the drama was about.

"I know you're worried about me," I finally said. "I'm okay. Really." Upon seeing my face, which I could feel had been drained of color, her expectancy to chat about what had just occurred dissipated.

Instead she nodded, giving me a knowing look, and afforded me solitude so I could focus and get back on task. I easily shifted into autopilot, measuring out the different parts to the compound to create more of our time traveling serum. Besides, it wouldn't be too much longer before Dakotah arrived for her shift. It would be easier for me to share with both of them at the same time instead of having to rehash it twice. I appreciated the peace, and she gained my respect for not prying.

As I predicted, as soon as Dakotah settled in to start her shift the familiar comfort she brought allowed me to open up with the two of them.

While Dakotah and Quinn eagerly listened, I replayed what I witnessed on the screen.

"He looked exactly how I remembered him." I poured the serum compound into a glass beaker and placed it into the homogenizer. "His confidence is still unmeasurable. Holding his space behind President Moore, he reminded me of the protective nature he always seemed to offer me."

"That's not how it was, though, Taden," Dakotah reminded me. "I saw everyone's memories of him and I have enough of my own. He wasn't trying to protect you, he was trying to isolate you and take your work."

"His eyes look different." I thought this was an important observation. "They don't hold the darkness that I remember there before."

Quinn couldn't keep up. This was all news to her. "Who are we talking about here?"

"We're talking about the man who used to have your job. It didn't turn out so well between him and me."

"Oh," she said. "I'm sorry to hear that." Quinn frowned as a sympathetic gesture and moved closer to the compound—assessing the mixing time left. "So, you saw this guy at the swearing in? That's why you got upset?"

"This guy is Marius Touma, and Taden is understating how badly it didn't work out. He kidnapped Taden, and took her into the past to be held captive by the terrorists he worked for in an attempt to get her to reveal the recipe for the time travel serum to them."

Quinn's mouth gaped open. "Are you serious?"

"Completely. When it didn't work out the way he'd planned, he strangled her. She was dead for hours. We figured out how to time jump ahead of her murder using a new DNA serum to inject her with to bring her to the present and bypass the missing time of her death from her time loop."

Lifting the beaker out of the homogenizer, she almost dropped the glass from shock. "He killed her?"

I wondered out loud, "What is he doing in this campaign? If he turned out different this time, maybe he's the mastermind of Mary's presidency. Dammit, but that means if he turned out to be the same awful person, we have huge concerns."

Dakotah continuously shook her head in dismay of the news, as if by shaking her head she could refuse his reappearance. Her green eyes validated the bewilderment I felt.

Quinn's body language had shifted from desperate interest to distraught confusion. If I didn't know better, Quinn was experiencing more than an empathetic response.

"Are you feeling okay? You look like you're going to be sick."

She didn't answer me. She might have thought I was talking to Dakotah. I realized my body was mostly directed to Dakotah, and I was making more natural eye contact with her. I could sometimes sense Quinn felt left out.

"Quinn?"

Startled, she looked up with a jerk.

"Yeah? Oh, I'm sorry. Did you ask me something? I don't feel very good. I'm going to run to the bathroom."

"Whoa, that was weird. I hope she's okay." Dakotah seemed concerned about her abrupt exit. "I'm going to check on her."

I nodded, not sure what had just happened. But my gut told me to dig into this thing with Quinn.

CHAPTER 12

RUTH

While I drove, lost in thought, I considered that if Taden found out I had gone to Abel with this first, she might feel betrayed. But Taden couldn't be trusted—as the sole proprietor of this detail—to act rationally in regards to Marius' reappearance.

Before I changed my mind yet again, I pressed her auto dial icon. "I was just about to call you," she said.

"You must sense I'm getting closer." It was uncanny how we always did weirdly well-timed exchanges with each other. "As we speak, I'm actually on my way into town for the weekend."

"Oh, thank the lord. I really need to see you." Her voice gave the indication that things might be less than stellar. My first thought was she knew about Mary. Maybe she was worried about telling me.

"What's wrong? Is everything all right?"

"Yeah. I'm just looking forward to seeing you." A terse silence filled the line. I drove, trying to pluck up my courage and tell her the news.

"You there?"

"I'm here." Before I could settle back into the silence, I plunged right in. "Taden, did you watch the swearing in today?"

I could hear my own thick hesitation. A part of me hoped she'd already figured it all out so I didn't have to be the one to tell her. This time, she became taciturn.

"Taden?"

"Yes. I watched it. I think I know what you're calling about."

Surprise and relief oddly paired together as I realized I didn't have to tell her my secret. "How're you taking it?"

"Initially, not great. The idea is settling in, though. It's not impossible, right? We saved him as a boy so he could have a better future. It appears he has. He's on the political party for the most heroic president we've had in modern history. It seems like we did the world a favor."

She hadn't mentioned Mary yet, and it gave me pause. Maybe she didn't need to know. Almost immediately, I felt guilty again. *Of course* she needed to know. I shouldn't have kept it from her this long. We should've learned by now that secrets between us never served us well in the end.

"Taden, there's more to it."

"What?"

"Okay, so, here's the thing. I'm about to tell you something I haven't really come clean with, but only because I didn't see any reason to cause alarm. Until today, when I saw Marius."

"Are you going to tell me or make me guess?" Taden easily slipped back into the sassy little sister act I had grown accustomed to ignoring whenever she handled her stress this way.

"President Moore. Doesn't she look familiar to you?"

"Oh my God, Ruth, just *tell* me already."

"She's Maria." I let that sink in for a moment. When she didn't respond, I restated it with more emphasis. "Maria! My best friend. Worked with The Reckoning. Made me leave L.A. Is now working with Marius. Maria."

Lingering silence.

"What are we gonna do?" I finally asked, followed with still more silence.

"Abel must already know. This is his department." I heard her shuffle around. "You and I need to stay far away from this. You hear me, Ruth? Do *not* get involved."

"Beyond reporting this information to The Patriots, I have zero intention to contact Mary. I *am* worried for her, though. She's working with Satan himself. Look, she doesn't even know who I am. I'm safe; it's *you* I'm worried about.

Don't you go putting your nosy science self into Marius' business. Take your own advice. Let Abel and his team handle this."

"Same here, sis—I'm not going anywhere near this mess. Like I said, we both stay out of it."

 I'd like to think it was an unlucky coincidence that the big account that landed on my desk a few weeks after my visit with Taden happened to be Mary's inaugural ball. I considered not accepting the event, but it was just too great to pass up. I would tell Taden in person, as soon as I met with President Moore's people and the account was official.

When it came to my career, I learned sometimes it's better to ask for forgiveness afterward than to ask for permission beforehand. I wanted this event, and I wanted to use it as an excuse to see Mary. Taden would know soon enough.

Perhaps, obviously, this made me question the intentions of our universe. I would not be able to keep my promise to Taden. How could I stay far away from Mary and Marius when I was the go-to woman in charge of the biggest day, thus far, of her career? Besides, The Patriots were aware of both Mary and Marius. I was certain they were watching them, which made the situation feel less dangerous.

The formal celebration of President Moore's succession was to be held at the end of the season. The entire planning process was rushed because of the whirlwind President Berthold's assassination dropped our country into.

Despite the rush, Mary wanted to keep with tradition as closely as possible to deliver the promises she had made to the people.

Our first face-to-face was meant to go over her vision for the party and obtain her invitation list. I was actually quite surprised she'd be conducting any of this business with me at all. I had justified accepting the job on the basis that I wouldn't see her much or at all. She had so many important issues to deal with as president, it didn't seem possible we would have many interactions. However, it became clear she wanted as much involvement and input as possible.

I was slated for her first appointment of the day. This meant I didn't have the entire day to psych myself up about sitting down with her like a normal client. All I had time for was my morning routine and the security detail ride to her New York headquarters.

Earlier that week, in an address to the nation, President Moore spoke about the business of her presidency and the upcoming inauguration.

"I am pleased to share with you, the people of this great nation, that I will be launching our fight for equality by beginning my presidency temporarily offsite until after my inauguration. We will be operating from the site where our nation's first president held his inauguration. If we really want to be true to our nation's ideals, we need to start over where our nation began."

Her metaphor led her to Federal Hall in New York City. She welcomed me into her office. As she did so, she rose from the chair at her grand mahogany desk. Standing at her side was Marius. He gave the impression of security detail. He didn't say a word. He didn't even look at me. His eyes were glued to the wall across from him. Throughout the meeting, I found it difficult to keep from glancing at him. It made me nervous to be defenseless in his presence. When I did manage not to be anxiously glancing at him, I was stricken by Mary.

The longer I sat in front of these perfect strangers, reliving vivid memories of each of them, the more my sanity came into question.

"To start, we need to settle on a theme," I said.

"Did you have any ideas?"

"I do, but please don't hesitate to share if you have any. I was thinking something like 'Back to the Beginning'."

"I like that. It references my choices here at Federal Hall and starting at the drawing board to move our nation into equality."

I beamed. She understood the intention of my theme. "If you like that, I was thinking we could have period entertainment—like people in costume dancing and historic food and beverages available during cocktail hour."

President Moore became fully animated at the idea. "I love it. I once read about Washington's procession. I've always wanted to ride in a horse-drawn carriage like that."

"No joke. I have that in my vision board. Look," I said, showing her the photos I had collected of Washington's coach drawn by four horses and accompanied by hundreds of officers. Oddly, the natural ease between us quickly birthed an excited vision of the event.

I guess it made sense in a way, since we had been such good friends for so long. When you know a person it's hard to un-know them, unless they are totally different from time passed on. Yet this experience seemed to prove that, even then, the core of who a person was didn't veer too far from the origin.

This thought triggered another nervous glance over at Marius, who still stood on guard—uninterested, unengaged, and blank.

"Ms. Barrett, I have to tell you, your name came highly recommended from many reputable contacts all over the city. It's not hard to see why. Your ideas are seamlessly classic, and I have every confidence you will have no trouble pulling off this important event in the few short weeks ahead. I am grateful you've taken the job."

"That's very kind of you," I said. "I'll put everything I have into making it your vision of success. Can I just say that I love your temporary move back here to New York? I'm sure a lot of people are probably not very thrilled at the change, but it feels right to me." The honesty in my compliment seemed to surprise her.

"Thank you for saying so, and I really appreciate the sentiment. It will require a lot of traveling between here and D.C. for a few months, but I agree with you. It feels right."

At the conclusion of our meeting, Marius stepped toward me with his hand out to officially embrace mine and thank me for my time. I was admittedly shaken by his sudden participation in the meeting. He surveyed me and returned a placid smile. It was a smile Taden might have melted for, but her enraged, revenge-filled sister wanted to smack it off his face.

She held up her phone. "I know I've got your office number in here, but can I get your personal number so I can text you if I have any ideas?"

Even though she had once been my best friend, in this moment she was the president. And it felt surreal to have the president ask for my phone number.

"Of course. Absolutely." I giggled. I told her my phone number, remembering a time when she was programmed in my own phone.

"It was really great to meet you and get the ball rolling. I'll start making phone calls and booking entertainment and catering." I reached my hand out to shake hers but she stepped in for a side hug. I became flustered and slipped into a goodbye I always used to say to her when I was being silly. "See you later alligator." Mortified, I turned to leave before she could see how embarrassed I was having said that to the president, but her response was uncanny and familiar.

"Bye-bye butterfly." I stopped in my tracks. That's how she always answered me when I would say goodbye to her like that. Then she said, "That was strange." She crinkled up her nose. "I just felt the strongest déjà vu."

"That was hilarious." I shook my head. "I just said 'see you later alligator' to the president and she came back with 'bye-bye butterfly'." Amused, I waved and excused myself from the office.

As I got into the car, I received a text from her. It threw me into nostalgia of a previous life—Maria used to be religious about sending me a text after we would have fun hanging out together. It was an act of love she'd pour into our relationship. I didn't realize how much I had missed it until I was staring at a message from Mary.

I had so much fun meeting you today! I'm elated you're hosting this event for me. I think you're just amazing, and I can't wait to get together again and do some more planning.

She closed it with a waving hand and butterfly emojis. I stared at the text, realizing the significance of our encounter, and thanked the universe for giving her back to me.

Our follow-up meeting was scheduled for the next week. When my brain wasn't consumed with the massive amount of work I needed to accomplish before our next meeting, I couldn't stop thinking about the next time we would get to sit and chat—and wished somehow Marius wouldn't be there.

Having sealed the deal on this event, it was time to let Taden know the exciting new account I had landed. Hopefully, I'd get a chance to do so before she found out from someone else.

CHAPTER 13

TADEN

Ruth walked into my office and instantly saw the photographs Abel sent me, displayed on my laptop. My brows rose in disapproval as I turned the screen to her. She could tell from my judgement that I had kept my promise and hadn't spoken to Marius.

"Okay, I can see you've been updated," she began. "You should know I did keep my word about not seeking her out. She just...landed in my lap. It's my job to plan events, Taden. I can't avoid these meetings."

I looked at her through squinted eyes. "Mmm. I get it." Even though I said so, I didn't particularly understand. "Why do our lives have to be so strange all the time? Seriously, of all the party planning firms and all the planners in New York, how did this come back to you? To us?"

"You're not mad at me, are you?"

"I wouldn't say I'm mad. This just all feels so foreboding."

She sank with relief onto the sleek tufted couch adjacent to me.

"I know. I keep waiting for our lives to settle into something resembling normal, but dang if we aren't crazy-magnets."

Her joke took the edge off the room, which I acknowledged with a small smile.

"So, I'm not going to talk you out of this event?" I asked in a hopeful tone.

"Sorry."

To be sure my message was sent loud and clear, I stretched a sigh out like I was practicing a three-part yoga breath. "I had a feeling. Abel's team is already carefully monitoring Marius. It should be fine. He told me to tell you that he is not asking, but *demanding* you keep him updated with any important details or concerns. Which I support. I don't like this, Ruth."

Before she could begin persuading me this would work out fine, Quinn bustled in. On her way in she gave a short, halfhearted knock on my door without looking up from the device she was busily tapping.

"Hey, Taden? I was just running the numbers in the half-second forward test and you have to see what I..." she looked up to find Ruth sitting across from me. "Oh! I'm so sorry!" She turned two distinct levels of red. "I didn't realize you were here. Am I interrupting? I am. I can tell. I'll come back later." She turned to rush out of the office, fully flustered.

Quinn reminded me of myself when I was starting out. It was painful to watch her squirm.

"No. No. No. You are totally fine," Ruth said, attempting to catch her before she ran off. "I was just telling my sister about my big new client—and twisting her arm to go celebrate with me."

Quinn slowed her rushed exit, turning back with a renewed excitement. "Oh, is it someone famous?"

"As a matter of fact, it is. I'm under contract not to release any names, though. So I can't verify anyone who might be throwing a huge political event this fall."

She waited to see if Quinn would be able to guess to whom she was referring. I happened to know that Quinn was just as enamored with President Moore as I was, so Ruth's clue was a giveaway.

"Honestly? You're hosting the inaugural ball?" She turned to me. "Are you okay with this?"

"So, you already know about the drama?" Ruth asked, unable to hide her surprise.

"I just found out. I don't really know much. I just know enough to know that Marius, the man working on the campaign with President Moore..." She paused, searching for the right words. "...played a painful role in Taden's past."

Ruth nodded, gathering that I hadn't divulged much detail to Quinn yet.

To my surprise Quinn took in a sharp breath, then exhaled and threw herself onto the empty chair next to me.

"You guys, I have to confess something. This is getting too weird, and the longer I refrain from telling you—" Her eyes begged for understanding "—I'm afraid, the more awkward it will become."

There was a pause as she folded her hands on her lap. Ruth and I looked at each other out of the corner of our eyes. What the hell was she about to reveal to us?

"I'm adopted," she blurted out.

Even though she wasn't aware of it, I already knew this detail about Quinn. Regardless, I assumed Ruth's face portrayed the same look of confusion mine did, because Quinn went on to clarify.

"What I mean to say is, I'm adopted *and* I have an older biological brother who I haven't seen in about fifteen years. My brother is Marius Touma. My name used to be Octavia Touma, but my adoptive parents changed it to keep me from being targeted as an immigrant, to protect me from harm or deportation."

I forgot how to blink in the moments following her confession. But she had even more to say.

"I didn't recognize him on the broadcast because I haven't seen him in so long, and we were both just kids when we were split up. But after you watched the swearing in—later, when you opened up to me and Dakotah—you called him Marius, and I put two and two together. He has to be my brother."

She paused, glancing between me and Ruth. Aside from our astonishment neither of us responded, so she took a shaky breath and went on.

"I just can't understand how he did those things to you. My brother took care of me, looked out for me, and genuinely loved me. How could he become the sort of man who murdered a woman he was supposed to love? It was all so overwhelming—please forgive me for not telling you straight out. As soon as I knew I ran to the bathroom to throw up at the thought of it, and then I couldn't figure out how to tell you."

Too often nowadays, reality left me gaping with shock. How could I have unknowingly hired the sister of my murderous lover? I couldn't make this stuff up if I tried. My eyes, still wide, scanned from Ruth's look of slow comprehension to Quinn's worried expression.

It was awfully brave of Quinn to out herself, taking the risk that I would no longer accept her as part of the team. She was beginning to crumble under the weight of her distress. Her chin quivered as warning before the first tear rolled down her cheek. Ruth did what she always did when someone was in need of comfort—she walked over, leaned down to hug her shoulders, and told her exactly what she thought.

"Oh, sweet girl." She sounded just like Dr. P comforting us as kids. "This was a really hard piece of news to reveal. You should feel proud of yourself for facing it head on like you did."

She released all of her built-up grief about her brother and all of her fear that I would reject her through heavy sobs.

"I am really grateful you saved him and gave him a second chance at life, Taden," she choked out through her tears. She sucked in a few gasps of air between her whimpers. "I don't know how you even found the strength to do that. I want to believe he turned out like the brother I knew." Her sobbing ramped up a level. "I want to know him. I'm scared, though. What if he did end up this awful person? What if he tries to hurt you again?"

Both of them looked to me, waiting for an answer.

"What should I do?" Quinn pressed.

I still didn't speak. It was a long few minutes before I did answer.

"It's not your fault. I just need some fresh air to process this."

Her confession caught me off guard. While I did admire her courage, I couldn't avoid the doubt that crept in. What if she was working with Marius somehow? The correlated timing of her hire and his resurgence was too odd. I didn't have a great response with my words, either. She was clearly distraught, and needed an affirmation of acceptance from me. I couldn't give her what she needed, though, because I wasn't sure myself. After all, she *was* his sister.

CHAPTER 14

RUTH

Leading up to my next meeting with President Moore, I found myself studying how to insert conversations that might suggest or reveal our alternate past together. She'd probably end up thinking I was a crazed fan of hers for even hinting that we knew each other in another life, but I couldn't help trying to figure out a way to address it. However, in every conversation I imagined, I couldn't shake the image of Marius standing behind her with his heavy, silent presence.

In our last text exchange, President Moore told me the security detail was trying to limit the number of cars coming into the property, so if I didn't mind they would be sending a driver to pick me up and bring me to our meeting. It seemed a legitimate concern that a president may need to take precautions, especially in the wake of the previous president's assassination.

The car they sent for me idled outside my apartment. I peered through the curtains, scoping out the driver. I wasn't the type of person who blindly entered a situation without feeling confident about what was coming. I always had a watchful concern in my toolbox, but it was definitely sharpened after my experiences surviving The Reckoning. The driver was glancing from his watch to my building. I could tell he was impatiently awaiting my arrival.

Gathering the tablet and bag containing all of my party detail plans from the coffee table, I headed to the car.

I hoisted myself up, climbing into the massive SUV. Once inside, the driver turned his face to greet me and—for the love of all things—it was Marius. How did I not place him when I stood at my window?

Hesitating to close the door and voluntarily shut myself in with him, I asked, "Are you the normal driver?"

He responded, short and frank, "I drive."

I must've been an extreme level of idiot, because I settled into my seat and shut the door like I was being reprimanded for bad behavior. I spent the ride internally yelling at myself for not listening to my instincts. I studied Marius through the rearview mirror, and he looked up at me at least a half-dozen times. It was uncomfortable to say the least, but I didn't look away.

Eventually, he penetrated the tense silence. "Ruth Barrett, right?"

"Yes. And you're Marius Touma?"

"I am. I don't recall introducing myself last time. You must have done your research."

"It's part of my job to know who's who."

"I see."

For the remainder of the ride, a strained quiet filled the vehicle. I looked out the window, purposely avoiding his eyes in hopes he wouldn't invite more conversation. Only a few blocks remained before I would be able to get out of the car unscathed.

He had become restless again, repeatedly looking in the mirror at me, each time followed by clearing his throat. Besides annoying me, it also felt like a signal he might have more to say. My stomach clenched, preparing for his next round of questions.

"You know," he said, narrowing his eyes, "I can't shake the feeling I know you from somewhere."

I kept looking out the window in an attempt to mask the panic growing inside. It never crossed my mind that Marius might recognize me from the night I helped Taden. He was just a teenage boy, but it was absurd for me to dismiss the thought altogether. We were the women who swooped in and rescued him from an untimely death. Of course it was possible our faces would be imprinted in his memory. It probably helped that our faces looked exactly the same as they did then.

My eyes searched the streets for evidence of Abel and his men tailing us. I knew they were somewhere. They had been watching his every move since the swearing-in ceremony. It was the only comfort I could cling to, that they were out there somewhere—hopefully listening to this conversation.

"I don't think we've ever met. I have a common face. People often mistakenly think they know me from somewhere." I forced a polite smile and returned my gaze out the window.

If the drive wasn't uncomfortable enough, being escorted into President Moore's office alongside a brooding Marius was possibly worse. I couldn't shake the feeling he was just waiting for a reason to use excessive physical force to remove me from the premises.

Relieved to be finally sitting across from Mary, my focus shifted away from Marius and his (I have to imagine) ill intentions. I was itching to lay the new foundation with my old friend so our paths would no longer diverge. If we weren't meant to be in each other's lives, fate wouldn't have thrown me this chance meeting for us to reconnect. Wanting to believe in her goodness, I first had to debunk any possibility she could be knowingly working for the bad guy.

Instead of assuming the bodyguard role he played in the last meeting, Marius was seated with us this time. In fact, if I wasn't mistaken, he was sitting unusually close to Mary.

"These are the two caterers I've been in contact with. Both are able to accommodate the rushed deadline and the size of our guest list," I told her. She leaned in to accept one of the bios I'd created. Marius reached for the other and bumped her hand. He withdrew but gently rubbed her arm in the process. It was so subtle, I wasn't sure if I had imagined it. But then, when I brought each caterer into the office so we could taste the sample menu, I caught him feeding her a tart.

Having the distinct memory of Mary's responses to suitors, I easily read the signs—she was pleased with his attention. Each time he would speak directly to her, she'd return his attention all doe-eyed. More than once she shimmied her shoulders in response to a food sample they both enjoyed, and it was getting annoying how she kept pointing out each of his favorites. I was concerned for a few reasons. First and foremost, this didn't relieve me of any doubts as to Mary's integrity. I'd seen firsthand this guy's ability to manipulate a person's moral integrity with the promise of love and affection. In addition, he wasn't Mary's type. She didn't love pompous, arrogant, controlling, self-absorbed people. If she was really into Marius—and I was getting the impression she was—I had to question if this was even still *my* Maria or if she was Marius' Mary.

I briefly excused myself to finalize with the caterer that Mary preferred. When I returned they had their backs to me on the couch in the center of her office, deep in discussion—unaware I'd entered the room.

"We still haven't located his body," Marius said.

"Is that reporter still planning to run with this story?"

"She gave us until the inauguration to dispute her claims."

"No one questioned the closed casket." Mary picked up a truffle still sitting on the table in front of them and slipped it into his mouth. "It still surprises me that this reporter is the only one on the scent. People can be oblivious when they want to be."

I couldn't believe what I was hearing and didn't want to be caught having eavesdropped on this conversation. I ducked back into the hallway, re-entering much more obviously so they wouldn't know I had overheard.

It was only our second meeting, and the sense of warning tiptoed up my spine. This was the kind of detail Abel and Taden expected me to report to them, even though telling them my concerns could sabotage my hopes of friendship with Mary and the biggest event of my career.

Regardless, keeping secrets from Taden never turned out better than if I had just told her the truth. I had agreed to work with Abel and Taden on this, and I had to follow through with my word.

Besides that odd conversation about what I assumed was President Berthold's body, I hadn't seen anything to imply Marius was up to anything nefarious. As far as I could tell, he was acting as President Moore's Chief of Staff. He also seemed to have absorbed the role of her personal body guard ahead of the Secret Service posted outside her office. Neither had shared his official title with me at our introductions, and my observations indicated he's a man of many roles for her.

My inclination to believe him to be shady came from a time now gone. I supposed he deserved the benefit of the doubt. At the very least, *if* Mary had turned down the wrong path following her desire for him, it wasn't too late for her to come back.

CHAPTER 15

TADEN

A heavy pit weighed inside my stomach. My thoughts swirled around saving Marius as a boy. What if he had essentially chosen the same pathway of destruction we'd hoped to save him from? I didn't want to entertain the idea. I wanted to remain naive about the possibility. If I was wrong, this would be my fault.

I risked the safety of hundreds of thousands—if not millions—of people to reconcile killing him. I sat in the chair at my desk and let my head fall back. Staring at the ceiling, mentally replaying memories of him revealing his true, monstrous self to me, I consciously lock-screened the images in the forefront of my mind. Moving forward, I could not be so generous. If he was still a danger he had to be stopped for good, and I needed to be ready to respond appropriately. Lifting my head, still heavy inside, I liberated the breath I was holding, ready to face my sister sitting across from me.

"You feel pretty confident he recognized you?"

"I do," she said. "He asked me point blank if we had met. When I denied the possibility, he stared into my eyes through his mirror. That guy really is creepy. I don't know how you ever dated him. I mean, for a split second I entertained the idea he could read my mind with how deeply he was looking into my eyes." She shivered. "You know I would leave you out of this if I didn't think it was worth reporting."

"It's not exactly my proudest moment, loving him." I felt shame wash over me. Every choice I had made while under the influence of Marius was painted with regret.

It wasn't good if Marius recognized Ruth. If he remembered exactly where he knew her from, it could be even worse. I didn't think she should risk continuing her business arrangement with Mary.

"In addition," she went on. "I've surmised Mary is…maybe dating him. Ugh, it's the worst idea she's ever had. Seriously, Taden, you're the smartest person I know and it was the worst idea *you've* ever had!"

"Oh no," I groaned. "Perfect."

"I'm not exactly excited about the prospect of Mary being part of some terrorist act. I'd almost prefer she *was* being blindsided by him, but I don't have good feelings about them either way. I walked in on them having a weird conversation, I think, about Berthold's dead body. Not much evidence to back up these claims other than my intuition, but I think we should tell Abel just in case I'm right. What do you think?"

"Absolutely. He's kept the tail on them and is still gathering intel, but we can't assume he knows more than you do when you're having these face-to-face sit-downs with them."

"Has he told you anything? What does he know about them?"

"I asked him to leave me out of the extreme details, but you know Abel. He doesn't like keeping me out of the loop. There's not much of a case built up pointing to Marius as trouble."

"Well, that's a relief."

"Abel thinks they're just being extremely careful not to leave any crumbs leading to their demise. Wiped records, that kind of thing. So he's keeping close tabs on both of them."

I had seen enough surveillance photographs of Marius and President Moore over the last month to have gotten the impression they might be romantically involved as well. Ruth's confirmation made it all the more likely. Instead of stirring up even more negative feelings about my past with Marius, I focused on Ruth.

"How are you doing with all of this? I know Mary is still important to you, even though…" I trailed off. Ruth didn't need me to hammer in the loss.

"This is hard. I don't like thinking she's making this huge mistake with Marius intentionally. But I also don't like thinking she's innocent in all of this and walking into danger with blindfolds on."

She didn't need my advice. My sister just needed me to hear her, to understand the pain she was experiencing. So instead of trying to come up with important words to suggest she follow, I simply locked onto her and leaned in.

I did need words, though. And only Ruth knew what they were. Without missing a beat, she gave them to me.

"Taden, listen. However Marius turned out, you made the right decision. He was just a boy, and he deserved a chance to live. You don't need to regret saving a child's life. Don't forget, I was there with you. I made the choice, too. If nothing else, you didn't do it alone."

I blinked heavy tears I had been trying to avoid. Once again I meant to be a source of comfort to Ruth, and she turned around to care for me.

I left the time travel adventures mostly unscathed; the only person I lost was Marius, and clearly that was a blessing. But Ruth lost so many people she loved: Maria, her best friend in the world; Trey, a friend she made in the midst of The Reckoning; and Jade, the woman who took her into her home before she got out of New York. None of them knew Ruth in this timeline, and I knew it must have been difficult for her to miss the people she connected with. It was of some comfort they were alive and well, but for Ruth it was its own kind of lonely torture to know people she loved and wanted in her life were living a life without her, somewhere else.

Swimming in the effects of time travel, I once again felt the overwhelming desire to stop traveling to the past. It pushed all my thoughts into future time travel. I still understood Danika's mission of intervening into the past to prevent the path of Berthold from unfolding, and I knew I didn't have the power to stand in the way of her mission. However, I sat across from my sister and felt the damage that an erased and unwritten past held. My objective had never been so clear. The changes we needed to make would have to be done here, in the present. We needed to get to the future so we could identify what changes to make.

 I was so close I could almost taste the answer, but I couldn't get it to form into a complete thought. I was sure part of the puzzle I needed was embedded in genetic lengthening, the process my team

used to add to my timeline and bring me back from the past before Marius had strangled me. The key to the future was somewhere in Ruth's DNA, and how it was able to pull me through the missing time my death left.

If I could just unravel this last piece, I would finally figure out how to travel into the future. I was confident the way the molecules moved within the serum relative to molecular movement within a person was what I needed to manipulate. The serum used to return home was slightly different from the serum used to go backward. The theory pinpointed the molecular movement used to return home from a time travel along with the DNA extension, which led me to recall the serum mixture I was working on for The Reckoners, in the past, at their lab in the mental institution. I had purposely altered the serum for a return travel home. That mission would essentially appear to fail, therefore making it an excellent stalling tactic. Funnily enough, that stalling tactic just might have been the missing ingredient.

A sudden flashback rushed my memory; hiding my notes in a ceiling tile above my workspace in the lab while Marius left to use the restroom.

It occurred to me that since those events happened in the past, I might be able to go back to the institution in the present, get into the lab, lift the ceiling tile, and find the notes I recorded still there.

A quick search online revealed the institution had been vacant for about fifteen years after closing its doors as a state mental institution. I knew better: the mental institution was a front for terrorist activity. With the terrorists killed, its facade of caring for mentally unstable individuals folded. I stumbled upon several videos of teenagers visiting the facility illegally to get wasted with their friends. Smirking at their carousing, I skimmed through a few videos to view the layout of the facility while mentally debating whether or not I should include Ruth or Abel in this adventure. Technically, neither of them could get too upset with me if I didn't. It's not like Marius could possibly be a danger to me there. He had no memory of that timeline, and so this place meant nothing to him. The most danger that could possibly await me would be some teenage boy trying to make a pass at me while stoned on LSD or something, and I knew how to take care of myself as far as that sort of danger was concerned. Looking at my schedule and considering when the least number of unwanted drunk kids would be there, I planned to head down to the institution early the following week on a school night.

CHAPTER 16

ABEL

There was no way I would ever agree to use Taden as bait. The Patriots were completely out of their minds if they thought for one second I would approve of their plan.

"What did you find in his computer history?" Mr. Richardson asked me.

"His web browsing shows he has done an in-depth search of Ruth. He definitely believes he knows her from somewhere. He was able to track down her hometown in Maryland."

"The shack he stayed in with The Reckoners was there," Mr. Richardson reminded.

"Yes. I think it's a leap to assume he's logically made the connection just from his web browser, but it's too risky to ignore."

"Agreed," he responded.

"I do have another lead, sir."

"I'm listening."

"Can I request that this remain confidential between the two of us, until I have something more definitive to go on?"

"Permitted," he said.

"Based on a conversation Ruth overheard between Mr. Touma and President Moore, I believe we have our first lead that they were working for Berthold."

"Continue your investigation, Dr. Mihal. But it's time to question Mr. Touma. Since we don't have anything concrete yet, lure him to us."

"Sir?"

"Let him see Dr. Barrett. He's already curious about Ruth. If he gets eyes on both of them, he'll need answers. Leverage, Dr. Mihal."

"I can't ask her to do that, sir."

"It's not your call. All we have to go on is that he Google-searched Ruth Barrett and has never even gotten a minor infraction. To be sure, everything about him feels suspicious, but nothing has backed these feelings up. We can set this trap and see what we catch. Beyond that, we've got to leave the man alone."

Marius was smart enough to link Taden's and Ruth's reappearance with the timing of his participation in what was possibly the biggest terrorist move our country had ever seen: Moore's presidency. I fully agreed they were right: Taden would almost certainly pull Marius' intentions into the light. However, I wasn't going to let Taden become his prey. Not again.

She sat across the table from me, listening to her leaders plan her downfall. She showed no signs of refusal, but her eyes were brimming and her fingers fumbled. Taden was going to agree to this plan. I could see it all over her face. She was going scared, but she was going.

"There is no way," I said. "I will not lead this mission. It is wholly unacceptable. We have taken enough from Dr. Barrett and her family. We cannot compromise her safety again."

Danika blinked slowly at me in a dare to challenge her leadership. When I didn't back down from my stance, she stared me down hard.

"No, Danika," I stressed. "I will not be a part of this."

"I want you to think for a moment, Dr. Mihal, because I am not asking for your permission. Once Dr. Barrett agrees, this mission will move forward with or without you. If you don't take the lead on this mission, you'll have to risk someone else—your new associate, Lt. Duncan, perhaps. He would successfully protect Dr. Barrett in your place, should you refuse, but do you really want to rely on someone else to guarantee her safety?"

I looked at Taden. Her face was unreadable. "You don't have to do this," I told her. "You've done enough already. Enough to last your whole lifetime. You do not have to do this. Please don't do this." Tears streamed down her cheeks, but she didn't falter. *Damn her. Why did she always have to be so headstrong?* I looked back to Danika. "Fine. I'll take the lead. I need a minute here."

Pushing my chair out, I escaped the room before my emotions got the best of me in front of every person I was charged to command. I needed to punch something, and since Marius wasn't in the vicinity I found myself in the workout room banging my hate out on a punching bag.

Taden knew where to find me, and it wasn't long before she had. I didn't even realize she was there until her hand was on my shoulder, causing me to still myself. I lived for the feeling of her touch and the heat that passed from her to me. My arms dropped to my sides and I turned around to face her. She put her hands on mine.

"Thank you for protecting me. Thank you for loving me, too." Then she placed my hands on the small of her back and released hers to reach up and hook behind my neck. We stood there for several moments, looking into each other's eyes, comfortable just to stay in the moment. Her tears returned and invited mine to join. The only thing I could see was us. Not wanting any space between us, I pulled her to my body and pressed my mouth to hers.

I would do anything to keep her safe and feel her warmth. That man would not ever hurt her again, not as long as I had life in me.

 Before long, the plan was in action. First, Ruth discussed the addition of her "assistant", who would be attending their next meeting with her so she could begin delegating the mountain of work. The inclusion of an assistant created the perfect role for Taden to adopt in order to set The Patriots' trap for Marius. The hope was that Marius would see the sisters together, fully realize who they were, and act on his initial impulse to know why they were back in his life.

I might not have had a say about Taden being the decoy, but I absolutely refused to allow this meeting to take place on *their* turf. The only way to secure the safety of Taden and Ruth was if I could control the setting. As ridiculous as it might have seemed, the president would have to agree to come to Ruth's office this time around. It was necessary to plant my team throughout the building ahead of time, and I could have multiple viewpoints on Marius every second of the meeting. It was easy enough to come up with an excuse for the switch of meeting location. Ruth suggested all of her materials were in her office and would be cumbersome to lug across town. She told us Mary seemed to have no problem with the location change and was looking forward to seeing her workspace. I wondered if Marius bought the story with the same ease as his counterpart.

My team was in place and ready much earlier than necessary. I didn't want one detail overlooked. There was to be no chance they might arrive earlier than planned and we would be unprepared. With the surplus of time I remained ready and waiting for his arrival, testing and retesting all the microphones and cameras. In the initial moments of his arrival, as he walked into Ruth's office, I felt an itch in my trigger finger. More than anything, I wanted to remove the threat he represented. He walked with arrogance into her office and my attention turned to the many monitors arranged to view him. My throat was already dry, sweat gathering along the base of my neck.

His eyes skated across Taden's face, and then danced over to Ruth's before landing back on Taden. On the night of her murder, Taden shared with me how she had dinner with teenage Marius and had tried to convince him to take a different path in life. Here in Ruth's office, as he registered her face, he had to be replaying that conversation with her in his head. He looked ill, like he had just seen a dead relative. I tensed, preparing to launch an assault if he took even one step in her direction. I couldn't bring myself to break away from him to observe how Taden was responding. My job was clear: do not let Marius near Taden.

Even though Marius looked obviously suspicious, he did not become defensive in any way. Instead, he flashed his famous smile and carried on with the meeting as if nothing was out of the ordinary. I knew him better than that, though. He was plotting. One room over I was plotting, too.

CHAPTER 17

TADEN

Every thought in my mind and all my muscle control was focused on playing it calm and nonchalant in front of Marius. It was difficult to pay attention to what transpired during the meeting, because my brain was hyper-focused. The length of time I allowed myself to view his face couldn't be too long and I had to use the exact smile I prepared ahead of time to convey how normal the interaction was, all while quelling my nervous laugh and simply staying calm. It exhausted me on a level I had not exercised in a long time.

I felt him investigating me with his eyes and sensed the tension pushing from his frame. I recognized the telltale signs of his defensive posture. My own body language was aimed toward my sister and Mary and this ridiculous party they were planning.

At the conclusion of the meeting, Marius rose from his seat rather quickly and stepped to open the door for Mary. He told the two agents outside the door to see her to the car. She asked if he wasn't coming with her.

"Madam President, go on ahead with your security detail," he said. "I have a few safety protocol guidelines I would like to run through with the ladies here. I'll be on my way afterward."

Ruth and I glanced at each other with wide eyes before quickly replacing our stunned responses with simple smiles. He smoothly returned to the couch across from us and sat down, crossing his legs. Marius looked past our faces at the door until it closed behind us. Then he moved his glassy stare to focus on our faces, placidly waiting for one of us to speak.

When neither of us filled the space of his intended silence, he said to Ruth, "I was sure I knew you from somewhere the other day when I picked you up, but you convinced me we had never met." He then turned his focus to me. "I am one hundred percent sure I know *you*. I can remember in vivid detail every word of our encounter. We spoke over dinner, half a lifetime ago." Marius ran his hands down his thighs until they reached his knees. "I know both of you. *You* are the women who took me from that house. Everyone else was killed that night, but you helped me escape to a refugee home. I'm alive right now because of you."

He looked back up at us, studying our responses. Neither of us broke our silence. I didn't look over to Ruth to see her face, but I kept mine as solemn as I could manage.

He couldn't leave the air empty of words. "I don't for a minute believe you are party planners. I would really like an explanation as to why you have not aged a day in fifteen years, but that can wait. What is more important is that you *will* tell me who you are and what you are doing here, and you will tell me right now."

I sensed Ruth turning her head to me. We'd planned for this. After all, I was the bait. He took it hook, line, and sinker. Ruth folded her hands in her lap and smirked, as if the game had been won.

"Marius." I offered him a warm, comforting smile, one a guardian angel might offer in time of need. Essentially, I *had* served as his guardian angel when he was a boy, and here I was again, in a precarious season of his life. "You do know me, and you are correct. I was there that night fifteen years ago. My job then is still my job today. I was placed in your life to protect you from danger." I paused for dramatic effect, noticing my courage increasing. "You are once again in danger, Marius, and I'm here to look after you as I did that night long ago." Reaching into my purse, I pulled out my phone and pinged his with a location. His body twitched just barely enough to register his phone buzzing in response to my ping. I followed the outline Abel had laid out for me, "I have sent a location to your phone. I'll be there tomorrow at midnight. If you want answers to your questions, come alone. I'll have questions for you, too."

I nodded at Ruth and we both stood, conveying to Marius this was the conclusion of our business. He looked rather shaken and slightly confused, but followed our lead out the door. He pulled out his phone and glanced down at it before leaving and releasing me from this encounter—my living terror. Ruth slammed the door closed behind him and pulled me into a hug. We held on to each other, knowing the hard part hadn't even come yet.

CHAPTER 18

ABEL

More than once, I could feel the tension in Taden's voice indicating her fear. Involuntarily, my mind revisited the image of his hands around her neck, squeezing out the last bit of life. My body remained in stealth mode, ready to engage if necessary. I couldn't fight the urge to be in the room with them much longer.

I've never been a huge fan of drinking, but I felt the need for a stiff drink right then. I needed to settle my nerves in order to not explode this thing in our faces. The second he was out of the building and the risk of blowing our cover had passed, I wasted no time getting to her.

"You okay?" I looked back and forth between Taden and Ruth, waiting for any reason to justify taking Marius out of existence. The sight of Taden, clearly shaken, pushed aside my instinct to hunt down Marius, replacing it with the reflex to comfort her. I put my arms around Taden and she accepted by burying her head into my chest. The sensation swelled through me, feeling as if it would burst through my veins. How did such an ache come with so much pleasure?

She pulled back enough to look up at me. "I didn't expect to be so afraid. I'm not sure what I thought I would feel. Maybe pity for the boy I saved, but that boy is long gone. This man could be capable of anything. I didn't really grasp that until seeing him in person."

"I've said it repeatedly—you don't have to go through with this, Taden," I reminded her. "You've done more than enough here. We can set the rest of the trap without you. All he has to do now is show up."

"No. I can do this. If I stay involved, it will go so much more smoothly. On the off-chance he did choose a better path of life, me being involved allows him the opportunity to prove his redemption."

"I know you like to face your demons head-on. But he may actually be dangerous. Especially if he becomes unhinged."

"He might've deceived me before, but with the distance I've gained I think I know him better than anyone. I can read him. My insight has got to be valuable during this meeting."

She wouldn't risk his safety, even still.

"I hate to break this up, but uh, what's the plan for tomorrow?" Ruth stuck her face in between the two of us, looking back and forth for answers. She had a tendency to want to lighten the mood whenever things seemed too tense. One of Ruth's many "hostess with the mostest" habits.

"Right. Tomorrow. Well." I sighed heavily. "If Taden insists on following through with this plan, she will be waiting for him at the location. We will be ready to intervene as soon as Marius is in position and boxed in. Taden will then be lifted from the scene and we will take over the interrogation from there."

"I'm not staying?" She looked at me with indignation.

"Correct. You are absolutely *not* staying. Do I really need to explain why?"

This immediately pissed her off. She pulled back from me and turned her face toward Ruth, nonverbally requesting her support.

"Oh! Sorry, sis. I'm with Captain America on this one." She wagged her index finger in my direction, indicating Taden had lost this tag-team effort.

"So, I am literally just the bait here?" she asked incredulously.

"I'm not sure why you thought otherwise. This was the plan from the beginning. Let him see you. Get him to sniff. Offer him a meet-up later. What'd you think you were going to do?"

"Right. I heard the entire plan. But it doesn't account for my ability to question him and read him. If you want the truth out of Marius Touma, I'm the best chance we've got."

"And I'm trying to tell you that your safety is not worth the risk of even having you there tomorrow, never mind anything else. He will show, regardless. We just have to be ready for him."

"What if he comes, realizes I'm not there, doesn't fall for the empty trap, and then you lose him?"

"We won't lose him," I said with certainty.

"What if you do, though?"

Her persistence drilled into my steadfast fear of her safety. I felt sure we wouldn't lose him, but I had to worry about Taden; whether or not she decided to follow through with The Patriots' plan. Still, I felt vastly more comfortable with the plan if we counted Taden out.

"The hours that would involve you waiting around for him to show like a sitting duck, you could be at the lab working on getting us into the future." She pursed her lips and narrowed her eyes at me. "You know I'm right. Your time is much better spent there."

"So if I decide to continue with the plan, you won't let me attempt to talk to him? I'll simply be the bait? Then I have to leave?"

"That's the plan." I could tell she was annoyed about the role she was to play, and I wanted to exploit her frustration to the fullest potential—hoping to lean her toward not participating.

"You do have a point," she said, beginning to waver. "I am wasting an entire night's work if I carry through with this plan."

She was thinking about backing out. I had to say something to seal the deal.

"Right. What if tonight is the night you get the inspiration you need to crack the code of getting into the future, and you miss it by choosing to play the role of an easy target?"

"I have to listen to my gut. It's the only way I ever make the right decision."

I really hoped her gut was in line with my need to have her not take any unnecessary risks with Marius Touma.

Ruth had already walked away to her mounting workload, but she interjected from across the room, "My gut says you should be at work, Taden. Besides, we already promised each other to stay out of their lives whenever possible. Here's your 'whenever possible'. Just go to work and be a genius, already. Abel's got this without you. Seems pretty logical to me. And obvious. But what do I know? I'm planning a party for my other-life best friend."

Taden huffed at her sister. "Fine. I'll go to work. I'm sure Quinn would prefer me being with her at the lab instead of gallivanting around, trying to set up her brother."

Relief flooded through me, giving way for easy breathing. She actually agreed to back out of this insane plan. Placing a kiss on her forehead, I managed to say, "Thank you," before ordering, "Now get on a plane to Maryland and get back to work so I can stop worrying about your safety."

Taden scrunched up her face at my obvious delight in her decision. "I hope Danika is all right with me backing out."

"Danika will be fine. She'll just be pleased you are getting her the technology she wants. Marius is insignificant to Danika. Now go." Once Taden got involved in her world of science, it was next to impossible to tear her away from it. I was banking on that.

CHAPTER 19

TADEN

Driving away from Ruth's office, I noted the calm that had taken over where a Marius-caused anxiety had been growing. It was the confirmation I needed that I had made the right decision. The clarity also allowed me to think about Quinn for the first time since she dropped the bomb that Marius was her brother.

That's the effect he had on me. I came face to face with him, and everything else became a blur. It was unsettling that he could still control my emotions like he had. This was different, though. This time it was a fear-based response, not one of love. At least I could hold on to some pride that I wasn't blinded by love a second time.

Quinn had expected to work alone with Dakotah all night, and I was pretty certain she was still uneasy about my feelings toward her, but I'd been contemplating her confession. Marius had blinded me with his charm. Why couldn't she be capable of the same? This question settled in my being until I finally became certain of the answer. She wasn't the same. She was genuine. Somewhere deep within myself, I knew Marius wasn't. I had ignored all of the red flags I had with him. Examining each of the interactions I had with Quinn, the warnings signs didn't exist. She was who she said she was.

It was time for me to be a friend and give her the words she needed. Finding her long-lost brother only to realize his corruption had to be traumatizing.

At the lab Dakotah was back in the memory analysis room, sifting through Abel's catalogue for inconsistencies. I poked my head inside the doorway. "Hey. How's it going?"

She was surprised to see me. "I thought you were playing a game of bait and switch tonight."

"Eh. I changed my mind. Decided to hang here tonight instead."

She nodded with approval. "Much better plan. I'm glad Abel talked some sense into you."

"I talked *myself* into some sense," I said, acting offended.

Dakotah looked up from the corner of her eyes as she scanned her computer screen. "Mmm-hmm. I bet you did."

"What, you can't believe I would walk away from the chance to spend a fun night out with my murderous ex-boyfriend?" My self-deprecation made her smile.

"Girl, I'm just happy you're here. We have a lot of work to do, and Quinn is running around like a chicken with her head cut off."

"How does she seem? I mean other than work-stressed?"

"To be honest, she's worried. Afraid you probably hate her. Afraid her brother hates you. You know, all the things." She looked up from her work to fully make eye contact, and in a stern, motherly voice suggested, "You should talk to her."

"Yeah." I paused, thinking about the awful conversation looming. "I'm just going to go work on some time travel first. I'll deal with my other mess later."

She smirked at me, knowing full well that I would continue to avoid the Quinn conversation as long as I could.

Turning the corner from Dakotah's work room I caught Quinn scurrying about the lab, fully engrossed in her work. I stood in the hallway, watching her for a few seconds before joining her in what appeared to be an exceptional way to spend my evening.

She already felt like family to me. I could anticipate her next move just by observing her. She was worth all of this. I felt peace about Marius for the first time since I took his life. In that moment, I was able to move forward without regret.

"Hey, there. Mind if I join you tonight?" She looked up from her calculations, startled by my unannounced entrance.

"My goodness, you scared me. I was so focused—I thought you weren't going to be here tonight?"

"I wasn't going to be, but I decided we have too much to do here for me to be playing hooky. What kind of an example would I be if I left the newbie all alone to do everything?"

I was trying to be funny. It sounded a lot more funny in my head. As I was saying it, it sounded dumb. She laughed anyway. It was generous of her.

"Quinn." My tone changed to a much more sincere effort. She stopped working and looked directly at me. "I want you to know I'm glad you found your brother. And I'm also heartbroken for you that he turned out to be…not who you remembered him to be. And you should also know I am elated to have you on our team. I feel responsible for saving Marius, and in turn saving you. If I could go back and do it all over again I would, because ultimately it's what led to you being right here, right now. I have your back."

She kept her eyes trained on me with every word I said to her. They were filled with tears by the time I finished. "Thank you for telling me all of this. I needed to hear those words more than you could imagine."

"Okay," I said, clapping my hands together. "We have work to do. Let's get the show on the road." Dakotah would have been so proud of my mature conversation with Quinn.

Wiping her eyes, she updated me on what she was auditing from earlier. "Do you see this calculation from the half-second interval data on our forward stops? I noticed them the other day when I walked in on you and Ruth, but then I obviously got distracted." She turned red again at the memory. "Anyway, I've been running repeated tests and keep getting this wonky response. What do you think?"

She showed me her tablet. I reviewed her simulations and the paired data results. On the fringe of an answer, my mind leapt back to notes hidden away at the asylum laboratory.

"Oh!" The exclamation jumped out of my mouth like a power switch.

"What? Did you find something in the data?"

"No, but I have an idea. I know I just got here, but I have to go. I might have the answer we need to solve this."

I grabbed my jacket and keys and made my way to the exit.

"Where are you going?"

"I need to grab my notes and I'll be back."

She grinned at me, understanding the compulsion that drives a scientific breakthrough in one's mind.

"See you in a few, then. Can't wait to see what you've got."

CHAPTER 20

TADEN

I peered through my windshield at the abandoned, menacing premises.

"Well, I'm here now. Follow through, Taden." I opened the car door and officially started my journey back to the abandoned mental hospital. Each step made an echoed crunch. My boldness increased with my mind's narrative that no other people could be here without making noise of some kind, which allowed me to refocus on getting inside to retrieve my notes.

Every door and window tested was locked, leaving me without the easy entrance I had counted on. Over the years of isolation, a few windows had been shattered. After a quick assessment it appeared they might be safe enough to climb through, but I would be taking a chance. I really didn't want to slice my leg open on a surprise shard of glass. I decided it was too dark to take that kind of risk.

Looking over the deserted building was more painful than I had anticipated. Marius had strapped me to a bed inside one of those rooms. Inhaling the fresh chilled air, I let my entire body feel those difficult moments before releasing them to the grounds of this place to hold on to.

Walking toward the back of the institution, I searched for the underground tunnels I had recalled a few teens stalking around in on some of the online videos. In the videos, it looked like the tunnels would be an easier entrance into the main building. I clutched my phone with its flashlight on and a can of Mace. Thanks to Abel, my self-defense skills had been polished to a higher level than I probably realized. I actually had to remind myself that if I did encounter drunk teenagers, I'd have to be careful not to hurt *them*.

A barren field of weeds and litter led me to a narrow path stretching into an overgrown grove of trees, guiding the way across a small, crumbling bridge. With some hesitation I went over the bridge, under which a long-forgotten stream of water quietly ran toward the river. Claiming the territory, branches hung low, forcing me to bow for passage.

Blood pushed its way through my veins, kickstarted from the adrenaline charging within me. I hadn't felt this alive since my last time travel. I missed the excitement. I missed having something to look forward to.

The conscious decision I made to not tell my sister or Abel about this visit to the asylum was so I might have this experience—these exhilarating spaces of time. The excitement surging within forced me to acknowledge what I had been ignoring: that I was tired of being treated as if I was fragile. I was sick of my quietly planned and cautiously monitored existence. I came here looking for something, but I wondered if my notes were really the trophy I sought.

However, not expecting the entrance of the tunnels to present as quite so creepy and formidable, I momentarily doubted my courage. Before trepidation could writhe into my thoughts, I reminded myself what I was capable of. Inching forward a few steps at a time, listening to each sound the night gave birth to, I found myself inside the dark cement tunnel.

The next level of adrenaline punched through my body. My controlled breaths echoed through the underground passageway.

Remnants of parties long ago were strewn along the sides of the tunnel, leaving a pathway just wide enough to walk through (with the occasional pile to hop over). Up ahead, I spotted what appeared to be a person, hunched over—sleeping. The nerve required to continue forward was almost more than I could summon. Tensely tiptoeing past the sleeping man was the pinnacle of stress when it came to my tunnel journey.

Once inside, I traversed up and down hallways and stairwells to different levels until finally I reached the floor holding the laboratory Marius had brought me to. The room looked how I remembered it, except for the fact that every removable object had long since been taken.

My eyes fell upon the exact spot where Vergard ran his icy fingers through my hair. I recounted how, to counteract the terror he intended to instill, I busied myself with mixing the serum, regulating my breathing with a concerted effort. I did not want to give him the satisfaction of sensing my fear.

Marius had returned at a moment when the interaction with Vergard might have turned into something I couldn't ignore. His return ended the private dread Vergard seemingly wished to cause. I remember the relief washing over me as Marius slammed my cup of coffee onto the counter in front of me, rescuing me from the grips of his evil boss.

Everything about Marius felt confusing, especially how he felt like safety to me one moment then suddenly like peril the next. Ultimately, I couldn't be decisive about my thoughts related to him, and it left me bewildered.

Lost in reminiscing, a noise from outside the lab snapped me back to reality. I wasn't sure what it was, and I didn't want to miss my opportunity to get the formula. Moving quickly, I rushed over to the ceiling tile I had shoved my notes behind so many years before. On my tiptoes, I slid it aside. Mounds of dust fell onto my upturned face, getting into my eyes, causing me to involuntarily curse through bouts of sneezing. Blinking rapidly, I tried my best to stay quiet on the off chance someone or something was out there.

I had no desire to meet anything or anyone alone in this daunting place. I stretched my arm up into the ceiling, feeling around through the layers of filth for my cobweb-covered notebook. Found it! I pulled it to my chest with satisfaction. I didn't even bother to put the tile back into place before heading in the direction of the tunnels. I considered trying to exit the institution through the main doors, but with the possibility that another living thing might be in the building with me I didn't want to take any chances.

Briskly walking down the hallway, I came upon a massive staircase with a wide bannister leading to the next floor up. Although I was in a hurry to leave I couldn't help but marvel at the expansive, undisturbed beauty. Looking up at its immensity, I caught a flicker of light out of the corner of my eye. I turned my head to get a better look, but saw nothing. As if the shake of my head could dismiss what I saw, I decided I had just imagined it. Forgetting to remain calm, my brain conveniently replayed scenes from horror movies I had filed away for a moment such as this. Motivated by what I might be dealing with if I stayed any longer, I sped up my getaway plan.

Gripping the notebook to my chest in one hand, I pointed my phone's light on the path out with the other. Entering through the cement blocks of the tunnels, I immediately dreaded the travel past the sleeping man I came upon on the way in. I hoped maybe he had woken up, and that it was he I'd heard in the building.

I took one last look over my shoulder before I left, and saw someone. My body responded before my brain registered its input. Every muscle felt rigid and tense, and my eyes widened. I looked directly at him, but he disappeared into the dark before my thoughts could catch up. Instinctively, I ran through the tunnels to escape.

What was Marius doing here?

This could not be a coincidence. I knew better than to stick around and find out Marius' intentions for me.

Almost to the end of the tunnel, I allowed a small feeling of relief to expand with the opening that was becoming visible off in the distance, but it was preemptive. An increasing sound of rapid footsteps trotted toward me from outside, accompanied by an approaching shadow from the tunnel's exit. I couldn't imagine how I would make it out of the tunnel and to the bridge before Marius, or whoever was out there, got to me. Instead, I doubled back and turned down an alternate tunnel veering to my right.

Tiny hairs stood at attention as thousands of goosebumps dotted my skin, alerting my sense of fight or flight to be ready for action. Running along the walls of the second tunnel were phrases that appeared to be in Latin. They reminded me of something cult-like, or ritualistic. The words were written in what I assumed to be blood. It occurred to me that my chances of survival might have been better off attempting to outrun whoever was after me in the previous tunnel, but it was too late.

I didn't have time to reconsider and turn around again. I had to push forward and hope this secondary tunnel led to a safe exit. Training my light on the walls, I saw the entire underpass was lined with the same terrifying graffiti. I convinced myself it was only spray paint used by some bored teenagers.

I slowed when I came across a small wooden table covered in a piece of leather hide. It displayed a large, chemically weathered copper chalice which held a murky, dark liquid. Next to the chalice lay a small, dead animal. Maybe a rabbit or a squirrel. I didn't stick around long enough to really investigate which. The looming face-to-face with Marius seemed less daunting than a possible meet and greet with whoever was responsible for this unsettling, ceremonial set-up.

Finally, the tunnel ended. The exit spilled open into a cemetery, and I tried my hardest not to believe it represented my symbolic outcome. Closing my eyes I shook my head with disdain, wondering if I could ever possibly exist in a timeline when I didn't feel the need to put myself in life-threatening scenarios.

Surrounded by badly weathered gravestones, I stilled my breathing as much as I could then assessed the area. I couldn't hear or see any evidence of my stalker having followed me, so I proceeded toward the front of the hospital grounds with caution. Each dark and deafening step through the graveyard reminded me I should have told Ruth about this. I should have told Abel. After each succession of three or four steps, I stopped to re-survey the area before continuing on again. Approaching the center of the plot, flanked with dead souls, I caught movement in my peripheral vision. Assuming a defensive stance I maniacally examined the cemetery in an attempt to identify the disturbance, but nothing came of it.

My stride increased the closer I came to the parking lot. My car was at last in sight.

I let go of the breath I had been holding, along with the mounting tension that kept it company. Simultaneously, I yanked on the door handle of my car and felt a cold, sharp slice of metal press against my throat. Releasing the handle I pulled my head back, away from the knife jabbed into me and toward the man holding it there. His free hand wrapped around my waist, followed by a heavy whisper in my ear.

"This time, I'm going to ask the questions."

Marius' voice was undeniable. I attempted to turn my body to face him, but halted as a stinging blow hit my head and filtered down my weakening legs. Attempting to remain steady on my feet, my vision blurred. As I tried to focus on his beady eyes, darkness took hold of me.

CHAPTER 21

ABEL

Looking out from the third floor of the office building, my satisfaction at having successfully removed Taden from this stupid plan to lure Marius was fleeting. To compound the intensity of waiting for Marius to show, we had spent almost the entire day preparing our strategy and setting up the perimeter so he would have no way to escape, even from a drive-up into the lot.

"You've cleared every floor?"

"All clear, sir," the soldier reported.

"I need eyes on—there," I directed, pointing to the neighboring structure.

Complying he spoke into his two-way radio, dispatching my order as he moved to his post on the floor above our office facade.

I expected Marius to arrive early in an attempt to thwart any subversive plans he might walk into. In response to my prediction, we set our trap in motion much earlier. When he didn't appear in the early hours I'd expected, I was disappointed—but when he didn't show as the agreed-upon hour approached concern took over.

"What's your twenty?" I asked into my transceiver.

"Fourth floor, sir."

"Anything to report?"

"Negative."

Each follow-up thereafter resulted with the same fruitless outcome. I paced, muttering, "*Where is he?*" until I eventually texted Taden to calm my nerves. She didn't respond, but it wasn't too unusual. After all, she was in another state entirely, at work and engrossed in what she was doing. Another fifteen minutes of idle time passed with no Marius or response from Taden. Calling her would ease my mind, but there was no answer. Still, I considered this wasn't too abnormal. Each assuring thought I conjured was only second to the more niggling idea that Marius was not actually going to show.

Accepting that we had been stood up led me to fear he was a no-show because he'd found Taden somewhere else instead.

"I'm on the move. Take lead."

"Ten-four."

Running up a mountain of stairs to the helipad, I called Dakotah.

"Does no one answer their phone?" I grumbled, throwing my cell onto the passenger seat of the helicopter.

On my way back to Maryland, I directed Lt. Duncan to assemble our remaining team. Before I could feed the desire to destroy Marius, I had to find Taden. Leaping from the landed copter, I ran down the NIST's rooftop staircase.

Exasperated, I stormed into the lab. "Taden?" Peering down the hallway and jogging toward her office, I continued yelling her name.

Quinn approached me with concern. "What's going on? Is everything all right?"

"Where's Taden?"

"She left a little bit ago. Said she had some notes she needed for what we were working on. She told me she would be right back."

"How long ago was that?"

"More than an hour. I was just about to call her and make sure she was okay."

"She went to her apartment, then?"

"I think so. She didn't really say, but I assumed that's where she was going. What's going on?"

"I'm not sure yet. Listen, if she calls you or if she comes back here, have her contact me right away."

"I will," she promised, wide-eyed and earnest.

On my way out of the lab I ran into Dakotah, who rushed to me with worry flooding her normally composed presentation. She didn't even have to ask me to know Taden was in danger.

"I'll have Quinn fill me in. You go. I'll handle things here," she assured me.

In those seconds, I was grateful for the history we had built at this place. A clear-headed moderator was needed, and I could count on Dakotah to take the reins.

I fled to my car, still parked at the lab from our departure earlier in the day. Furiously I tapped at my phone screen, pinging Taden's cell. So much time was wasted not checking her location as soon as I left New York, but I was sure I would find her at the lab.

A chill ran down my spine as I stared at the signal. It was blinking on the location of the abandoned hospital. Marius had held her captive there in the previous timeline. Swallowing the heaviness that came with knowing he took her there again, I got into my car and sped across town to find her.

Her car was there in the parking lot, and I spotted her cell phone on the ground next to it. I bent down to retrieve it and noticed an old notebook sticking out from underneath her driver's side. Looking around for signs of a struggle, there was nothing else notable. Filled with concern, I alerted Lt. Duncan and my remaining crew of our rendezvous point.

A building of that size was going to require a full and thorough search. I hunched down, peering through her car windows, taking inventory of what had been left behind. In the console were her sunglasses (I had a memory of her putting those on and pursing her lips, raising her chin as if she were a movie star in disguise). Next to the sunglasses, an open pack of spearmint gum. My chest hurt at the everyday items she left behind, not doubting she'd return to them. Her laptop sat on the passenger seat, and even her purse was still inside. She wouldn't have left all of this out in the open in an unlocked car, which meant she didn't intend to leave any of this behind.

If I hadn't had such tunnel vision related to my Marius subterfuge, I would've entertained Taden's doubts that he might not show. I would've made sure someone was with her, preventing this very situation. I couldn't wait any longer for my team to arrive. If she was inside with him, time could be the only thing that might save her. I had been too late before, and I'd be damned if I was too late for her again. Running to the nearest window, I picked up a sizable rock and threw it with the intention of busting as much of the remaining glass as possible. After swiping my gun across the shards left from the shatter, I leapt through. A piece stuck into my forearm, and it reminded me of what pain he might be inflicting upon her.

The first locations I searched were the rooms near her last stay in this godforsaken place. After I checked every room on the floor, I heard some bustle from below. It was my team arriving. "Up here, third floor," I yelled down the main stairwell.

"Roger that." Lt Duncan sent some soldiers around the perimeter of the building and the remaining followed him up the stairs to meet me. Together we ascended, heading in the direction of the lab.

I wanted her to be in the lab more than anything. If she was on the other side of the door, this could be over and she would be safe. If she wasn't there... I couldn't even entertain the idea. Standing outside the door to the lab, I took a deep breath before we busted through.

The room was completely barren. Furniture removed, ceiling tiles disturbed. Still, we entered and searched every corner. I fell against the counter and stared up at the ceiling. Like the tile that had been removed, debris fallen to the floor, I felt gutted.

"No one's here. Comb the rest of the building. Contact me if you find anything. *Anything*. Got it?"

"Loud and clear."

"I'm going to Taden's place to look for any sign of her. I'll let you know if I get another lead."

I knew this feeling. The loss of Taden. Her absence from sharing the same air with me. But this time it wasn't the same. She was alive. I could feel it in my bones.

At Taden's apartment, I alternated between pounding on her door and ringing the doorbell in rapid succession. Her neighbor came out to check on the noise I was making,

"Is everything all right out here?" she asked me.

"Oh, hi there. Yeah, I'm looking for the woman who lives here. Taden."

"She hasn't been home all day. Is she in some kind of trouble?"

"Um, well, no one has seen her in a while and she's not answering her phone. Her friends and I are starting to get a little worried."

"Do you want me to call the police?" Her voice was filled with concern.

"No, not yet. But thank you for keeping an eye out. Can I give you my phone number in case you see her?"

"Sure. I've seen you two together," she told me with approving eyes. "She's smitten with you."

I politely smiled at the old lady, knowing she was trying to make me feel better. But the thought of Taden being smitten with me and the knowledge that I had let her down once again made me feel sick.

I didn't want to disturb the neighbor any further, and I knew I shouldn't have wasted even those few precious minutes I already had. I remembered she kept a spare key hidden in the courtyard of her complex, and ran around outside to find it. Frantically searching under an overgrown bush, I felt doom take hold of me again. *What if she wasn't inside? Where would I look next?*

I finally located the key and jammed it into the lock. With my gun drawn and ready to serve Marius his deserved ending, I cleared each and every room, corner, and hiding space of her residence. As I suspected, she wasn't there—and neither was Marius. I called Dakotah to be sure she hadn't returned to the lab.

"She's not here."

"She's not here, either," Dakotah said, having completely lost her even-keeled temperament. "I'm worried about her. I've tried texting and calling but she hasn't answered."

"I know. She doesn't have her phone. It was left behind. Okay. I'll keep you updated."

Before I could hang up, she injected a plea. "Abel, you have to find her."

As soon as I hung up, I was convicted with the all-consuming thought that I had failed her. If Marius had her, it was because I left her alone. Why didn't I send a detail to the lab to keep watch over her? I could've gone one man short. Closing her front door behind me I took one step down on her porch and collapsed, wracking my brain for where to search next.

I tried to think clearly and figure out my next move, but I felt helpless. I had never felt so frozen in place before. I should have been able to come up with a plan of action, but I couldn't.

I had lingered too long. I needed to keep moving forward, and I needed to find her. I lifted my head, preparing myself to re-engage with the world around me.

I will find you, Taden. I won't let you down again.

CHAPTER 22

TADEN

Blinking hard, my eyes adjusted to the dark room I found myself in. I lifted my head from the table I was hunched over. As I attempted to rise from my chair, I realized I was handcuffed to the table. Yanking my arm in an attempt to free myself, I tried to take in my surroundings. It felt like an interrogation room at a police station, but I'd never actually been in one. My experience was solely from television, so I couldn't be sure.

Marius entered the room, closing the door behind him. He handed me an ice pack for my head, which hurt an incredible amount, so I took it from him without hesitating. He set a glass of water and two aspirin on the table in front of me before he sat down across from me. With one eyebrow raised, full of suspicion, Marius watched me swallow them down. He was ready to get some answers.

"Who are you?" he asked, then quickly added, "And what are you doing here?"

He got up from his chair, stalked over to me, and bent down in front of my face. I could smell his familiar scent. Instinctively, I leaned back and turned my head to maintain my personal space. "What I know: you pulled me out of that house." He closed the space I'd created. "What I don't know: why you look exactly the same as you did then. It doesn't make sense."

He tried to put his finger on time travel, but he had no idea that was what he was circling around. The general public didn't know we had that technology, and I couldn't let him find out. I saw what it did to him last time.

"It is not possible that you are the same woman who saved me. But you have her face. Tell me why."

He looked hard at me, like a man willing to exact pain on anyone who might thwart his present progress—not at all like a man willing to thank the person who saved his life. I became convinced Marius did indeed have a plan that my presence threatened.

I didn't rush to respond to him. The hold-out would either demand respect from him or trigger him to reveal more information. Even though I didn't know *this* Marius, I was certain his inner monologue was similar. Wait-time would make him doubt himself, which would make him nervous.

"Why were you following me, Mr. Touma?" I eventually asked. "Better yet, why am I here against my will?" He seemed put off by my questions. After all, he'd planned on asking the questions and I still wasn't answering them.

"I didn't trust you would show up at our meeting, so I staked it out—from a distance—earlier this morning. Wasn't it a surprise to learn, as the afternoon progressed, that an entire unit of soldiers was preparing for me, but you were not? No, you were not even in New York. My sources indicated I'd find you here," he stated, lifting his hand, "in Maryland. Coincidentally, not too far from the site where you rescued me."

I couldn't help feeling an 'I told you so' moment on the horizon. I'd tried to explain this outcome to Abel. If nothing else, it confirmed I still understood how Marius operated.

"I'm sure the disappointment was palpable when *I* didn't show *either*. Well, I was too busy tracking you down." He sat back in his chair. "A perk of having presidential access to private records. How *was* your flight home this morning?"

I glanced at him sideways, keeping my mouth downturned, and waited.

"I have to say, after that military display I didn't expect to find you all alone without even one soldier as a precaution. Maybe I got lucky and tailed you before they thought of it. Not too smart on their part. Good thing for me you decided to have a solo night adventure in an abandoned hospital. I don't imagine anyone knew you were planning your little escapade. What was that all about, anyway?"

I wanted to kick myself for ignoring my intuition. I knew I shouldn't have gone there alone. I wished Marius was wrong, and I wished Abel hadn't left me alone to my own devices. I wanted to believe Abel was right outside this place, getting into position, ready to storm the building and rescue me.

But then, right in the middle of my self-chastisement, a more sensible version of myself rose above the damsel in distress narrative. She told me to sit up straighter in my seat. Although Abel was someone who would do anything to rescue me from a situation such as this, I was someone who could rescue myself. From the surge of self-empowerment, I locked my eyes on Marius.

"I did save you that night, and Ruth helped me." I let it sink in for him, watching him swallow hard. "We aren't back in your world by coincidence, Marius. It's just like I told you back at Ruth's office. You are in danger, and we want to help you."

His face contorted. He tried to convey he didn't believe anything I was saying, but I could see he was struggling to refute my story.

In an attempt to distract his fixation with my lack of aging, I simpered, "I can't justify why we've aged so well. It must be in our genes. I will tell you, however, you are not the only child we saved." He was listening. The questions he desperately wanted to ask poured from his eyes.

"Octavia is safe."

I was nervous to say her name out loud to him. He was unpredictable when it came to his sister. I had seen him morph into a madman at the mention of her name—but I'd also witnessed an incredibly vulnerable and soft version of Marius when she was mentioned, too. He wasn't immediately violent, so I went on.

"She is happy, and has a beautiful life. Once you're out of danger, we want to reunite the two of you. We can't do it yet. It wouldn't be fair to Octavia if we brought your current threat to her door. I'm on your side, Marius. I always have been. Asking you to trust me is a big request. I know it is. But I am going to ask you to trust me anyway."

He looked at me like I was speaking a language he didn't understand. He could see I was studying his response, and turned his back to me in order to process everything I'd said.

"You're not lying to me." It was a statement he made to convince himself this was real. "How would you even know about my sister if you weren't telling me the truth?" His question hung in the air, the stillness broken as his hands reached toward me. My mind replayed the last time Marius lifted his hands to me. Instinctively, I winced in preparation of the same. With my eyes shut tight, I felt the handcuffs unhinge from the table.

"I choose to trust you," Marius said. "But you should know—whether you saved me that night or not—if you screw with me, I'll kill you."

I scoffed at his threat. "For some reason I believe you."

"You haven't yet told me who you work for," he stated.

"It's classified."

"I can make a few guesses. Tell your people you won't taint our vaccine launch."

Confusion took hold of my face before I could hide it. He must've registered it, even if subconsciously.

"I'll be in touch. You can go." He didn't need to tell me a second time. I was quick on my feet, eager to find the exit. It was late and I didn't even know where I was. Without my phone, I wasn't able to address the issue. I'd settled on the unfortunate outcome that I'd be walking, but a car was waiting for me outside the building. Its driver said nothing as he opened the door for me.

"Is this ride for me?" I asked, looking behind me. I worried I might not make it home again but then, before I knew it, I was dropped off near the parking lot of the institution. Walking through the tall grass on the side of the road, I started to make out lights from armored vehicles in the parking lot. As I approached, one of Abel's soldiers recognized me.

"Ma'am; we've been looking for you all night," he said when he got close enough.

"Is Abel in there?" I nodded toward the hospital.

"No, ma'am. He left a while ago, in search of you. I'll radio him now and inform him you're safe. Wait here. I'll drive you home." He reached for the walkie-talkie attached to his chest. "Dr. Mihal, do you copy, over?"

I stared at the transceiver, waiting to hear his voice.

"Loud and clear, Sergeant," Abel replied.

"I have Dr. Barrett, sir."

"Repeat soldier," Abel commanded.

"Dr. Barrett is safe."

"Escort her here immediately."

"Understood, sir," he told Abel looking up to me as he pointed toward his vehicle.

"I appreciate the offer, really, but I need to be alone," I said.

"Ma'am? Are you sure? He wouldn't approve of this…"

"I'm sure. Please. I'm fine."

He wasn't comfortable with the position I'd put him in, but nevertheless Abel's soldier turned away and sent transmissions to the rest of the unit that I had been recovered.

Driving home was a challenge through swollen, tear-stained eyes. I'd released the fear that I'd kept at bay. The way the evening played out forced me to relive the terror Marius had once put me through. I was playing with fire, but it was the only way we had to learn his true intentions. Plus, he had said something about interfering with his vaccine, and that was perplexing.

I walked to the stoop of my apartment to find Abel sitting on the steps, anxiously talking on his phone. His knees were pulled into his chest, his free hand running through his hair, leaving scattered pieces in its wake. "Yeah, she's on her way here now. I'm not sure where she was." He paused, fixing his gaze onto the pavement.

I saw him first. His unmoored appearance stopped me cold. I took in the scene and gathered my emotions which threatened to spill out again. Just being near him washed me with the relief of safety.

"I know," he said into the phone. "I found it next to her car." Another pause. "Thanks, Dakotah. I'll make sure she calls you. Can you update Quinn? She's got to be a wreck, too."

I must've cued him to my presence, because he looked from the ground up to me and jumped up, rushing me in the same breath. "She's here. I'll call you right back."

"There's my phone. I couldn't find it anywhere. I wanted to call you…"

"You're safe. I was so worried."

"I'm okay. I'm so glad you're here," I said weakly.

He closed the distance between us and put his arms around me. The next breath escaping my body felt like it weighed more than my entire mass. In its absence settled a much lighter feeling of calm. This was how Abel made me feel when his arms were around me. Every time.

"He didn't show tonight. We lost our tail on Marius and haven't been able to locate him. I didn't know what to do. I could only believe he was headed right to you. Did he find you?"

"He did."

We stood on the sidewalk. Abel held me in his protective embrace. Neither of us knew how to handle the words to come. I lost sense of time and didn't feel particularly rushed to withdraw.

This time my eyes were filled with gratitude, and I wondered if anyone had ever studied whether tears were structured differently when they were of joy.

Waking me from my reverie, Abel put his lips to my forehead. At the same time, he gathered my hair off my shoulders and tucked it behind my ears. The mix of how tenderly he moved my hair back and how slow and gentle he kissed above my brow felt more intimate than any love I'd ever received from a man.

Filled with ardor, I mentally catalogued every detail. I wanted to remember how he smelled, what his face looked like, and the sensations in my body. Lifting my eyes to take him in, a stray tear fell down my cheek. His thumb caught it with a gentle swipe. I thought of the kiss we exchanged the other night after I found him in the gym, getting out his frustration. Before my thoughts fully unraveled, I took his lips with mine. His kiss was warm and soothing. It made me feel soft and delicate, and it released a passion that unfurled itself within me until I became light on my feet.

We had already kissed twice before, but in that moment, having waited so long to fully know him, his kiss changed the depths of my soul. For the first time, I understood and accepted what it meant to be wholly loved by a man. To be enough. As I was.

Even with magic dancing between the two of us, just below conscious thought, already I was preparing for one day when I would lose him. Life had taught me early on that no one lived forever. Choosing to ignore the pain his love would one day bring to me, I opened myself fully to receive what he offered on my doorstep. Indeed, this love was worth whatever was to come.

My knees buckled under the desire that filled my body. In response, he pulled me closer. With barely enough breath in my lungs to push out a whisper, I imposed words upon our solace. "We should go inside."

An excessive amount of built-up energy left me fumbling with my keys in an attempt to unlock the door. I worried my awkward self might ruin the magic of our moment. In answer to the hope I clung to, at the opening of my door, Abel swept me up and carried me inside.

I woke to the rain pounding on my window. My head still ached from the blow I received from Marius. I rolled over to find Abel asleep next to me. I wanted to watch him sleep, but he sensed me and awoke. His eyes connected with mine and, without speaking a word, we moved into each other's arms. It was as if the world would stop its rotation for us as long as we held on to one another. I wanted every morning for the rest of my life to start this way.

"I suppose we need to go to work today?" he asked me. If I said so, he would skip it all—but we had to return to the responsibilities we'd committed to. No matter how badly we wanted to stay in bed.

Going into work that morning was bittersweet. My life felt reborn with the love we had given to each other—but I felt mournful of his absence, however brief it was, from my side.

We had an urgent update meeting with Danika, Bernard, and Joseph about the previous night's events surrounding Marius. It was a lot of information to take in when my brain was muddled with flashes of Abel touching my skin and kissing my body. I hoped the flushing of my face would appear as a result of the business with Marius. I couldn't even look at Abel throughout the meeting for fear everyone would read my thoughts.

The lovesick spell I was under was abruptly halted by Danika's words. I hadn't even noticed she'd begun speaking.

"I want to respond to this promptly. I don't like that he abducted my scientist. Whatever his intentions, his comment about the president's vaccine is enough of a concern that I'd like to know the full story of Marius Touma. Dr. Barrett set up an easy target by dangling the carrot of Mr. Touma's sister. Let's build on her initial plan. Did you have any follow-up ideas?" she enquired of me.

I took a drink of water from the glass on the table, hoping I could wash away the fog in my head. Everyone was waiting for my plan to be revealed.

"When I told Marius about his sister, I didn't really have a plan. I just knew the person he cared more for than anyone else in the world was Octavia, and I knew it was my leverage."

"I see. Okay, Dr. Barrett, you and your team are dismissed to get back to work on your immediate goals." She looked to Abel. "I would like Dr. Mihal to stay behind."

I looked at Abel for the first time during the meeting. He subtly nodded while holding my gaze with his. I passed him on my way out of the conference room, and he grabbed my hand with a quick squeeze as I moved toward the door.

I paused in the hallway before heading to the lab to find Quinn. I had a lot to catch her up on, and I didn't know how to start.

CHAPTER 23

ABEL

I sensed Danika sent Taden out of the room with a purpose. She didn't want to deal with both of us as she laid out her plan.

"At first, it seemed like President Moore's interference with the Berthold reign was going to help us avoid a mission to the past in order to eliminate the threat of Berthold from office. At the very least, I thought Moore might buy us some time here in the present. But with the assassination of Berthold leading to Moore's dramatic placement in office, and the tension rising around Marius, we have reason to believe there is more concern than before."

The tension in the room hinted that Danika wasn't seeking to give me news I'd respond to positively. Mr. Richardson held a mug, sipping a steamy liquid which caused him to instinctively pull back and set the drink down. Pushing it forward, he said, "Recent intelligence has uncovered information that Berthold is still alive." I narrowed my eyes at Mr. Richardson to convey my surprise that he would announce this after I'd asked him to keep it confidential. "It appears the assassination was staged. We don't know if this means Touma's people are holding him hostage or working *with* him." Mr. Richardson finished and looked back to Danika, whose face filled with irritation.

"We need to move forward with our original mission, and we need to fast-track it," Danika said. "Dr. Mihal, you're being sent on a reconnaissance mission."

"Understood."

"I have targeted three reference points in time that I want you to go back through. In order of importance, your first deployment will be nine months prior to the handover of power from President Berthold to his son."

Immediately, I had questions. Would I travel to that destination in time, collect intel, and then return home? Or would I try to stop what happened? After that, was she sending me on two other missions? How long were each of those?

She folded her arms. "During the duration of your mission, I want your team to closely monitor every meeting that the father and son share with each other."

"Are you suggesting this will be a nine-month mission?" I asked.

She looked annoyed that I'd interrupted her. "Yes, Dr. Mihal. Is that a problem?"

I didn't respond, not exactly thrilled about the length of the mission but also not clear about its goal yet.

"Don't worry, everything here will be managed in your absence. I have Lt. Duncan assuming your command while you're gone."

This time I folded my arms. "How often will I return to check in?"

She raised a brow. "Dr. Mihal, your TRB will send us all of your intel in real time. You won't need to return to the present for that purpose. Clearly, if you find out something pertinent, you can inform us through your TRB."

I looked to Mr. Richardson, my direct commander. He shrugged and folded his hands on the table. "I've sent you a file with the names of who we suspect to be colluding with the president and his son."

"How will I know if my mission changes while I'm there? So I'm not wasting time if something affects what you know in the present? Shouldn't I at least have checkpoint returns to the present?"

"That's not necessary either. Dr. Hughs has implemented an alarm on your TRB. If it's triggered, that will be your signal to abort the mission and return to the present."

I was getting the distinct impression that Ms. Farkas wanted me out of the picture. I did often question her stratagem, and it was obvious that it annoyed her. She, in particular, was pretty open about her disapproval of my feelings for Taden, too. The Patriots' goal was to perfect time travel in order to salvage our democracy, and Taden was the direct line to that. They didn't want her distracted from her goals.

"With all due respect, wouldn't Lt. Duncan be better suited for this mission? As it is, Dr. Barrett can't seem to avoid potentially dangerous run-ins with Mr. Touma. I'd like to be here to assure her safety and our progress."

"I recognize your concern. I share your sentiment." She pushed her chair from the conference table. "I feel confident in Lt. Duncan looking after Dr. Barrett while you're deployed. In fact, I think it actually might better serve both of you."

I asked, "How's that?", my face pinched.

"By providing space and distance from each other, which seems somewhat necessary in order to refocus your purpose here at the NIST."

That pissed me off, but I chose not to respond to her comment. "Is it then even possible the mission *may* take less than the tentative nine months?"

"Anything is possible," she said.

Mr. Richardson unfolded his hands. "If you find intel that serves to bring you home sooner, we'll trigger your alarm and get you out of there."

"What if I learn something that leads me to a different reference in time? Since I'm apparently not returning for check-ins to get approval, do I just jump to that event?"

Danika rose from her seat. "You will under no circumstances jump to any other points in time without approval," she said firmly. "If you discover a lead to another time juncture, report it. We'll investigate, and if we deem it worth attending we will either pull you out of your time location or deploy a different team."

"Yes, ma'am." I still wasn't on board with this mission. "With respect, why don't I just go to the night Berthold was supposedly assassinated and make sure it really happens. That way, I'm only gone for one trip to the past and we've solved the issue."

"Dr. Mihal, this is not a kill mission," she scolded. "The intention is to gain intelligence so that we can use the information to prevent Berthold from taking office, while also learning what other misdeeds took us down this path. Sources have pointed to several indictors that his leadership was coming. We need you to find these indicators. If we can identify the moves both Bertholds made to manipulate how the power exchange unfolded, we can then devise a plot to prevent them." She moved closer. "Meaning, Berthold will never succeed his father. The next stage of the plan will be to plant a new candidate to succeed Berthold Senior's last term. That should get us back on track." She turned from me and moved next to Mr. Richardson. "We will finally have a president worthy of our great country."

I couldn't deny that altering the events of our past without murdering anyone *was* a better choice. I wasn't exactly pleased with a nine-month mission, but deployment was a part of my military expectations.

"Are you accepting the mission, then?"

"Yes, ma'am. You can count on me." I swallowed my personal feelings, thinking about the night I'd just shared with Taden. Nine months wasn't forever, but each day without her by my side would feel unbearable. "When does my team depart?"

"You will travel back in time tomorrow morning at six. Say your goodbyes today."

"Affirmative." I left the conference room, avoiding the magnetic pull toward Taden's office, and instead headed to the gym and my punching bag.

 "You're leaving in the morning? That's sudden," Taden said surprised.

"I know." Had she noticed I was avoiding eye contact? She had no idea this was a real goodbye yet.

"How long will you be gone?"

There it was. Right out of the gate. How would I tell her, now that we finally figured out how to be together, that this mission would be almost a year? There would be no more lingering in the smell of her skin, working alongside her, or laughing at her adorable awkward tendencies for months. The role I accepted with The Patriot Party came with the huge benefit that I would get to be with Taden every day. I didn't foresee it would result in separation.

I tossed around the idea of declining the mission. I could let someone else play the part of hero this time. I could transfer all of my memories over to someone else. I wished to have a life with Taden. It was the only desire in my heart. Our relationship was so new, I didn't want to risk losing it due to distance. But I had to go, and I had to do whatever was necessary to stop our country from falling into corruption.

"Abel? How long?"

My silence communicated my dread. I watched her face arrive at the realization that I was telling her goodbye.

"It's a long mission, isn't it?"

"Nine months."

Her face fell. "Wow. You've never been on a mission that long before."

"I know. Because of our TRB updates, I don't need to return for checkpoints."

She raised both brows in understanding. "Well, that sucks. It seems like my technology just bit me in the ass."

"Taden Barrett, will you do me the honor of going on a date this evening?"

She bit her lip, mulling over the news. "You're right. We shouldn't waste our last day before you deploy having a pity party." She grabbed my hands. "I say let's squeeze as much as we can into this night."

"Like, a night full of dates?"

"Yes! I love this idea!" she exclaimed. "Let's wrap things up here so we can head home to get ready. I'll make all of the arrangements. You just come prepared for anything."

"What? You want to leave work right now? It's only afternoon, Taden; what are you going to tell everyone?" I asked, chuckling.

"I don't even care. I'm not going to tell anyone anything. We have a lot to live tonight."

Taden didn't stretch out the normal, tedious tying up of daily loose ends like she normally did. With the exception of Dakotah, she didn't tell anyone she was leaving. I marveled at the uncharacteristic, who-gives-a-shit mentality she'd adopted for our agenda. With vigor she pulled me out of the office building, leading me hand-in-hand to the parking lot before she firmly kissed me on the lips and said, "I'll see you in a little bit." She rushed to her car, and promptly sped out of the parking lot.

I arrived to our Night of Many Dates in casual jeans and a plain white t-shirt underneath a blazer. I hoped I looked more or less casual, depending on where we went. Stalling at her door, holding a pot of forget-me-nots and a wrapped package, I couldn't believe how high-strung I felt.

The flowers were for her kitchen windowsill. I wanted her to look at the bright blue blooms and remember I would never not love her. The other gift I held had been a work in progress for years. It was supposed to be for her big birthday next year, but with this sudden fork in our road it seemed more appropriate to give to her now.

One afternoon in college, close to Valentine's Day, we were studying in the library and the topic of romantic gifts came up.

"The best gift a man could ever give me would be his favorite book. But I'd want him to give me a copy he'd read many times—well, at least twice." She laughed at her fast acceptance of only twice. I couldn't think of a single book I'd read more than once. "He would have the margins full of anecdotes about his favorite lines and what different passages made him think about. Oh! Oh! Maybe he even points out parts that he feels like I might enjoy, or parts that reminded him of me." She glanced at me suddenly, like she remembered I was there, and her cheeks flushed. "I don't know. Maybe it's a dumb idea. I just think it would be the ultimate insight into his life. So intimate. So personal."

"I don't think it's dumb at all! I'm totally stealing your idea. I'll woo some girl right off her feet with it someday!"

We both laughed and returned to our studies. For days after the library conversation, I painstakingly focused on picking the right book to one day give to Taden. At first I couldn't even decide on a genre, but I needed to choose one I enjoyed that would be worth re-reading and writing my thoughts in. Finally, I settled on *The Great Gatsby* by F. Scott Fitzgerald. It held a decadent setting, warnings of chasing after love, and it was a classic.

Exactly one week following the most-romantic-gift conversation, I started my first read-through of *The Great Gatsby,* after inscribing the date on the inside cover and a reference to our discussion about the gift. I'd waited since then, reading and rereading, until the day I could give Taden her gift.

Taden,

I am looking forward to the day I can give you this book to show you the many ways my thoughts return to you and the depths of my love. Until then, I will read it and talk to you within its pages. You are worth more than the time it takes for "at least two readings".

I read the book every year after that. Almost every page had been written in on the margins, passages highlighted throughout, and the only thing left was to scribe the closing message.

Inside the back cover I recorded the current date, followed by words I knew meant a great deal to her. The book was wrapped in our first co-authored research paper. Hoping she would open the book with impatience, I scribbled a note onto the gift tag. "Don't open right away. Open this when you are desperate for me."

I stood outside her door, wired with nerves. I'd planned on giving her the book for so long by that point that actually giving it to her turned out to be a little frightening. What if I picked the wrong book? Over the years, as this book became more personal to me, I discovered many people disliked *The Great Gatsby*. How had I never even thought to ask her opinion of the story? In addition to my doubts about the book, the forget-me-nots were starting to feel like a silly gift—and I was reconsidering the choice of jeans for the evening. I should've worn something nicer in case… My brooding was cut short at the opening of her door.

"Ohh, gifts!" she squealed as she wrapped her arms around my neck and wildly kissed my cheek. She smelled like a candied breath of sugar. "Are these forget-me-nots?" She reached for the small pot of blue blossoms.

I nodded. "For your windowsill. I thought they might brighten up the kitchen."

"They're beautiful! You picked the perfect flowers. Let's go put them in their new spot."

I followed her inside, still holding onto the book, considering how I might hide it so I didn't have to embarrass myself by giving it to her. She looked over her shoulder at me with a crooked smile that made my chest twinge.

She spotted it in my hands but didn't ask about it. After she placed the flowers on her window, adjusting them just right in admiration of their beauty, she sauntered my way, allowing me to feel every step, until her breath swam across my lips and hers met mine in anticipation.

I raised the wrapped package from my side and Taden turned her focus onto it. "Another gift? Abel! I didn't get you anything. I feel like a jerk."

"Don't be ridiculous. You've planned this big night for us. That's your gift to me."

 Once in her hands she brought the carefully wrapped package to her nose, inhaling it with her eyes closed. "If feels and smells like a book." She read the tag and dramatically performed aloud the part, "Desperate to have me near." Her bright smile caught my heart and I promised myself to never forget the mental picture I took of her. "Okay, I won't open it until you're gone, but I can't promise I can wait until I'm desperate."

She grabbed my hand and pulled me into the living room. The lights were turned off, welcoming the orange glow of evening to sift through her bay window. Dozens of candles were strategically placed throughout the room, glimmering in turn with each other. The mix of early dusk with the radiance of soft, flickering candlelight bounced from every reflective surface and moved around Taden perfectly. I could not take my eyes off her dazzling silhouette. She stepped aside, revealing her giant coffee table pushed to the center of the room. It was also decorated with shimmering candles and surrounded by what looked like every pillow she owned, arranged for us to sit on the floor.

"Come on, dinner's ready," she said, waving me toward the table with a beaming smile.

"You *made* dinner? Are you sure that was a good idea?" Self-amused, I watched her lips curve to acknowledge my jest. Taden could mix a compound to send humans into time travel, but her ability to mix ingredients for a meal was less than stellar.

"Actually, I *do* know how to make *one* dinner rather well. Prepare to be shocked and amazed."

"I already am. This is quite the turn of events, Dr. Barrett. I can't wait."

"It was the first and last meal I learned how to cook from my mom. I don't make it very often, though, because why would I eat an entire lasagna by myself?"

"Lasagna? That is my *ultimate* favorite pasta dish!"

She presented the tray to me like it was the capstone of everything she had ever created. The most intelligent and beautiful human on the planet was holding a dinner she'd made for me. There was no man more lucky than I was.

"It smells amazing. My mouth is watering just looking at it," I told her in earnest as she beamed back at me.

Throughout the meal, the mood of the room tiptoed from the light-hearted banter we were used to, to the heaviness of our impending separation. We both felt it. We were trading easy smiles for long, desperate, knowing looks.

She refused to let our night become hijacked by the heartache which would be waiting for us tomorrow.

"Enough of this. Finish up your last bite, and let's go," she instructed me.

"Where are we going?"

"Don't you worry about it. I have the whole night planned. You just follow my lead."

She loved this, and I was in my glory. As she drove us to our second date spot of the evening, she couldn't help bubbling over with energy about her plans.

"Are you going to give me a hint?"

"Hmm," she pondered. "Okay. Here's a hint." She cracked up at herself, which was a good indication she was about to tell a joke. "We'll kick art the evening at our first stop."

"Did you say, 'kick art the evening'?" I planted my hand to my forehead, groaning at the awful pun. "So, my clue is art."

"What? It was a good joke."

"The Glenstone Art Museum." I pointed at her.

"Abel! You guessed it on the first try." She scrunched up her face. "That's no fun."

"I thought they closed at five," I said, glancing at my watch.

She raised a single eyebrow. "I've got connections."

"Oh. Nice. An after-hours visit."

"I almost forgot." She tapped the radio in her console. "I made a playlist for us to listen to." Pressing play, she cued the first song. I watched her hum along until the chorus hit and she belted out the words of the old song.

"If you're lost you can look and you will find me." She turned her gaze from the road to me and raised her head into the next lyric. "Time after time."

Her playlist was our soundtrack until we pulled into the museum's lot. I'd already felt gratified and the night was only starting.

"Milady," I said, bowing my head as I opened Glenstone's door.

"Thank you, kind sir."

Taden had arranged the visit with her friend earlier and he was already awaiting our arrival, welcoming us in and handing over a map.

"You have an hour to enjoy," he said. Looking me over with approval, he added, "You got yourself a good one here."

"Oh stop," she told him, swatting at his hand.

"I'm a lucky man. Believe me, I know it." And it was the truth.

She slid her fingers between mine and we walked in the stillness of the closed art museum, side by side. I followed her lead into a gallery where she began more urgently pulling me with excitement.

"Around this corner," she said, looking at the map. "Is…ta-da."

I was looking at three white shelves of pharmaceutical packaging. "Whoa. It's a Damien Hirst. I have one of his pieces in my office."

"I know." She beamed. "I always thought it was rather odd. Odd enough that I looked into his other artwork. That's when I found he had a piece in our very own Glenstone."

I kissed her hand as her friend arrived carrying a canvas and easel. He opened the easel and set the canvas on it so that it was stationed directly in front of the Hirst exhibit.

"The best way to enjoy an exhibit," he said, "especially one as unusual as this, is to draw what you see." He handed us both small charcoal crayons.

Taden giggled, accepting the crayon, and looked to me with skeptical eyes. "I can't draw."

"Neither can I."

Her friend chuckled at both of us. "Have fun. That's all that matters." And left us to our own devices.

Taden and I did our best sketching Mr. Hirst's exhibit, and while it might not have even come close to any resemblance of his masterpiece, we laughed so much during our attempt that the sketch we created together will forever make me smile.

Our next stop was a hole-in-the-wall local establishment with a live band. It was packed with people who all appeared to know each other. I can't explain the pride I felt walking into the place with Taden at my side. I wanted to announce, "She's here with me."

As directed, I followed her lead again, this time right onto the dance floor. By the fourth song we'd perfected our rhythm, no matter what song played. Fast-paced, we showed off our footwork. When it was slow, we pulled in close. The place was hot and we were sweaty.

She gathered her hair up, exposing her neck. I gently kissed her back, along the base of her neck to her shoulder, pleased with the myriad goosebumps I caused on her skin. Between the dancing and teasing, my internal temperature rose. To avoid overheating I removed my overcoat, pretending not to notice Taden's hungry eyes. But she wasn't holding back from me, either. Her hand found its way onto my sweat-covered shirt, hovering over my heart until she had moved in so close that there was no space left between us. The song didn't match our assumed tempo. It was a fast and snappy beat, but we were slow and smooth, not a single care for our surroundings. She rose onto her toes, leaning into my ear, and I could feel the warmth of her breath.

She whispered, "It's time to go," with a slight upturn of her mouth. She was joyfully driving me to the edge before, once again, leading me out the door to our next date.

The cool night air renewed my senses, while the darkened sky made it difficult to see. Taden held a blanket retrieved from the back seat of her car, as well as a flashlight, which she powered on and pointed to her chin.

"*Woooo*, so spooky." She imitated a ghost, giggling at herself.

"Stargazing, eh?" I asked.

"I got us front-row tickets to a sold-out show." She spread the blanket on a bank of dirt, overlooking the glassy lake which shone bright in the moonlight. Turning the flashlight off, our eyes adjusted to the glow in the sky. The cool air was laced with Taden's marshmallow scent, welcoming me into a high the likes of which no drug on earth could ever rival.

CHAPTER 24

TADEN

I would've used up my last moments alive to stay in his arms under the moonlight, frozen in time. A memory forever to be imprinted on my soul. We made a pact to go to bed with the moon, which meant Abel would be deployed having only had a few hours of sleep in exchange for a night together.

We made love next to the shining water. Fresh gusts of lake-chilled breezes burgeoned goosebumps but Abel's touch denied them, lighting a fire that could only be tended with his love.

As a young woman, I believed I would make many romantic connections throughout my life. As an adult, my understanding sharpened to appreciate that the connection Abel and I had didn't often happen. We were friends first. We learned each other's strengths and weaknesses. Witnessed tragedies and celebrations. We respected each other's boundaries. I could be myself around him. And then, there was this unexpected desire to be seen and loved by him.

I was grateful to the universe for guiding us together when we were younger and the slow path that led us to this moment. I also wondered if I would still feel as grateful for his love once I had to live without it for the next nine months. He could send updates through his TRB, but I wouldn't be able to communicate with him until this was over. Our love was so new, I couldn't help but worry. Would we make it through the long distance of silence? Was briefly knowing and then going without worth the inevitable pain? Or was it better if I had never known it at all? Under the moonlight, I swore he was worth every bit of heartache I would soon know too well.

CHAPTER 25

RUTH

In my meetings with Mary following the failed entrapment of Marius, I felt even more on edge. I cared a great deal about the possibility of renewing our friendship, but that need came into question after Taden had been abducted by Marius. How was I supposed to sit in meetings with the two of them, thinking about the threat he was to my sister? And, possibly, to me?

For God's sake, Taden currently had a gash on her head from Marius. He had released her, but only because she had something he wanted: his sister. Interacting with him, pretending I wasn't privy to Taden's abduction while discussing which plate chargers to use at the gala, felt like I was playing a deadly game.

Taden had made me promise not to act on my desire to exact vengeance.

"The Patriots have decided we go ahead with the inaugural plan. You are still in play as an important go-between with Marius and President Moore," Taden informed me, in as convincing a manner as she could summon.

"You can't be serious. He hit you on the head and knocked you unconscious. You could've been killed."

"You don't think I know that? We may not have hard evidence yet, but there are enough strange outliers with their actions, paired with who they both were in the old timeline, that it's worth keeping you on the inside. I don't want to put you in danger, though."

"I'm not worried about me, Taden. I'm worried about you."

"Then do this. Keep up appearances. Don't let your anger dictate the meeting. There's a very real chance Mary knows nothing of this entire situation, which means you still have an in with her."

I clicked my tongue and sighed. "You got it. I'll keep up the charade."

Marius still wasn't certain of what our history together entailed, but he knew enough to guess my intent to be a menace to his objectives.

What I wasn't totally sure of was whether or not he had informed Mary of any details regarding myself and Taden—and his sordid childhood trauma. It appeared throughout our meeting that she was blissfully ignorant of the conversation my sister and I had with him at the end of our last meeting. It also appeared she was oblivious that Marius had once again abducted my sister. Unfortunately, this added to my list of concerns. Instead of worrying solely for Taden's safety I included Mary's safety as questionable, pertaining to Marius, as well.

CHAPTER 26

TADEN

On the first morning after Abel left, I stared at my puffy reflection in the bathroom mirror. While I didn't want to draw attention to the evidence of a night spent sobbing alone, I didn't have the motivation to apply makeup. Instead, I splashed my face with ice cold water. Trudging downstairs for a cup of coffee, I pulled my hair into a bun. I'd already skipped a shower and brushing my teeth. I stared out my kitchen window while the coffee percolated. Leaning in to smell my forget-me-nots, I sucked in the sharp reminder.

As I pulled into the parking lot of the NIST, I realized I didn't even recall driving here. I was on autopilot the whole way. Walking into the building was a different experience. My heart didn't race with excitement like it used to. Instead, every step closer to my lab felt like fire pressing against my skin, branding me with his absence. I considered driving away from the lab and heading to Dr. Pasterski's instead. I imagined she'd make me a hot cup of tea and we'd both sit on the couch and listen to my dad talk about popular science. He'd be able to tell I was sad and really juice up the interest level.

I didn't have the luxury to nurse my heartache. Our work was paramount, and nothing could've made it more clear to me than Abel's mission.

The only good thing about today was that my other main project, Marius, was going all right. It had only been a couple days since he learned Octavia was alive, and because I was the only one who knew where to find her he seemed to be behaving, not wanting to blow his opportunity.

On this particular morning Ruth had a meeting with Mary, sans Marius, which most likely meant he was still lurking somewhere close, waiting to contact me again. Ruth was to join our meeting with The Patriots, virtually, to get her directives going further. Her meetings with Mary were the simplest opportunity to keep tabs on Marius, if he did turn out to be an issue.

I bypassed my office, still avoiding the workload guaranteed to be on my desk, and headed straight to the coffee.

"How you doing?" Dakotah waited for the truth as I poured an exuberant amount of sugar into my cup.

I shrugged my shoulders. "As good as can be expected, I guess. A lot to do today, so I should forget I even have a name pretty soon. I hope so, anyway."

"I'm coming to stay over tonight. You cool with that? I don't think you're ready to be alone yet. Probably should've forced my company last night."

"I don't have the energy to tell you no. So, you're probably right. Did he send an update through his TRB yet?"

"You know he did. I didn't watch them because they were left for you. I forwarded them to your account and deleted them off my drive. Maybe, though, don't listen to them until you're ready to go home tonight," she suggested, raising her eyebrows to accent her advice.

"Yeah. You're right. It'll motivate me to get through the day."

Finally, I'd wrapped up my daily report and sent Quinn home for the evening. I sat at my desk, clicking on each application until I opened the one from Abel. I hesitated before pressing play. I don't even remember actually starting the thing, but once I had I couldn't quench my need for more and replayed it over and over. He sat on the armchair in his hotel room, speaking directly into his TRB.

 "Hey Dakotah, I know you're receiving this first. I'm actually recording this update for Taden. If you wouldn't mind sending this to her. I'll post a second update for you after. Thanks, buddy."

Then he shifted in his chair and brought the camera closer to his face.

"Finally, we're alone," he said to me.

For the first time that day, I actually smiled. He hadn't even really started talking yet, and already I felt approximately eighty percent less sad. "Want to check out our digs?" He scanned the hotel suite with his camera. "I get the room. Josh gets the pull out."

The Patriots had sent him back with arrangements for food and lodging as they had on every mission he'd gone on. With this one being so long-term, I'd expected his room and board not to be as nice as they typically were. I was pleasantly surprised to see otherwise.

"So, how was your day?" he asked. Then he dramatically paused, aiming his ear at the camera as if he were listening to me share my answer. So, I did.

"My day sucked without you," I said sullenly to the computer screen.

"Really?" he said with wide eyes.

"No joke. It sucked," I confirmed.

"Do you want to hear about my first day?" he asked me.

"Of course," I muttered again to my computer. Sucking in my bottom lip I hunched onto my elbows, resting my chin in my hands.

"Well, for starters, I sat in my car outside Berthold Junior's place, listening to the tap we installed. I had the radio on and you'll never guess what song came on." He displayed his toothy grin, waiting for me to guess. "You guessed it—that Cyndi Lauper song. I could practically hear you singing off-tune." He laughed, wiggling his finger in his eardrum.

I joined him, wishing we could replay the other night on an endless loop.

"I already miss you and am counting down the days until I can see you again. I've gotta send a report for The Patriots now. Have a good night." He blew me a kiss and ended the transmission.

I drove home that night, with 'Time After Time' on repeat.

 For weeks, I came to the lab just so I could get my work done as fast as possible and then allow myself to watch the videos Abel sent. But as the weeks progressed, his tone became more apathetic.

"Hey Taden, I miss you so much. I wish I wasn't here. I was thinking, you know, I could get a different job. I don't have to work for The Patriots. If I had a normal nine to five, we could at least see each other every day. I don't know. I'm probably just tired. I got on the inside. I've been hired as a Secret Service agent for Berthold Senior. Listening to these guys talk about our country makes me physically ill." He sighed. "I've gotta get a few hours of sleep before my night surveillance starts. I miss you."

He was struggling. I was struggling, too. I felt his absence like crazy. He was all I thought about. But as bad as I had it, Abel had it worse. Besides his team he was all alone in a world he didn't belong to, strapped with the responsibility he'd committed himself to. I was worried about him, and pressed Dakotah for information I might be able to send to his TRB.

"The TRB isn't set up to receive messages from this timeline. All I've coded it to do is trigger his alarm. Which he knows is to abort his mission," she reminded me, trying to re-instill logic.

"Potentially, we could set the alarm to go off in a series, though, couldn't we?"

"What do you mean?"

"You know. Like, Morse code. I could send him a message that way. I'm certain he would figure it out no problem."

"And when he comes back thinking it was his abort mission alarm? And Danika finds out? Is it worth the heat from her?"

"Then do it. Abort his mission. She can send someone else. She only sent him to separate us so I wouldn't become so distracted by him. She easily could've sent Lt. Duncan. I don't want to live my life without him. He's considering quitting."

I wouldn't have been able to admit how much anguish I'd succumbed to, to anyone other than Dakotah. Subconsciously, I counted on her ability to hold a mirror to my despair.

"He can't quit the NIST. Just no. This isn't going to last forever. Okay? Taden, you have to figure out a way to let him be. He's gone and he's not coming back any time soon. I get it. It's hard. But he *will* be back. In the meantime your work is important, and you have to get out of this funk. Your lack of interest in Quinn is making her feel isolated. Have you even spoken to Ruth, *really* spoken to her? It's time to stop this. I realize your pain still feels raw and fresh. But life here is going on around you and you have to participate in it. Just like Abel has to participate in the life he's living."

It was tough love from my best friend, but I knew she was right. I've felt loss before, and I got through it. My survival strategy was always to drown my brain with science. It would have to be my coping mechanism once again.

I imagined Abel was confiding in a friend on his team who gave him similar advice, because as more weeks advanced he sent fewer updates to me.

Eventually, he wasn't contacting me at all anymore. I told myself what I needed to hear: he missed me, he loved me, but he had to survive and live his life. I wanted him to be happy. I just wanted him to be happy *with me*.

Grief had given me a powerful sense of courage to do things that would normally cripple me into cowardice. I suddenly felt willing to participate in whatever The Patriots deemed necessary related to Marius.

I still reserved an amount of hesitancy on behalf of Quinn, though. I hadn't completely gone off the deep end, willing to dangle her out into the danger zone, but I welcomed the strategy of using her as a pawn in this game. As long as she wasn't accessible to him, I didn't see why we shouldn't use her as bait.

"We had eyes on Mr. Touma leaving a vaccine plant in New York. We looked into the medical group and found ties to Berthold," Lt. Duncan reported.

"How so?" Ms. Farkas asked.

"One of their lead engineers was on Berthold Senior's National Vaccine Advisory Committee."

Mr. Richardson brought his hand to his chin. "Do we know what Mr. Touma was doing there?"

"No, sir."

"Dr. Barrett, I want you to fly in for a visit with your sister. Remind our old friend, Marius, he'd better be good if he wants to meet his sister."

"No problem," I said.

"Lt. Duncan, I'll brief you on the details and you will escort Dr. Barrett. I want to know if Mr. Touma is trying to hide anything."

Almost a month had passed with no word from Abel. Once again I'd gone into his reports, hoping for some sign of communication hidden in his messages for me. There was nothing. I felt so far away from him, and the distance was eating me up. I thought about going to the past. I could easily leave after everyone went home for the day. No one would even know I'd left. I fantasized about finding Abel and sharing the stolen time with him. But reality pulled me back. The last time I used time travel for my own personal agenda, I almost died. Technically, I did. Besides, if Abel had wanted to see me, he wouldn't have stopped sending me messages.

It was another lonely Friday evening, home alone, sitting on my couch. I was staring out the window, wishing for Abel. I needed to feel something, and before I could even consciously decide how to make that happen I was in a cab headed to the bar he and I went to on our last night together. We had spent the night dancing together there, so I went in search of him in that place. I had never gone to a bar alone before, and walking into the dimly lit room by myself, feeling the eyes of lonely men size me up, was the first sense of fear I'd felt since Abel left. It wasn't enough, though, for me to turn around. And, to be honest, the uneasiness stirred by their watchful eyes felt better than the loneliness I had come to know so well.

The dance-floor was mostly covered with tables, lending to the live entertainment of the evening: a solo piano man. With my newfound independence I sauntered to the front of the room and sat at the first open table, right next to the piano. Once I reached the front row seating, it felt safer than being hidden in the back of the bar and more distant from predatory eyes in the dark.

Halfway through my first drink, I looked up from my intent focus on the glass of liquid painkiller for the first time. My object of observation was the ruggedly handsome musician in front of me. He sang to the melody tapped out on the keys under his massive fingers. His voice broke through to the emptiness inside me and felt like a welcome guest to my pity-party of one. To my surprise his coffee brown eyes caught mine, and at that moment I finally noticed he was in the same room with me. I blushed at the fact that he'd seen me being pulled by his voice. I immediately looked back down at my drink, but I didn't feel the urge to escape my awkward moment. I remained because even this wasn't as bad as sitting at home, alone and full of loss. As the evening continued his set list continued, and he played several of my favorite songs.

I'm sure the alcohol encouraged me, but it felt like he and I were hanging out together and the rest of the bar just happened to be there, too. With a solid foundation of liquid courage, I joined him in singing along to many of the songs I knew word for word. Convinced we were becoming fast friends, I wondered if normal people made friends this way. I didn't have a ton of experience making friends outside of work, so I wasn't too sure how weird I might have been coming across to the piano man.

I was almost finished with my third or fourth drink when he announced he was taking a short break.

"Be sure to stick around for the next set," he said in his honey voice to encouraging applause.

He walked over to the bar, and I felt alone in the room again. I turned around to see, for the first time since I'd entered, that the bar was indeed full of people—yet I felt so naked, and so solitary. I lifted my drink to swallow down my last swig, when I saw through my glass that the piano man was standing in front of me. I tried not to choke on the large gulp I had just swallowed and set my glass back down on the table.

"Is this seat available?" he asked.

"Sure." My face flushed again, and I was thankful for the dark room.

He set his drink down, and a second drink in front of me. "I asked the bartender what you've been drinking. I'm impressed. The lady drinks whiskey."

He sat down in the chair next to me. I could smell on his breath the whiskey he'd already consumed. I was thinking about Abel, but Piano Man took the edge off.

"I hope you don't mind me asking, but what are you doing here alone? From where I sit, you're way too...*everything* to be sitting here alone."

"I'm *not* sitting here alone. You're here."

He laughed. "So, I've walked right into your trap?"

"It would appear so." I felt a tinge of guilt. I wasn't blind. I could see he was hitting on me. I could also see he was an attractive and charming man with broad shoulders and an easy smile. I could feel the attraction, too, but I didn't want him. I would give up nothing for a conversation with Piano Man. I would give up anything, everything, for one conversation with Abel.

"What's your name?" I heard myself asking him. I didn't even know why I asked. I didn't really care what his name was, I just wanted him to return to making music and helping me forget how lonely I felt.

"Where are my manners?" He held his hand out for mine. I laughed, a nervous response I detested giving to people. Obliging, I placed mine in his and he kissed it. I couldn't decide if his chivalry made me swoon or irritated me.

"My name is Michael."

"Nice to meet you, Michael. I'm Taden."

"Now that we're friends, Taden, would you like to hang out with me for a little bit? I have about ten more minutes before my next set. I'd love to show you around the joint."

"Really?" I looked at him through skeptical eyes.

"I'll be a well-behaved man. Truly. I just want to be in your company."

"No funny business, Michael. I'm not that kind of girl," I warned him.

"I wouldn't dream of it. Scout's honor." He held up three fingers.

"I can't imagine what's to see on your tour. This may be the tiniest bar I've ever been to."

"There's actually quite an extensive musical instrument collection, with all of the live performers they support on a regular schedule." He pointed to the ceiling. "You might even be impressed—I play most of the instruments here."

I followed him to a staircase.

"I don't think I've ever seen you here before," he said to me.

His comment sent me into the memory of the last time I had come, and who I was with. How much I would've traded this moment for that one. Instead, I opened the door for mindless small talk.

"How long have you been a musician?" I asked him as he led me up the narrow stairs.

"I have no memory of ever not being a musician," he replied over his shoulder, one step above me.

"I feel the same way about science."

He stopped and turned around to face me. "Nice. You're into science? What do you do?"

"I work over at the NIST. Physics department." He nodded his head in approval. I could tell he was impressed with my career status. His response, paired with the steady flow of drinks I had ingested by that point, made me feel pretty cool about myself.

On the second floor, we entered an open space crammed with various instruments. It vaguely reminded me of the music room at my high school. I didn't play any instruments back then, but my last hour of the day was Office Aid and I'd visit the room, lugging forgotten instruments to students after their parents dropped them off. Each time I would appear with a forgotten instrument a room full of musicians would greet me, exploding fanciful sounds from trumpets, flutes, and timpani—and somehow, the collective effort would form together into music. It was a foreign language to me, but one I loved to hear.

"We practice here before gig nights. We even give lessons up here, too," he told me, walking over to the piano in the center of the room. "Do you know how to play?"

Shaking my head, I replied, "I can play "Twinkle Twinkle Little Star". Does that count?"

Michael couldn't contain his laughter. "Yes, it counts. Come on." He nodded his head toward the piano. "Let's play."

I saw through his offer as a means to have closer proximity between us, and felt a matching tension emanate from him. "Look, I don't want to waste your time, so I'm going to be straight with you. My life is messy right now, and I'm not interested in bringing anyone into my world. I just came here tonight hoping I could feel something different for an evening. Tomorrow, I fully plan on returning to my life of despair." And I laughed the same, stupid, nervous laugh.

"I promise you, my time is not being wasted. I would be more than willing to help tonight feel absent of despair with you," he said smoothly.

Damn, this guy was good. I reminded myself he was working at charming me, and that this was a facade of a connection.

"You've already done a nice job," I told him. I wasn't intending to involve him any further in my quest to forget how constricted my heart beat without Abel.

He looked confused. "How have I helped?"

I wondered why this ten-minute intermission felt like forty. "Watching you perform. Feeling the music you make. The way you're looking at me right now doesn't hurt, either." To lighten the heaviness I brought into the atmosphere, I added, "I've all but forgotten my sadness, for an hour, because of you."

I smiled lifting my hands in surrender, and his whole face lit up. I was flirting! I couldn't even believe myself. I hadn't intended to send poor Michael the wrong signal.

"It's only fair you should know," I blurted, "I love someone else. I just wanted to feel something good for a while. Besides, I'm sure you bring women up here all the time, and have them eating out of the palm of your hand, so…" I was word vomiting, and couldn't stop myself. "I've never even walked into a bar alone. I've certainly never followed a man upstairs and, I don't know, flirted with him, awkwardly, apparently." I paused to sink into the embarrassment I'd created. "I can go."

I couldn't believe how uncomfortable I had made this situation. I turned to leave but he reached his massive, elegant hand toward me and gently wrapped it around my lower arm.

"No, stay. We still have "Twinkle, Twinkle" to play." He gestured to the piano. I replayed every ridiculous word I had just uttered to this complete stranger. Sure, he was attractive and talented and bold. *What about the chance that he could be crazy? Had I not learned my lesson about crazy men?*

Michael interrupted my overthinking just as my brain prompted me to leave before I did something I'd regret. "I really want to keep making you feel good tonight. You've already made my night a million times better. I still vow to be a gentleman." He tilted his head at the piano and snuck in his own joke to lighten the mood. "But you could never want me, huh? That's a hard one to hear."

He smiled in a way that I felt heat up my entire body. There should be a word for grieving the living. I was exhausted from mourning Abel every single day. Everywhere I looked, there was a memory—and it was beginning to make me sick. *Maybe*, I thought, *tonight I can escape the pain of missing Abel and let this gorgeous man make me feel something that didn't hurt so much.* On one hand it felt like betrayal, but on the other hand Abel had shut me out.

While I was knee-deep in my Abel reverie Michael was intently watching me, assessing my decision to stay or go. He sat on his piano bench, an arm's length from me, and put his hand out so his finger just grazed the edges of mine, sending a jolt of electricity strong enough to pull me back to the moment. My face contained a brewing heat storm. It made him smile that he'd embarrassed me with an insignificant touch.

"C'mon. Sit down. Let's play."

This time I obeyed, and sat leg-to-leg with this god of a man. He instructed me which keys to tap while he melodically played along on the upper keys. I couldn't keep from smiling at the silly song we played, with the dive bar under our feet. I hoped it wasn't audible downstairs. He reached across the keyboard over me and tapped a key once, letting the note ring out. Then, with his other hand, he cupped the back of my head, preparing to kiss me. He waited the shortest pause to let me stop him.

I didn't.

Between the way he held my head in his hand and the way he gently pulled on my lips with his, I felt dizzy with sensations that didn't feel anything like heartache. I was hungry, maybe even desperate for more. I swung my right leg over the piano bench so I straddled it, facing him, and scooted my body closer. The strong hands I had watched move along the black and white keys all evening were pulling my lower back even closer. Like a power switch, we suddenly couldn't get close enough to each other. I released my hands from behind his neck, pulled just far enough from his lips to look into his eyes. He was carnality personified.

"Don't you have to get back on stage?" I asked him.

A sigh of disdain left his body. He squeezed my bottom now, his hands pulling me in again. I could feel his desire. I stood, still hovering over the bench. He grabbed both of my dangling hands from my sides and wrapped them back around his neck and pulled my waist to him again. This suave move left me straddling him instead of the bench. Immediately, I felt fire move through my legs. I sighed into his mouth as he kissed me again, once more, with an extra charge before he used his strong body to lift us both from the bench, me still wrapped around him, and gently set me back to my grounding.

"You are going to do some damage. I can already tell," he said.

It was as if his words were the stroke of midnight. I snapped back to reality. *What had I just done?* I didn't want to do this. I didn't want to be here. My mind was drowning with immediate regret. Almost out of body, I followed Michael back down the narrow staircase to my table in the front of the room. He stepped onto the stage, resuming his magic of musical transformation—but this time, nausea swept through me. Every sensation screamed at me to leave. I forced a smile at that beautiful man, mouthed "thank you", and retreated before I could do any more damage. A cool breeze hit my face, eyes burning, and my thoughts were suddenly more clear than the sky. I went there looking for Abel. I couldn't find him there, but I knew where I could.

Swiping my badge I walked the empty halls of my lab, headed to the room where we collected Abel's TRB data. I logged into the computer to obtain the access needed to view his vitals. My eyes fell upon the picture confirming his identity and agent information. Then the data feed from the band on his wrist was live. A green circle confirmed he was there; his heart was beating, and his blood pressure was steady. He was living and breathing. I was overcome with relief and anguish. He was there. On the other side of a green dot. I touched the screen, desperate for him.

All at once I was reminded of him standing at my front door, holding Forget-Me-Nots and a wrapped gift. I still hadn't opened the gift. The note attached was scribbled with the words, "Open this when you're desperate for me".

The next thing I knew I was sitting in a car at a red light, muttering, "C'mon, c'mon, turn green already."

An unknown amount of time had lapsed between kissing the piano man's lips and the drive home with more purpose than I'd experienced in months. When I was finally running upstairs, into my bedroom, satisfaction settled over me to hold the still-wrapped package in my hands.

Carefully removing the tape so as not to damage the gift-wrapped words Abel and I had written, I opened it to find a worn out copy of *The Great Gatsby*. I knew it was a book!

On instinct, I brought the book to my nose and inhaled it deeply, hoping it held a trace of Abel—and like the relief of rain quelling a drought, it did. Droplets fell onto the cover and I wiped my eyes with the back of my hand, not wanting to damage any traces of him left behind. I climbed onto my bed, pulled the blanket around me in place of the hug I so badly needed, and set the magnificence of his book down in front of me.

For the longest time, I just looked at it in all its splendor. Eventually, I gently lifted the cover as if it was the most delicate object I'd ever touched. Inside, Abel wrote me a snippet of a conversation we had so many years ago when we first became friends. He had loved me from the beginning. All those years. I never knew. All that time we'd wasted.

I wished, for the second time since creating time travel, to go back in time to a specific moment and change things. This time my regret was to undo my ignorance so the two of us could have spent every day after that moment together, in love with one another. How different my life would've been. First and foremost, I never would have experienced Marius the way I had.

Already, those first few minutes with Abel's book assuaged my torment. It moved my soul. It made me feel less lonely. I flipped through the pages to see them filled with his handwriting. Tracing my finger along his words, I released the desolation of my evening through sobs into the night. Each time I regained my composure, I'd return to thumbing through the wonder inside his gift. Near the end of the book, he'd underlined a passage that caught my attention: "The afternoon had made them tranquil for a while, as if to give them a deep memory for the long parting the next day promised." And in the margin next to it, Abel wrote, "This lover's goodbye is so powerful. I've read this line so many times, yet tonight it popped into my head and I quickly skimmed the book again to find it. I'm heading to your house soon and we will spend this evening creating deep memories for our own long parting."

I'd come to the back of the book, where I read the last words he wrote—dated the day before he left. They leapt off the page and cradled me the way his hands did. He used my own words, words I once put into a sentence meant to self-comfort in the absence of my mom. They were the words that gave me the courage to let go of my pain and accept her memory as evidence she'd loved me. He was giving them back to me, to use again, this time in absence of him. He wrote,

Taden,

I ardently love you.

In all of my timelines.

Beneath it he drew a symbol. It reminded me of a variation on a Celtic knot I've seen in my dad's heritage artwork. Abel's symbol included two closed oval loops which crossed paths in four locations, where they weaved over and under each other. Inside each separate oval, he'd filled them in to appear like separate galaxies. The caption he added beneath it said, "We are forever entangled, you and I, no matter the distance. Whatever happens to one, affects the other."

CHAPTER 27

ABEL

My mission was to gather intel, to bring back the names and dates of each major interaction that acted as a domino to Berthold's presidency.

According to history, in seven months he'd replace his father and begin his task to even more deeply dismantle the foundations of our country.

"Help me attach this wire, would ya?" I asked Josh, my roommate.

I'd gotten inside working undercover as a Secret Service agent for the president. That morning, he was to have a meeting with his son and an unnamed businessman at an offsite location. My team had been tracking this meeting as possibly being the initial exchange regarding their major move to side-step an election.

"We've got the radio receiver set up in the van," he said, taping the tiny microphone to my chest. "We're ready to go."

Fastening the buttons of my crisp white shirt, a vibration from my TRB advanced through my arm. Caught off guard, I accidentally ripped off the button between my fingertips. I'd never actually experienced the alert before. It meant I was to return home to the present timeline immediately.

"Josh."

"Yes, sir?"

"I've been called home. We'll need to plant a bug for this meeting."

"That's bad timing," he said.

"It is. I hope it's good news."

"We carry on until told otherwise."

"That's correct. I'll either return or send an alarm for the team to come home."

"The van's ready. We'll drop you at the time-jump checkpoint."

Standing in the lab that I had no idea when I'd get to see again, I was torn between the joy of being there and the anticipation of what horrible news had brought me. It was surprising not to find Taden waiting for my arrival. The initial sting of her absence was immediately replaced with concern. Had something terrible happened to her? Before I reached panic, Dakotah burst into the room.

"Oh my God, I'm so glad to see you! Come with me."

In stride, we headed to the data collection room. "What happened? Is everyone all right? Where's Taden?"

She didn't answer my questions, which did little in calming my fears. Once we were inside the small office where she had, at one time or another, probed me about every living memory I'd ever held about the world, her concerns met mine.

"I found something terrible in your memory, Abel. I haven't spoken to anyone yet. Taden's with Ruth, helping her prepare for the inauguration. Lt. Duncan is there to monitor. Quinn's running the lab, but this doesn't meet her clearance level."

"What? What did you find?"

"As soon as I stumbled upon it, I triggered your bat signal and texted the others using our emergency code. I've been tapping into the memory further to isolate it enough for viewing." She clicked her keyboard rapidly before stopping to glance at her clock. "It's official, though… time travel is the fastest mode of travel. *Where the hell is everyone?*"

"Dakotah! What did you find?" I couldn't honestly think of anything urgent enough to threaten the mission I'd sacrificed so much for.

"You have a memory of the government mandating a compulsory injectable data tracking device."

"Yes, the mandate was released in a news conference with President Berthold just before The Reckoning went down. But it never happened. After The Reckoning, the issue fell aside."

I waited for her to fill in the missing link I couldn't connect.

"Your memory indicates our government explained each injection would include a microscopic chip to be implanted into our fingers." I nodded. "They sold the chip as an easier process to carry each of our personal data. No longer would we need a driver's license, social security card, birth certificate, or passport. All of our health care information, etcetera, would be stored in our chip."

She stepped away from her work station over to me. "The chip could be accessed through our devices to update as necessary. A simple convenience for us." Attaching the memory braces to my head and wrists, she glanced at the clock again.

"Berthold's chip, it turned out after further exploration, was actually meant as a force of fear repression," Dakotah continued. "The Patriots' intel learned that the chip, once injected into a host, could release a deadly disease upon being triggered."

"...yeah? I mean yes, it's scary, but it never happened."

"Actually, that's what caused me to sound the alarm. His chip was designed by several members of The Reckoning terrorist cell. No one else has the timeline memory of this, besides you and your team. While you've been gone one of the platforms President Moore rolled out for her presidency is this technologically advanced immunization, so small it can be injected into the tip of a finger." Dakotah paused for effect. "Sound familiar? Plus, we linked an engineer from the immunization plant where these are being created to Berthold."

"So, Moore might actually be working Berthold's plan," I thought out loud.

"She boasts her vaccine will prevent three different strains of a modern virus looming on the horizon. There's been no mention of a chip as part of the injection, but that doesn't mean it's not in there. They've been flaunting how every attendee of the inaugural ball will get to volunteer as the first to receive the immunization at their event to kick off the campaign, 'Stop the Spread'. But this is too much of a coincidence. We have to entertain the idea that, in this timeline, the people in charge are withholding information related to these injections.

"So, you're concerned this might be a tactic ultimately meant as a power move," I said.

"You have to brief The Patriot Party on every detail regarding the injection from the previous timeline. We need to get a handle on this before the president's inaugural event, when her vaccine goes live. Then the following day they will be available for the public to volunteer for."

I agreed with Dakotah's decision to abort my mission; this issue felt damn close to an emergency.

Dakotah nodded. "I've finished with your memory analysis," she said as she unhooked me from the monitors. "I imagine you're probably anxious about being back so suddenly. It could still be at least a half-hour before everyone else arrives and we can start the briefing, if you want to take some time…" I'd never appreciated Dakotah's insight more than at that moment.

I had only been gone a few months, but in my absence I'd effectively cut Taden off, believing I needed to make a choice between the NIST or being with her. I'd become depressed and didn't want to distract Taden with concern. I decided to stop sending her video updates so she could fully focus on time travel, as Ms. Farkas had pointed out. Once this mission was over, I planned to return home and make the decision with Taden about our future. Now, here I stood, minutes away from sharing the same airspace with her once more. I presumed she felt every bit of heartache I felt, with the added pain that I'd stopped communicating.

I was back, but I still couldn't see a way for us to be together while my mission was still active. We were worlds apart. Even then, standing in the timeline I belonged to, I was acutely aware it was temporary. I would get to see her, smell her, and listen to her voice, but it would still be unavailable to us. How was I supposed to handle this? Continue to give her reason to hate me, so she could go on living her life without the idea of me holding her back? I wanted her to be happy. I didn't want her to be angry with me, but I wasn't sure it was fair for me to swoop in and steal more of her love just to leave her again.

I needed to clear my head and focus on what I was actually here to do. This immunization issue could be the best way to expose Marius and President Moore to the people—if we played our cards right. I for one was all for handling our world issue in the present, rather than relying on jumping backwards in time.

Indeed, maybe—just maybe—if we could fix the present here and now, I could abort my current mission. If all was well, I wouldn't need to go back into the past again. It was a small chance, but it was one worth going after.

After all didn't Gatsby, too, have a small chance at a beautiful future? He went for it. I would, too.

CHAPTER 28

TADEN

Dozens of round tables surrounded us in middle of the Grand Rotunda. Ruth had begged me to come in for the big event and assist her with setting up.

"These buttons look authentic," I said, placing one on each setting of the table. "They look like they're from the first inauguration."

"That's because they were designed to look just like Washington's commemorative inauguration button," Ruth said, pleased with my impression.

"That's an eagle, right?"

"Yes, it's been used throughout history because of its great…" My phone signaled a text. Ruth's eagle knowledge faded into the background. Looking at my screen, I nearly fell over. Ruth reached out to catch me as I set my phone on the table and sat down in one of the grand chairs.

"Jeez, Taden. What's going on? Have you eaten today?"

"Sorry. I'm fine. Just a bit caught off guard." My face was surely a picture of shock. "I just got a text from Dakotah."

"What'd she say?"

I picked up my phone again to re-read the text, not sure I saw it correctly. The words were clear. Abel was back. Reading it aloud to Ruth elicited a free-flow of emotion only to be abated after I excused myself to a more private location.

I didn't know why he was home. All that mattered was that he was here. I beamed with joy in the mirror... until I started to doubt if it mattered to him that he was back. He hadn't contacted me in weeks, and he wasn't even the one who'd informed me of his return.

In a flash of worry, I texted Dakotah. "He's okay, right?"

"He is. We're waiting for everyone to arrive for a debriefing."

My brooding deepened at the idea the chasm between us might be permanent. I stared deeply at my reflection, trying hard to find any trace of the woman he'd loved. I loved that version of myself, too. I splashed my face with water. Patting it dry I then returned my gaze to the mirror, speaking affirmations to move myself forward.

"Even if he doesn't love you anymore, you are loved," I said. It sounded fake. I tried again: "You are *loved,* Taden. If everyone else on earth left you behind, *you'd* still be here for you. You are going to get through this. You are intelligent and funny and valued."

I took a great big breath, trying to ignore the sharpness in my chest, and left the restroom to find Ruth.

"There you are," she said, rubbing my back and pulling my cheek into hers.

I stiffened. Not because I didn't want Ruth to comfort me; I wanted to crawl on her lap and let her pet my head while I cried myself to sleep. But I was a grown woman who had a responsibility to attend to, and in order to function as such I couldn't be a blubbery mess of emotion. Therefore, Ruth couldn't rub my back or give me hugs or look at me like a puppy dog.

"I have to go," I told her firmly. "Dakotah's text said it's an emergency. This must be why Abel's back. I'm so sorry."

"It's okay," she assured me. "There's plenty of people here to help. Don't even worry about it. But come back tomorrow?"

"I wouldn't miss it for anything." And I didn't intend to.

CHAPTER 29

ABEL

I felt her enter the room before I saw her. Every cell in my body migrated in her direction. My pulse felt heavy in my throat. Still not sure how I should interact with Taden, I kept my eyes down. She was already looking at me, I could sense it. Unable to resist returning the contact I looked up, surprised to find her reading the briefing for the meeting and not looking at me at all. No matter. It gave me pause to study the outline of her face and take note of the changes it'd undergone in the months since I last saw her. Those changes might go unnoticed to the untrained eye, but mine knew that when Taden hadn't been sleeping well, the corners of her mouth took on a subtle droopiness and the skin under her eyes became darker. To conceal it, she put on makeup she normally didn't wear. Her bright red lips, faintly moving as she read the briefing, put me into a trance.

Dakotah started the meeting by explaining why she made the call to urgently bring me home from the past. It was enough of a distraction to pull me away from Taden's lips and my worry about her difficulty sleeping. Sooner than I expected, it was my turn to debrief everyone regarding my memory of the chip injection from the previous timeline. My hands were clammy and I still didn't know how to respond to the imminent eye contact we were undoubtedly soon going to exchange. I tried my best to speak to each person in the room, but once I turned toward Taden I was powerless to break away. She became my sole audience. As I spoke, she furiously tapped notes into her device. She couldn't avoid my eyes forever. Before long, she'd return her unfiltered attention back to my presentation and back to me. During the question and answer session following my briefing, she asked several important questions. Taden asking questions was a sign she was listening. The fact that she was listening felt like a positive.

"Do you recollect how a microscopic chip had been designed to release a virus?"

"I do have the memory of the chip's design. It will have to be finessed from my mind, though, because it's of a photographic detail."

"We've bugged the chip's designer," Lt. Duncan asserted. "It might be more efficient to bring him in for questioning."

"I'm sure Ruth could get access to the lancets. We could have her snag a few to study." Dakotah had wanted to get her hands on this immunization since we found out it was their move.

"Or we could do all three: scope my memory, get our hands on the immunization, *and* track down the chip's designers."

Ms. Farkas rubbed her temples, listening to us launch ideas. Clearing her throat, she sat back in her seat. "We won't expose our position so close to the finish line. We can always go back in time to fix this if it doesn't turn out a success."

I blinked with disapproval at how cavalierly she suggested time travel as a solution.

"Lt. Duncan, I want you on post during the event. We'll remove the samples for Dr. Hughs at that time." Then she looked squarely to me. "Dr. Mihal, it's good to have you home. You will remain until we've handled the emerging event."

"Are we thinking that President Moore is linked with Berthold?" I asked.

"If we make our conclusions based on what we've gathered so far about Moore's injections, it isn't looking good. Let's reconvene tomorrow at our rendezvous point in the city."

As soon as Ms. Farkas left with her entourage, Taden stood to follow her out the door. It never usually went down like that. We always stayed back as a core group and talked about how the meeting went, without our bosses present. Clearly, Taden did not want to be in the same room with me.

I didn't want to cause her any more torment, and if this was what she wanted I would respect her wishes.

My office already had a new tenant, Lieutenant Duncan. I tried not to acknowledge the sting, because I was an adult and it made sense. Why would they keep an office empty for months if Ms. Farkas had more missions planned for me, maybe years on end? But the feeling of so easily becoming a shadow in my present life was unsettling. I no longer fully belonged to this place which used to be my home. I'd never belong to the timelines I traveled to.

With no office to retreat to I ambled back to the conference room, now empty. It appeared this would be my space for the duration of this mission, so I resumed my work of clearing my mind. I sat at the table, looking to each empty chair, void of my friends. With my head in my hands, I thought through a plan to confront Marius.

CHAPTER 30

RUTH

A friend of mine used to say, when she was excited for something but also scared that she was *skited*. Going into this inaugural ball, I was certainly skited. This was the biggest event of my entire career. It would be seen nationwide, and even beyond. People around the world would be watching President Moore officially celebrate the world-changing event of her inauguration, of her leading our country out of tyranny and returning to the democratic process.

Building hype, commercials of her 'Stop the Spread' campaign aired non-stop.

"I was raised to take action. Growing up, I witnessed the hardships resulting from poor health care. I've promised you this would change. I will be putting my words into action during my inaugural ball." She held up a fingerstick device. "This vaccine delivery system was modeled after the same instrument conveniently used daily by diabetic patients around the world. Inside, it contains a technologically advanced microscopic injection of a vaccine that will protect you against three contemporary viruses. The research into this cutting-edge immunization has been years in the making, and it's finally ready for volunteers, like you, who want to be included. Tune in on inauguration night, when I will be the first to volunteer."

Every detail of the event mattered. I needed to consider the impression the media would make with the images sent into people's homes. I also had to think about the impression left on the guests in attendance.

I hadn't slept properly in weeks.

It wasn't enough that this event was going to catapult my career into an entirely new ballgame, but also, despite every red flag, Mary and I had developed a wonderful new friendship. We texted back and forth on a daily basis, and I couldn't help but wonder if this would continue after the event. At the moment all we talked about was the event, but I had been paying attention to any open doors to normal discussion. If she welcomed anything personal, I was quick to pick up her cue and carry the conversation through.

"Are you inviting your sister?" Mary asked.

"I was hoping I could."

Mary looked down at the invitation list, adding Taden's name. "Of course. I see your dad on the list with a guest—Dr. Pasterski. What about your mom?"

"My mom passed away." My heart still pinched whenever I revealed my loss to someone new.

"Oh. I'm sorry. I didn't know. I wouldn't have suggested—my mom passed away, too."

"She did?" I asked. This was surprising news, because when I knew her before her mom was alive and well. This must've been an outcome affected by the changes of The Reckoning. "Do you mind if I ask what happened? I mean, for my mom it was cancer. Did your mom die from cancer, too?"

I could tell it still caused her the same type of reaction to talk about her own mom from the painful smile she forced. "She died giving birth to my little brother. In my home country, we didn't have access to the health care she needed to safely deliver him."

Again, surprise. Maria and her family came here before her brother was born, but Mary didn't come here until after her brother was born. "That's awful," I said, gently touching her forearm. "Your brother's okay, though?"

"He died as well."

"Oh!" I covered my mouth. "President Moore, I'm terribly sorry to bring this up."

"It's okay. It actually feels good to talk about them. People don't like to hear about personal tragedy."

Fervently nodding, I sucked in my lips. "It's so true. Whenever I talk about my mom, people become uncomfortably silent."

This led to a lingering silence that was anything but uncomfortable.

"Tell me what you miss most about your mom," she said.

"So many things. Umm, I'd say I miss how she used to tuck my hair behind my shoulders when she'd tell me she loved me. How 'bout you?"

"Oh, my mom used to spin me around our living room listening to salsa music," she said, shimmying her shoulders.

Our mom talk was the single-most important conversation we'd had, beyond the inauguration. Each meeting after felt more and more familiar. Marius was no longer present on a regular basis, and when he was around he didn't remain for the entire meeting. The deeper we delved into party details, the less likely he was to stick it out. His interests were merely related to safety and procedural notions. If he made me uncomfortable, I used my observations about this to get rid of him.

"Mary, you have to see the linens. They just arrived, and I brought samples of the tablecloths and napkins." Gathering them from the bag I had left on the couch across the room, I glanced at Marius out of the corner of my eye and caught him checking his phone screen with itching boredom.

"It appears you ladies have this under control. I'll be down the hall." He took measured steps to the door, looking back to Mary as he left. "Call if you need me."

She giggled at his haste to escape, returning to me and my weapon of linens.

"Not everyone appreciates the details," I said to her, sure to carry on poking fun at him.

The fact was, he had no reason to believe I would pose any threat to her. All he knew about me was I had helped rescue him from death as a teenager and that Taden, who actually did the rescuing, had the missing link to finding his sister. If anything, I appeared as an ally to Marius. Not blind to the rapport Mary and I had built, he was smart to let it lie and refrain from stirring up trouble. He seemed to have the intelligence to lay low with Taden as well. Since the interrogation he forced upon her, he took great care not to antagonize or even contact my sister. At least for the time being.

As far as I was concerned, Mary was completely naive about Marius and his tendency to lean into the darkness. I'd done my fair share of digging into our talks, trying to get her to admit any romantic notions she felt for him, and although she wouldn't outright confirm they existed her body language told on her. She reminded me of Taden, lovesick under his spell. There were times I wanted to take her by the shoulders and shake some sense into her. Other times I would watch him interact with Mary and I could swear he wasn't putting on a show, either. He really expressed genuine care and admiration for her. Sometimes I forgot he was the villain in this story.

At night when I couldn't sleep, these were the moments I'd get hung up on most often. With all I knew about this man, I still found myself forgetting what he was capable of. At times, I even bought into his charm and seemingly authentic self. It haunted me in the sleepless dark. His ability to hook his prey increased his potential to be especially dangerous.

The topic that drew the most attention from Marius concerned the procedures we would use in announcing and distributing the immunizations at the ceremony. He felt strongly they were to be the backbone of President Moore's legacy. This was the strategy they needed to get her officially elected the following November. It was Marius' idea to have Mary reveal the highly anticipated injection toward the end of her speech, when her chief doctor on staff would enter left stage to give her the injection on live television. She'd say something along the lines of, "As you can see, it's as simple as that!" and then identify the areas in the ballroom any interested volunteers could go for theirs.

I demonstrated for them the application my company's engineer created for keeping a record of who received injections and who declined.

"This is good. Simple and efficient," Mary said.

"I want this app to link the data live to my network," Marius told me. "Is that possible?"

I thought it was weird that he wanted that information himself. I was under the impression that aside from my application there was some type of data being collected from the test group for scientific purposes. I thought my simple app was only meant for smooth delivery and inventory tracking at the event.

"It will be useful data to give the Centers for Disease Control and Prevention."

"Of course," I told him, doubting his intentions.

I hadn't been honest, though. The data application was developed for The Patriots to have access to these records.

Abel wanted to know every single word exchanged regarding this portion of the evening. It'd gotten to the point where I couldn't provide the verbatim he required, and so in the final days before the inauguration he'd wire me to a recording device.

At first I felt intensely justified playing an integral role in the defeat of Marius, but this was eventually followed by soft feelings of guilt. I was worried about when Mary found out I'd been a double agent of sorts. It'd destroy any chance of getting her back in my life—if she wasn't guilty of misdeeds herself.

Also—and I hated to admit this—I had the tiniest seed of doubt that Marius was actually not a bad guy in this play. Sure, he had followed my sister to an abandoned hospital and then taken her to an unknown location to interrogate her, but didn't she seem like the bad guy in that scene from his point of view? Wouldn't anyone have responded similarly in his position?

I read once that deep undercover agents can get so caught up in the alternate role they play that they begin to lose grasp of who they really are. Instead, they find themselves buying into the world they were meant to take down. I was starting to have real concerns I might be too deeply involved with President Moore and Marius Touma. At what point did I stop seeing Marius as anything other than my sister's murderer?

Regardless of anything else, the turnout for President Moore's Inaugural Ball was straight from my dreams. Every detail met my expectations.

The saucer-domed ceiling and Corinthian columns easily transported me to imagine our country's first inaugural ball. Each table was set just as Martha Washington might've done. Silver candlesticks surrounded by teapots and elegant serving pieces. Each eggshell napkin folded with precise corners. Servers wearing either knee breeches and coats or elegant brocades carried pewter trays of trifles.

It was a sight to behold, and amid all the chaos of the event I found a quiet corner, hid myself behind a large tropical plant, and soaked in the moment. With age, I'd learned to appreciate these small gifts of time which often go unnoticed marching through the business of life. It's the seemingly insignificant events that become the very seconds our mind replays when threats loom.

I took in the bustling room filled with elegance, laughter, and human proximity. Reflections of light danced on beverage glasses, and soft music subtly filled the background. My vision felt as though it was experiencing synesthesia, as the colors throughout the room both stirred my appetite and satisfied my cravings. That night was surely the pinnacle of my career, and I lingered in those last few satisfying seconds before President Moore took to the stage to give her history-changing speech.

"Ms. Barrett! There you are. I've been looking all over for you," my young assistant shrieked as she rounded the greenery in a tizzy. "She goes on in ten. Shouldn't we do another quick sound-check? To be sure her mic is connected?"

"Relax. The sound has already been tested three times. We're ready for this. Take a look." I turned her around and spread my hand across the expanse of the room. "We've done it."

The young, wiry, up-and-comer just looked at me as if I was cracking a little. "Are you all right? Can I get you a water?"

"I'm good. We've got this. Okay, you know what you can do? Do a second check of the four immunization stations. Make sure they are ready and prepared for our guests to begin filing in. Once President Moore's speech is finished, those areas are going to be the hot spots."

I smoothed my hands down the skirt of my dress and walked into the reality of what this event actually was.

"Good evening," the event's emcee said into the microphone. "I am excited to start the part of the evening we've all been waiting for."

The anticipation of the main event replaced the soft chatter in the room. Every pair of eyes settled on stage, awaiting President Moore's speech. The sense they were witnessing history was evident. As the emcee announced her Mary walked onto the stage, and the room erupted in cheers and thunderous applause. Beaming, she stood poised, waving at her audience until the room settled.

"Thank you all—" She took in the moment and placed her hand to her chest. "—for being here to support the long-overdue rebirth of our country's democracy. Thank you for spending your evening with me and supporting my presidency." She waited as the crowd cheered again. "We have great work laid out before us. President Lincoln said it best in his 1865 Inaugural Address: 'With malice toward none, with charity for all, with firmness in the right as God gives us to see the right, let us strive on to finish the work we are in, to bind up the nation's wounds, to care for him who shall have borne the battle and for his widow and his orphan, to do all which may achieve and cherish a just and lasting peace among ourselves and with all nations.'"

I watched her, overcome with emotion, wondering if the quote from President Lincoln was personal to her in some way. She dabbed at the mist forming in her eyes and waited again for applause to simmer before launching into her own words.

"Our country has been engaged in a war against our human rights for too long. It is time we rebuild. It is time we re-lay the foundation of our democracy. It is time for poverty and illness to be buried in our history. It is time for peace and prosperity to blanket our great land. It starts now!"

With every sentence she uttered her voice crescendoed, and the crowd matched it with their own cheers. Gasping wonderment preceded a crackling of applause that rose to a standing ovation at her finale.

Her speech ended with the moment every guest had been talking about for weeks. No president had ever used a platform such as the evening of her inaugural ball to deliver to her citizens the promise of her campaign. She stuck her index finger out, and the medical doctor who would be serving as director of physicians for her presidency took to the stage. She carried what looked like a pen in her hand. She held it so the audience could clearly see the instrument. Her excitement spread from her face throughout the crowd, and a collective hush stifled out the preceding noise. The doctor removed the cap on the lancet pen and pressed the tiny, double-edged needle into President Moore's upturned finger.

Mary tapered her response to the sudden pinch. Only wincing her eyes slightly before rebounding with a gallant smile, she shared her surprise for what little discomfort the poke provided. Then she raised her still-pointed finger in the air for everyone to see, the tiny droplet of blood forming where the injection was made barely visible.

"Simple and easy. As promised, those who wish to be a part of this advancement, it's your turn. Available now, you will find a designated site in each of the four corners of the ballroom. Dance, dine, and get your spot in line!"

I looked over at the injection site closest to my right to find the beginning of the end for my perfect event. Jaxson Duncan, my sister's new head of security detail, was working the station near the entrance. I can't say I was shocked to see him there. I expected The Patriots to have infiltrated the evening in some way, but they hadn't given me the inside information of their strategy.

We'd met enough times over the last few weeks that I understood the gravity of what could result from the party. I was their source. The one who leaked every detail of President Moore's free vaccine program. Even though I felt fully responsible for The Patriot Party's presence in the room, for the briefest beat of self-interest I wished that, whatever their plan was, this event could be untouched by it. That maybe the mission to thwart Marius might be done in stealth mode.

My initial scan across the remaining three stations allowed me to easily identify an undercover agent I recognized from NIST at each one. This confirmed their mission was already in motion, and all I could do was wait and see how it would play out. I turned my attention back to President Moore, who was fully engrossed in interviews with reporters. Their cameras panned the room to show viewers how easy and painless getting the highly sought-after injection would be.

I hadn't located Abel's presence in the room yet, and it became an anxiety-suffused mission to find out where and what his role might be. My eyes darted back to Mary, realizing I hadn't spotted Marius near her. His absence gave me a queasy turn. Abel and Marius were both MIA, which likely meant they were somewhere around the event together. The outcome that would result from the two of them in an encounter at this very public event, for which I was responsible, left me dizzy.

"Ms. Barrett, excuse me?" The young intern was stressed about details again. "Station three seems to be running out of lancets. There were more than enough boxes to handle the lines an hour ago. We counted and recounted, but now they are missing more than half the supply." I stared blankly at her flustered face. "Ms. Barrett? Did you hear me?" I blinked in response, but words escaped me. "Are you okay? You look pale." I summoned a minuscule nod.

"Check the other stations' supplies."

And so it seemed The Patriots' plan for the night was to hijack injections from the premises. It was going to reflect badly on me, regarding a security breach, but it seemed like a minor fallout considering what else could've been on their agenda. Already I spun into problem-solving mode: how would I address the disappointment that the most anticipated part of the evening was to be cancelled?

I could already imagine the juicy story this would serve for the media outlets. I needed to tell President Moore what happened without them hearing. My walk to her, while only a few steps across the room, felt like slow motion. Action around me seemed to continue at a normal rate, but the crawl to reach Mary felt endless.

She caught my approach out of the corner of her eye and reached out her arm to acknowledge me while continuing her conversation.

"Please let me introduce you to the genius who put this entire gala together: Ruth Barrett, my event planner."

I graciously smiled to hide my building concern, and extended my hand to greet the socialites before me. After receiving high praise and politely thanking them for their kindness, I turned to Mary and mouthed the word *problem* while tilting my head toward the corner.

"Please excuse me," she said, dismissing herself from the huddle of important people. "What is it?" she asked once we'd broken away.

Her concern matched mine. "I think we might have an issue with the injections. It appears a large supply has been stolen."

She closed her eyes and sighed before addressing her predicament.

"That does put a damper on the evening. Where's Marius?" She looked around for her counterpart.

"I can't find him. I was hoping you would know where he might be."

"No, the last I saw him was before my speech."

"I have my people checking the lancet supply at each station as we speak. Hopefully only the few we are aware of are gone, but you should be prepared to address the crowd in a few minutes either way."

"What should I say?" she asked me. I didn't have a good answer for her, but I didn't think she should tell the truth.

"I would avoid suggesting a heist and simply imply that an error in inventory was made."

"What if more are missing? It'll be difficult to pass off as an error."

"If that's the case, we'll have to…"

"Excuse me. Pardon me."

I turned to the source of our interruption. He didn't seem to actually notice or be concerned that we were in the midst of a serious discussion. "I am an associate of Marius Touma's. I regret to inform you he's in some trouble, which may negatively impact the evening's ceremony."

My eyebrows rose and my jaw dropped. I'd been correct assuming Marius' absence indicated a problem.

"Who are you?" I asked, desperately looking around the room, hoping to locate Abel.

"That's not important, and time is of the essence." He looked to President Moore. "You must come with me immediately if you wish to avoid further disruption of this evening."

"What do you mean, 'further disruption'?" Almost as soon as the question left my mouth, a scream penetrated the air. I whipped around to locate the source. Fear trickled through the crowd; I was unable to identify the woman who released the scream. However, I spotted a man dressed in a similar black suit as the one who'd approached us. He was holding a pistol with a silencer on it. Dismayed, I looked back to the stranger standing next to us.

"Let's go." He grabbed President Moore's arm. She in turn reached for my hand and he led us from the ballroom, through the swinging kitchen doors.

"Where are we going?" I demanded, pulling at Mary's hand.

"We aren't taking another step. Tell us who you are, right now," she asserted.

"Madam President, I already told you who I am. I work for Mr. Touma. He's in trouble, which means you are, too. We have to leave before his trouble catches up to you." He flicked his hand in reference to the ballroom. The ballroom which still held my family.

CHAPTER 31

ABEL

The surrealness of driving away from the building with Marius unconscious in my backseat set my critical thinking skills haywire. I wiped the blood from my lip. He'd hit me with a strong uppercut. I wasn't meant to remove Marius from the event. However, he saw me poking around the vaccines while President Moore was giving her speech and confronted me.

"Excuse me," he said. "Can I help you?"

"No. Sorry. I was just double-checking the inventory for Ms. Barrett." I pointed in Ruth's direction.

"I don't recognize you." He slid his hand into his pocket. "I'm sure I've met each of her employees. What is your name?" He raised his chin, peering at me with his eyes low.

I lifted my hands. "No problem. Let's go talk to Ms. Barrett now." I started walking away and he grabbed my arm. I pushed him off of me. "Don't make a scene here, buddy."

Before I knew it we were fighting, which led to him being in my backseat.

It was difficult to resist my imagination, which was concocting fifteen different ways to get rid of him, but I'd been directed to keep him alive. He had information we needed about the phony immunizations.

Since I'd been home, I had something nagging at me that I kept avoiding. Admittedly, there wasn't much time to dwell on my thoughts and pinpoint what was bothering me. But upon leaving the disarray of the inaugural ball, I wondered why it seemed as though the man holding a gun knew we'd be attempting to remove the lancets. The only people who were privy to that information were those of us sitting in the conference room developing the plan in the first place.

After I'd informed The Patriots that I had him, Ms. Farkas determined that once we got Marius to confirm their plot or at least divulge information we didn't yet have, we'd use time travel to undo another one of his messes. I for one had spent so much time in the past already, I didn't understand what we were waiting for, and Ms. Farkas had seemed so cavalier about using time travel when I'd first returned. I couldn't argue; she was right, we needed a clear strategy before we time jumped to fix this. Still, if Marius had useful information, it was worth keeping him alive for the time being.

The immense satisfaction it gave me to put him in restraints gave me pause. I couldn't help but feel it was karmic revenge for his past behavior with Taden—even though this version of him technically never harmed her.

His head slumped forward, still unconscious from the benzodiazepine I injected him with at the gala. It took three men to help me drag his large body to and from the car. I trusted Marius so little, I partially doubted he was truly unconscious. I considered he might be faking and attempting to stall for time.

Right on time Ms. Farkas entered the room, followed by Mr. Richardson and Mr. Warren.

"Wake him," she ordered.

Opening the box on the table next to me, I pulled out a syringe of Flumazenil to counteract the sedative and injected him with it. Within a few minutes he inhaled a deep breath through his nose, squeezing his closed lids tightly together. He put his hand to his neck, wincing from the sting of the needle. Breathing out, he began to choke. I offered him a glass of water, which he warily accepted. Placing the glass to his lips, he complied by tilting his head and allowing a gulp of it into his mouth. Clearing his throat, he studied the others who were seated against the wall like eager spectators. He'd gotten his bearings and replaced his confusion with anger. His nostrils flared through punctuated breaths, resembling a predator—reminding me of who I knew Marius to be. He made it easy for me to hate him.

"Good evening, Mr. Touma."

"I think you're overestimating your evening," he retorted.

I let out a sardonic laugh. Only Marius would be tied up in a room this inhospitable with an audience seemingly intent on watching his destruction and remain overconfident.

"It's going pretty well so far." I was being completely honest as it was quite pleasing to have him sitting in my interrogation.

"What do you want, asshole?" he demanded, clearly not entertained by my witty banter.

"We know who you are, and who you're working with. We've invited you here this evening to tell us what you know about President Moore's vaccines."

This time *he* scoffed.

"I don't know what you mean." The smirk that settled on his face didn't have the effect he wanted it to have. Instead of returning his anger, I pitied him. He was so predictable. First, he would try to intimidate. When that didn't work, he was going to go for a reverse interrogation in an attempt to gain power. Lying would be his next play. I was already three steps ahead of him, waiting for him to catch up. Leaning against the wall, I folded my arms and glanced over at Ms. Farkas to assess her level of patience. She was thoroughly engrossed in our exchange, which meant I had time to break Marius down.

My eyes traveled back to Marius, who was still working his menacing stare. I couldn't help but return his attempted intimidation with another smug grin.

"Look, we can play this game all night. I've already targeted every injection site across the country." I was bluffing. The scale of dispersal was so great that even if we could get ahead of half of them, there would still be at least two percent of the population injected. From the information we'd already gleaned we understood the potential for disaster, but we didn't yet know exactly what about the injection was lethal or why killing mass numbers of people was even their strategy. Dakotah was already busy studying the stolen vaccines, but we wanted Marius to reveal their end goal.

"I can assure you, you don't have all night." He was still trying to give the impression he had the upper hand.

"And why is that?"

"First off, my people are on their way if they aren't already here. But more importantly, you'll never be able to stop President Moore's vaccine program from launching."

"I can't wait to meet your friends. I do hope they arrive soon," I said, still taunting him in hopes of moving him along to his next tactic.

"Who *are* you?" He flared his nostrils again and clenched his jaw to assert dominance.

"Forgive me. I didn't introduce myself. I'm Dr. Mihal. My friends," I pointed to the three stoic agents seated behind me, "are Ms. Farkas, Mr. Warren, and Mr. Richardson."

"Who do you work for? What do you want?" he fired rapidly in response. "I demand to talk to your superior."

A demand. Classic Marius: an order laced with an insult. It was his standard method for asserting dominance. His communication style was on target with the Marius I knew. I wondered what else might still be intact. It was a big leap, but I was zeroed in on finding any evidence that he was who I remembered.

CHAPTER 32

RUTH

"You are in medical danger," warned the man in the suit. "The injection in your body is deadly."

"You're insane!" Mary exclaimed.

"Listen to me. Your injection was hijacked by Berthold's people. It doesn't contain an antidote to fight against his virus. Instead, it *contains* his virus."

"President Moore," I said, closing my eyes, wishing none of this was true. "I think he's telling the truth."

Fury ignited within me. I hadn't been told any of this. Here I had been gathering vital information for The Patriots. They were so interested in the details surrounding the vaccines, I should've questioned it. They never explained I could be watching my friend die.

"Why would Berthold's supporters care?" Mary asked. "About any of this? He's dead."

"He's not," the man claimed.

Mary paused, narrowing her eyes. "What are you saying?"

"Ma'am, with all due respect, we're running out of time. Please, for your safety, cooperate. We need to leave."

Looking back toward the doors still flapping, I didn't want any of us to face the man with the gun. "We should go," I urged.

Unfortunately, the gunman wasn't alone. Two more were waiting for us outside the building. From the parking lot, our hidden attackers shot at us the instant we stepped through the exit. We followed the man in black, ducking and running between parked vehicles, hoping he wasn't leading us to a worse fate. He barked commands into his cufflink and within minutes a car appeared, its doors flung open for us to jump inside. The driver peeled off, but the car took several more shots before we made it onto the street, headed to the highway.

Police were everywhere, swarming neighborhoods, evidently already searching for President Moore. We ducked low in the backseat to keep from being spotted. Once we were in the clear, the man turned around from the passenger seat. "Buckle up. We're on a time crunch."

Before my belt clicked into place the driver accelerated at a jolting pace, forcing my head back in the seat. I looked down to Mary's hand and noticed she was holding the vaccine-injected finger. My gaze moved to her face and found her bleary-eyed.

"I know you must be terrified right now, about what could be happening in your body."

"I am, but actually I'm thinking of all those other people who allowed this into their own bodies because of me. I'm thinking about how the health of each and every one of them rested in my decision. I have to inform everyone and stop the vaccine from being dispersed tomorrow. If any single person is harmed through this injection, it will be my fault."

She began searching her pockets. "Where is my phone?" Her innocence in all of this was obvious.

"This is not your fault. You didn't know. It was Marius. He fooled you. Just like he fooled my sister."

"Marius?" She froze with dismay. "How did Marius fool me?"

"He's working for Berthold. Don't you see that?"

The man in black scoffed. "Mr. Touma working for Berthold? Lady, you're all sorts of confused, aren't you? Marius Touma is working *against* Berthold. Berthold stands for everything that is the antithesis of Mr. Touma. Marius has been working with a network of people devoted to the dismantling of the Berthold empire for at *least* the last decade. The question I have is, who are *you* working for?"

My brain flooded. Despite all of my doubts about his intentions, how was I supposed to reframe my mental process to accept Marius was a hero in this timeline? And also defend myself against the possible accusation that *I* could be the enemy.

"Me? Who do *I* work for?" I laughed at his ridiculous notion. "I'm an event planner. I work for President Moore this evening."

Of course I *had* taken a side, and it wasn't Mary's. While The Patriots told me nothing of their intentions or their plan of action, I'd been giving them details after every single planning session. I didn't know the injection Mary freely allowed into her body would endanger her, but did Abel know? Worse than that, did Taden know? How could they know the risk and not tell me? Not warn me Mary was in danger?

"Ruth, are you hiding something from me? What did you mean when you said Marius fooled your sister?"

Dammit, I shouldn't have said that. How was I to explain my blunder? Sighing, I plunged into my best confession...without revealing too much.

"A few weeks ago Marius followed my sister, who you met at one of our last planning meetings." She nodded that she remembered Taden. "He followed her to a remote location and then cornered her and knocked her unconscious," I emphasized, with the intention of highlighting his violent tendencies. "When Taden came to she learned he'd taken her to another location, where he questioned her. She was afraid for her life, and felt desperate to say anything to keep him from harming her." Mary kept her eyes on her hand. "Did you know any of that?" She continued to appear unaffected by my claims. She must've known. It left me stunned. "You knew?"

"Yes, I knew. Marius told me about the night he questioned your sister. He was concerned the two of you might be working for Berthold. He had theories the president wasn't actually assassinated, but had faked the whole thing as a move to stop me. I thought Marius' concerns of treason were extreme, but it appears I was wrong. I suppose I shouldn't have doubted him; it's not like he's ever let me down before."

I shook my head in disbelief. Not only was Mary confirming Marius most certainly wasn't working for Berthold, but she was making it quite clear that he suspected Taden and I *were*. He abducted Taden under suspicion that she was colluding with the dictator.

"So all this time, you knew Taden was my sister and not just an assistant?" She nodded. "Why didn't you confront me, or say something, if you thought I was lying to you?"

"Marius told me not to worry. He said your sister was clean. After that, it really wasn't an issue. Why would it matter if your working relations include family?"

"I suppose. But it didn't make you wonder why I didn't just introduce her as such?"

"No. Everyone has a right to privacy, and she passed security checks. Your sister is a highly respected scientist. It didn't strike me as odd she'd be helping you with such a big event."

"I mean, I guess not. I thought we were becoming actual friends, though. It's something a friend would expect to know." She didn't respond. Instead, she looked back to her hand.

"We are friends. Aren't we?" she asked.

I brought my hand to hers, gently sliding it under the injected finger.

"We are. I'm not going anywhere." I may have lost Maria, but I found her in Mary. If everything she believed about Marius was actually true, with every passing second her life was in further danger as the injection worked its way through her body.

In addition, Marius himself was in a precarious situation. It would seem the alliances of Berthold were hunting him down, as well as the misguided Patriot Party. I felt complicit in the latter. Every bit of information I'd passed along to them in the last few months had been tainted with my perception of Marius as a villain. It washed away the distinct purpose of Taden's rescuing him. I'd just wanted to punish him for hurting her.

I wondered if I would ever learn a life lesson free from turmoil, or if this was the only way I was capable of understanding. So far every lesson I was meant to learn about friendship, loyalty, and love had been loosely tied to danger, loss, and trust. Just once it would've been nice to learn a moral simply from a book.

"I need to tell Taden about Marius," I realized, reaching into my pocket for my cell phone.

"And I need to tell the people the truth about this vaccine," Mary asserted. "Can I please use your phone?"

"You don't understand. Marius could be in danger, because she believes him to be a threat to us all."

"I've looked in to your sister," Mary confirmed. "She's a scientist for the NIST. How could she possibly endanger Marius? Unless...there's something you're keeping secret?"

She was asking me to come clean.

"I can't tell you specifics, but my sister has ties to an organization seeking the same justice for Berthold as you are. They believe Marius to be involved. That's all I can say. Truthfully, it's about all I know."

I felt a twinge of guilt because there was a hell of a lot more I knew. How could I reveal any of it to her, though? It would've been a betrayal to Taden and to The Patriots, one I could never recover from. I didn't even really know Mary, or have a deep enough history with her in this timeline to share that kind of information.

"Do they have him? Is that why he disappeared tonight?" she asked with a new level of concern.

"I don't know if they have him, but one of their head agents who should have been present at the event was also missing. I can assume the two of them went missing together, and therefore it's logical to assume they have him in custody."

I dialed Taden. As the phone started to ring, the man in black tore it from my hands. "Is this thing's GPS-enabled? You know they can track us with this, right?"

She shot a worried look to the man in black. "I want her to be able to contact her sister right now, and clear his name. If anything happens to him—"

"Absolutely not, President Moore. I need to disable its GPS and location accuracy immediately. If anyone is tracking Ms. Barrett here, they've got us."

CHAPTER 33

ABEL

As the interrogation proceeded, the initial satisfaction I had from capturing and detaining him dwindled. Every question I asked, he responded with a question. Even though I was fully aware of his antics, he still managed to get under my skin. After an hour of his stonewalling, Mr. Richardson took me into the hall.

"I think it's time we employed some more aggressive tactics. We don't have the luxury of letting this guy jerk us around all night," he said.

While I found the concept of torturing Marius enticing, the morality meter I tried to live by didn't condone it. I had to at least first try another method to get him to talk, and I was sitting on a massive countermove.

"I have one more idea before we go down that route," I suggested.

"I'm giving you half an hour. If he doesn't budge, we will force him to talk."

Mr. Richardson made himself crystal clear, which probably meant Ms. Farkas' patience was wearing thin, too.

"Agreed. I have to go get someone. I'll be right back."

Mr. Richardson returned to the room. I sprinted to the waiting area of the building where Quinn was sitting, busily working through time travel equations. Next to her Taden anxiously sat on her hands, repeatedly tapping the floor with the ball of her foot.

"We're going to need you," I said to Quinn.

She looked up from her device, pursed her lips, and nodded. I stole a glance at Taden and, to my surprise, her blue eyes were already settled on me. I felt it all the way down through my toes. She made no move to look away, either.

Quinn set her device on Taden's lap and rose from her chair, following me back to see her brother. Taden placed her hand on the device in acknowledgement of Quinn, but her eyes stayed on me. She meant to force *me* to be the one to break away first. I didn't want to. Not a single muscle in my body cooperated. We were frozen, neither wanting to leave. It required an immense amount of self-control not to abandon everything regarding Marius so I could take the seat next to Taden. I wanted so badly to implore her to see me, touch me and love me, but I had to try to work this scenario so that I wouldn't have to leave for the past. If we could get to Berthold through Marius, I could take him down here and not have to leave again. If I didn't succeed in the present I would be gone again soon, and she didn't deserve to have to revisit this emotional push and pull.

"All right, then. Let's do this."

I moved away from Taden, escorting Quinn back toward the locked room where her brother waited.

Before we turned the corner, I peered back at her to get one last glimpse. She didn't know I watched her pull her knees to her chest to calm her trembling body. She couldn't know how much it destroyed me to walk away.

"Are you ready for this?" I asked Quinn one final time, giving her a last chance to opt out.

I hoped she was going to be able to pull this off. I knew she was about to step on a land mine of memories, and from what I'd learned about Quinn in the short time I knew her she really did strive to do the right thing.

She bobbed her head up and down with conviction and walked through the open door. I followed closely behind her and guided her to a seat across the table from Marius. With fascination I watched him scan the woman opposite him. No one said a word. Quinn's eyes filled with tears. Her response to seeing him was the giveaway. His face contorted into a look of disbelief.

"Octavia?"

He stretched out her name and lifted the inflection at the end to punctuate his revelation. The room remained still amid the unexpected tenderness of their meeting. Even I couldn't deny a powerful stirring of emotion at their reunion. Marius repeatedly cleared his throat in an attempt to dissuade his emotions. There was no way he would've been able to stifle them. Not unless he was void of feelings. I gave them a few minutes to soak in their reunion.

Even though I hated him with all my heart, I was still human and so was he. He cleared his throat again. "Octavia?" This time, she confirmed who she was with her own freely flowing tears.

"Can I go to him?" she asked me.

"I'm sorry, no."

"I understand," Quinn responded, wiping her eyes with the back of her hand.

"You are beautiful," he whispered in wonderment. She smiled at him and wiped a few more tears from the corner of her eyes.

"Thank you. You turned out pretty good yourself."

"How are you?" He stretched his hand across the table. "I searched for you everywhere. I'm so sorry I couldn't find you."

His care for her was evident. I was already primed from seeing Taden in so much pain, but watching the two of them together again after so long further softened me.

"I'm good. My life is actually really great. I'm a physicist following in my big brother's footsteps." She beamed proudly at Marius. "I have a wonderful family who loves me. I'm good."

With her simple life update, Quinn eased years of pain and worry from her brother. I could almost see the heaviness lift from him right before me.

"Marius?" she said.

He leaned in, wanting to give her whatever she needed from him. The earnest way he looked at her when she said his name was unmistakable.

"Please tell them what you know."

CHAPTER 34

RUTH

"We're here," announced the driver.

In a whirlwind, we were whisked into an unmarked building.

"My phone," I reminded the man in black.

He handed it to me and I furiously typed out a text to Taden. "Marius is innocent. Call me ASAP."

"We need to alert the media!" President Moore exclaimed, reaching for my phone.

"And say what?" asked the man in black. "Tell them you could be dying? Tell them they could be dying? We don't even know what this is yet. Your celebration is over. No one else is getting a vaccine there. The testing sites don't open until the morning. We have at least a few hours to gain some insight before launching a media crisis."

She didn't like that he was suggesting we sit on this time bomb. I texted Taden again. "The vaccine is a virus. Did you know?" I noticed my first text was unread. Why wouldn't she be reading her texts? She had to be worried, too.

Two doctors advanced in our direction, guiding us down a hallway into what resembled a clinic. Skipping introductions and niceties, one of the doctors said, "We need to get you into X-ray. Come with me."

I dialed Taden's number. It went to voicemail.

"Taden, I'm worried about you. Where are you? I've texted you twice. Marius isn't guilty and that vaccine is a virus. It looks like they were set up. Call me back as soon as you get this."

I dialed Abel next. It also went to voicemail. "Ugh, c'mon. Someone answer the damn phone." I was concerned—if they weren't answering, could they be in danger themselves? "Hey Abel, it's Ruth. Marius is innocent. He's been framed or something and the vaccine is going to kill people. Call me back as soon as you get this."

I was just about to call Dakotah when Mary returned to get me from the waiting room.

"They're reviewing my X-rays now. Do you want to come back with me?"

Sliding my phone back into my purse, I joined her immediately. I sat across from Mary, staring at the images of her hand and upper arm. We were searching for evidence that the very same injection they celebrated could be taking hold of her life.

"It has already attached to the tendons. It hasn't gotten to her hand yet, though I can see the beginning of it. If we wait much longer, the entire hand might have to be removed."

This medical conversation took place between her doctors as if neither Mary nor I were in the room. She was in obvious shock, blank and uncommunicative, as if she never heard the implication of what they had just said. I, however, heard everything.

"Are you saying you want to remove her finger?" I felt sick even asking it aloud.

"Unfortunately, yes. But removing her finger is better than removing her entire hand," the doctor assured.

"Why can't you just open her finger up and surgically remove the foreign material?"

The first doctor became irritated; he sighed and looked imploringly at the other doctor.

"Do we really have time to sit here and answer these questions?"

I stood to my feet, ready to engage both doctors in a battle of wills, but Mary gently grasped my hand and nodded for me to sit back down. It was her life on the line, and her finger they were talking about cutting off, so I obliged.

"I have questions," she said calmly. "And I would prefer you take the time to answer them. I understand the risks involved with waiting. I'm willing to chance it."

Another heavy sigh came from the impetuous doctor ready to amputate. "Very well, Madam President. What would you like to discuss?"

"I understand whatever was implanted in my finger will spread through my hand." Both doctors nodded, encouraged she understood and believed the urgency of the situation. "Will it continue to spread through my body? Am I going to start feeling some kind of pain? As it is, I don't feel anything."

"It's unknown. We know next to nothing about its trajectory. We can only assume the worst, that it will not stop at your hand. I don't expect you'll feel any type of pain while the virus remains inactive."

The other doctor chimed in, "The little information we do have about it was hacked from its engineers. We don't know the final stages of its outcome. Our plan is to be proactive, and stop it before we find out. Your safety is our main concern."

"There are already dozens of people who have also been exposed this evening. We need to contact them."

"I'm certain that's being handled. Our job right now is first to prevent danger to you, Madam President, and in doing so hopefully learn how to address this issue for the others who've been infected."

Mary was devastated. She'd delivered Berthold's Trojan Horse.

"I want to wait."

"Ma'am?"

"If my people are at risk I should be, too. I want to know more about what is in my hand before we do this surgery. I know it means I may lose my hand completely. How long do you predict it will take to spread?"

"My prediction, based on how fast it has traveled through your finger," he paused, "would be an hour. By then I suspect it will be past your finger and into your hand. But please, let us do this."

"I've made my decision. I'll wait. You find out everything you can about this injection. Take samples from me and get started on studying the behavior of this thing." She looked over her shoulder directly at me. "I want to speak to Marius. We need to get this information into the hands of the people. Stop the sites from opening tomorrow. Can you make that happen?"

"I'll do what I can."

Checking my phone to see if Taden or Abel had gotten my messages, I found them both unanswered. My final call was to Dakotah. I was flushed with relief when she picked up on the first ring.

"Hello?"

"Oh, thank God! It's Ruth. Are you with Taden or Abel?"

"Neither is here. Everyone's gone. I'm holding down the fort."

"They're wrong about Marius. He's not working for Berthold. They have to know!"

"Are you sure?"

"I am *completely* sure. President Moore wants to speak to Marius directly. I need your help."

"I'm on it."

"You can get us in touch with him?"

"Yeah, your sister is with him now."

"Dakotah, the immunization is a virus. It's going to kill a bunch of people."

"How do *you* know that?" Something in the way she questioned me made me think she already knew the vaccine was a problem.

"I'm looking at the president's hand imaging, and a virus— through the vaccine—has already spread."

"I've been studying it myself since the team gave me the stolen lancets from the inauguration. I've already figured out its half-life."

"I don't know what that means, but you should be *here* working with *this* staff. They could use your insight. You're hours ahead of them."

"I'll track down Marius and get over to your location."

"You are a lifesaver. Literally."

Ending the phone call I nodded to Mary, confirming her request was in motion. She thanked me and fell back into her chair as the medical team finished collecting more samples from her hand.

CHAPTER 35

TADEN

I was a shell of myself. My purpose in life had been embedded into time travel, until losing Abel to the past forced me to question the very thing I'd created. I was disappointed over how much I missed him. I wasn't supposed to need a man this way. I was hell-bent on being a woman who thrived from her work, knew what motivated her, and went after it. But according to my recent history I'd been duped by a narcissist and almost put the world in jeopardy, and then I'd fallen hard in love with one of my best friends who promptly left. I didn't feel like a strong, independent woman. I felt like a failure.

I wanted to completely abandon the invention I'd spent my entire life working to create. It only left a hole. My remaining motivation to get up in the morning was to figure out how to get to the future—but then Abel came back. It sidetracked me almost to a halt.

I kept his book with me at all times. Just knowing it was in my bag gave me a feeling that he was with me. I stared at my bag sitting on the floor next to me, and fought the urge to reach inside and pull it out right then. But I didn't want to be embarrassed if Abel somehow caught me.

I should've pulled myself out of my state to call Ruth. She was probably learning the truth about the vaccines. If so, she wasn't going to be happy. It was classified, but she wouldn't see it that way. Understandably. Even so, it's not like President Moore would've injected the actual virus into herself. We didn't see her putting herself in any real danger.

Every minute that passed I knew was a wasted one. I should've been in the lab working on the future, but instead I sat in a waiting room, wallowing. It had come to this: Marius being questioned by The Patriots. Quinn, my dream protégé, was actually his sister. Abel, the man I wanted to spend my life with, was out of reach. Ruth was working for a possibly corrupt president who claimed to be the Second Coming.

CHAPTER 36

ABEL

"You want to know who I am?" Marius asked punitively. "You want to know what I know?"

Quinn looked at me with apprehension.

"When I was fifteen years old I came to this country with you, Octavia. We were separated at the border. I searched for you. My search led me to a group of men who took me in, gave me work, and promised to find you. Not too long after I began working for them, a raid of the house left every single person inside dead. I only avoided getting gunned down with the rest of the men in the house that night because I was whisked away by two women who brought me to a refugee care group. These two women have recently, mysteriously, popped back up." He looked all of us square in the face. "The next three years I spent learning English, continuing the search for my sister and avoiding detention camps. It wasn't as easy as it sounds, hiding from corrupt government officials who were constantly hunting for those of us deemed less than human."

I concluded that Marius learned to hate our government just as he did in his previous timeline—the one resulting in Marius being a key player in The Reckoning.

"I didn't know if my sister was even still alive. Every year, I was unable to find her. I imagined the worst, and began to believe it was true. It wasn't difficult to match my experiences to my imagination." Although his sister sat safely in front of him, I saw his anger reborn. "Eventually, I connected with a network of others similarly oppressed. As our contacts grew, so did our reach. We're going to dismantle the broken operating system of this country. We will bring to this land what every living human deserves."

It was clear Marius believed the same about our government that he did when I knew him: he believed it to be evil. He saw this country as controlling, harmful and destructive to the world, while claiming to be the force of good in it. It occurred to me that The Patriots shared the same viewpoint. Was it possible that Marius' feelings about our government didn't justify the conclusion that he was involved in the misdeeds that were going on?

"The people with whom I work are done allowing this country to carry on with business as usual. It's time for a wake-up call."

"While I appreciate the history lesson, we are here today regarding some more pressing issues than your life story," I snapped.

His face flushed at my slight. I heard the callous words coming from my mouth. Was I any better than what I viewed Marius to be? Who would I be if our roles had been switched? I caught Quinn watching me through disappointed eyes.

The issue still remained that an incredible number of lives were at stake, and I needed to get the information from Marius that would give them a chance at survival. I folded my arms, contemplating a tactic that would work without betraying my moral standing. Danika's impatience grew, and Mr. Richardson glanced at his watch. I resigned myself that we would not torture Marius. Unsure about him, I was certain torture should not be an option. Stepping into his line of sight, I contemplatively rubbed my nose before running my hands through my hair.

"Listen man, I'm sorry. The thing is, your life was shitty and it drove you to become who you are now. I get that. But those immunizations, filled with deadly viruses, are going to kill a whole lot of people. Good people. Bad people. Senior citizens. Kids. I just can't see how this act of terrorism will deliver the wake-up call you're hoping for."

He looked at me incredulously. "You think the injections contain a virus? That's insane."

I crossed my arms in a defensive stance. How was he going to deny information The Patriot Party had already breached about these vaccines?

He continued, "What they *do* contain is an antidote for a disease Berthold already unleashed into the population months ago. A disease which remains dormant until a trigger is activated. I'm guessing this is information I don't need to tell you, since you are clearly working for him."

"*We're* working for Berthold?" I looked back to Danika, dismay on my face. She raised her chin, encouraging me to continue my line of questioning.

"*Pfffft*. Right. Acting surprised should convince me otherwise. How stupid do you think I am?" he scoffed.

"You *must* be some kind of stupid if you think we're buying into your piece of shit story. The vaccines are the actual virus and you, my friend, are the one who is working for Berthold."

"Sure, man. If you say so." He clenched his jaw tight. "Well, whatever. It doesn't matter. You can't stop this. Every citizen who wants this injection will obtain the antivirus, and neither you nor Berthold can stop it."

"Berthold is dead," I reminded him.

"I'm sure you'd like me to believe your assassination story, too. Look, I've told you what you want to know. Can you please just let me and my sister go?"

"Marius," Quinn stated, "I'm not being held against my will. I work with these people. They *are* the good guys."

"You're wrong, Octavia. I'm the good guy and they have me tied up. What does that make them?"

She squinted at him, trying like hell to believe what he was telling her. Her elbows rested on the table as she slid her hands behind her neck in an attempt to massage away her doubt.

"I want to look at you and believe you're on the right side. You're my brother, and everything I've ever known about you confirms you are good—or however good you can be. But I haven't seen you in fifteen years. A lot can change in a person over such a long time."

Marius closed his eyes. The pain her words brought him was palpable. His eyes still closed, he nodded his head slowly at first and then increasing in vigor before they popped wide open. "I want you to understand what I'm saying to you. I've spent the last fifteen years believing you were dead or hurt somewhere, and living my life to avenge you. I've spent these years becoming a man who would never let this sort of mistreatment be deemed as acceptable behavior. I've fought for outcasts, and prevented mass human rights violations. I've helped defeat the most heinous man ever to come to power, and I've done it all in your name. You don't believe I am who I claim. That's okay. I know who I am. I can prove to you who I am. You'll see. You're my sister, Octavia, and I love you. None of this matters, really. I'm just so happy you're alive and safe and healthy. That's all that matters."

Quinn was still holding the back of her neck as tears streamed down her cheeks and onto her arms, collecting at her elbows against the table. I didn't know what to think. I'd never seen a genuine, self-sacrificing emotion from Marius before. I wasn't sure if it was just a terrific act. If it wasn't, I understood how the loss of his sister made him into the monster he was in the other timeline.

Either way, we all needed a break.

"We're going to pause here and give the two of you some privacy." We could hear everything they discussed in our absence. If Marius was lying to us, he might reveal himself to Quinn while we were out of the room. Quinn didn't know for certain the room was monitored either, but she was too smart to assume otherwise.

I needed some fresh air and to talk to Taden. Putting aside the tragedy which was us, we had to speak frankly about Marius. I was beginning to doubt he really had any insight about the fraudulent vaccines. She was right that she knew him better than anyone. She could read his gestures, maybe even push him to the brink of snapping to reveal something he might be hiding. At the very least, it gave me a great reason to speak to her.

CHAPTER 37

TADEN

I can look back on years of my life and find it difficult to identify periods in which I was sad enough to cry. The type of whole-body crying that causes my core temperature to drop. The crying where awful sounds emerge from my throat. The crying that leaves my face blotchy and my nose alternating between drippy and stuffy. After years of avoiding this type of emotional exorcism, I was overdue for a release. In the year surrounding The Reckoning and Berthold's epidemic, I cried more than I had in my life.

In the waiting room, I emptied myself of tears. It'd take years to replenish the feelings needed to cry again after that. Sitting in the vinyl-covered visitor chair, finally vacant of emotion, I tried to match my mindset to my feelings. In the stillness, my thoughts went to the lab and Dakotah. Last I'd been updated she had just received the stock of immunization lancets from President Moore's inauguration, tasked with studying its make-up.

I reached down to grab my bag. Now that I'd gotten my emotions in check, I was prepared to talk to my sister and, if she didn't already know, tell her our concerns about her friend, our president, and the vaccine she's promoting. I also needed to check in with Dakotah to see where she was with the virus.

Just as I reached for my phone, it buzzed. I looked at the lock screen to see Dakotah's face light up the incoming call. It was spooky when that sort of thing happened.

"Hello?" I answered.

"Hey. I've got some, uh, interesting news. You sitting down?" She sounded apprehensive.

"Mmm-hmm." I didn't want her to know I'd been crying. Having her be disappointed in me would be more than I could take.

"I don't know how to say this delicately, so I apologize for my bluntness, but you gotta get Abel to back off Marius."

"What?" Was she serious? Like a bucket of cold water had been poured over my head, in an instant I forgot my tragic feelings.

"I know this is going to sound out of left field, but listen. I just got off the phone with your sister."

"Is she okay? I have to call her."

"She's all right. Listen. Marius is actually working against Berthold, and for the greater good this time. President Moore's immunization plan was legit."

"Ruth told you this?"

"Yes. I'm on my way to the clinic where she's with the president, to bring what I've got so far about the vaccine. President Moore was injected with the virus. She didn't know. And I just updated my news feed. It looks like Berthold's people infiltrated several of the test sites due to open in the morning. Crowds were already gathering to be first in line. They've started opening them early. I think they're trying to infect as many people as possible."

"Did you find out who the guy with the gun was? At the inauguration?"

"Our people had taken the lancets as planned. The gunman was trying to stop our agent from leaving the premises with the vaccines. We think he was working for Berthold, trying to ensure the vaccines were delivered to everyone who was willing. As things were getting physical, Berthold's man pulled out his gun. A woman in the crowd saw him and screamed, drawing attention to the gunman. The chaos gave our agent the chance to slip out."

I had no words. My only reaction was to blink.

"Taden? You got all that?" she asked.

"Yes. I'm heading to Abel now." Out of body I was on my feet, still holding the phone to my ear. I needed to understand what Dakotah really meant. "So, everyone who got the vaccine at the inauguration is infected?"

"That's what it looks like. I'm in contact with the medical team who've been studying President Moore's response to the injection. Between what I've isolated and their data, we'll know more soon. I'm heading out the door now. I'll talk to you later. Oh and hey, call your sister. She's freaking out because she can't get a hold of you."

"Got it. Thanks, Dakotah. Keep me updated."

My phone screen showed dozens of missed calls and texts from Ruth. I dialed her number as I walked back to the interrogation room. Not looking in front of me, I collided smack into someone coming full on in my direction.

"Oh!" I exclaimed, rubbing my forehead. Ending the call before Ruth picked up, and already embarrassed, I looked at him to apologize for my distraction—and saw Abel. I resigned myself to believing the universe just hated me.

"No, I'm sorry." He put his hands on my arms, and it felt like the easiest thing to do was to bury my head in his chest. Instead, I forced my eyes to meet his. They were smiling gently. My cheeks flushed. He seemed to find it entertaining that I could still get embarrassed in his presence. I shook my head, refocusing on the insane matter at the forefront.

"I just got a phone call from Dakotah. Marius is innocent. He's telling you the truth in there."

Unresisting while Abel's hands remained, I recapped Dakotah's message.

He didn't seem surprised. "I know this is going to sound crazy, but I was beginning to consider his innocence. Actually, I just left the interrogation to come get you, to see if you would join us in the room and verify what I was thinking."

"We don't need me to do that now. You know. I'm going to head back to the lab and get to work. There's not a whole lot for me to do with this, and I feel like what I've got going on there might better serve all of us."

"Taden..." His face told me everything I needed to know.

I interrupted him. "I know, Abel. I opened the book. I know." We stole a few seconds in the midst of the madness, just to stand there. Then he pulled me to him, like he needed the exact same thing I did. When we separated from each other we both knew what we had to do, and we both knew our love meant something greater than our surroundings, greater than our words, greater than time.

On my way to the car, I finally got my call through to Ruth. At this point, she knew more than I did.

CHAPTER 38

RUTH

"To stop this from spreading any further, we have to do this right now," Mary's doctor demanded. "We've already gone well past the allotted hour and you've had all *night*. The virus has undoubtedly moved through your arm. Once it's passed beyond, we won't have any limbs to remove in order to save you."

"Doctor, please tell me what you've learned." She ignored the blatant plea they made to save her life. She bordered on nonsensical, and I wondered if the virus was in her brain.

"The injection contains a DNA disruptor that, once injected into the body, begins mirroring and attaching to DNA strands. This is how it spreads. It doesn't cause any damage; its only function at this stage is to replicate."

Mary turned from him, folding her arms across her chest.

"Ultimately, I don't need to be the president of this country for it to come to grips with the terror Berthold brought upon us. If I die fighting this viral attack on our citizens, then it will have been a worthy death."

"Are you saying you're just going to let this thing kill you?" I asked, trying to mask my horror.

"I'm saying it's my *job* to die for the people of this country."

"Not necessarily. You could fight the virus inside you *and* save your people."

"I won't have my arm removed to prevent the replication of this foreign substance within me. I'll allow it to travel as it will. I'll be exposed to the same outcome that I unknowingly unleashed upon my people. If they die, so will I."

I was going to lose her again. We'd just found each other and just started to re-forge our friendship, and now she was being torn from me a second time.

"Using me as a warning may prevent millions from getting the vaccine tomorrow. I want the state of my condition made public immediately. We need to tell everyone the vaccine is a subterfuge of Berthold's. Too much time has already been wasted. If they can watch me die before they get their own finger poked, maybe they'll stay home tomorrow. Shut it down before it's too late."

She was right. This was an urgent need. I just wasn't qualified to make this news public.

"I could get in touch with a few of the contacts I have in the media," I offered.

"Yes, do that. Please. Also, I really need to speak to Marius. Why haven't we heard from him yet?"

"I left my sister dozens of messages, and Dr. Hughs said she would be sure to have Marius call my phone as soon as they released him."

I checked my phone for the zillionth time. It wasn't like Taden to not respond to me, especially when I was so insistent about her calling me back. I set my phone on the counter next to me just as Mary's doctor returned to take her for more monitoring.

"After you've identified how fast this is spreading, I want you to trigger it," she told him.

"Wait," I said, getting to my feet. "You want them to try to activate the disease? Why would you tell them to do that?" I looked imploringly at the doctor, asking him with my eyes not to trigger the virus.

"We have to begin to understand it," she said with presidential assertion. "We need to know how it's set off and how quickly this thing takes over the body, so we can be prepared to address the scenario for the dozens of others who were infected this evening." She folded her hands together and brought them to her chin. "Well, I guess we should get started." She didn't sound as assertive with her final directive walking toward the doctor.

"I'd like to do another image of your hand to see how completely the replication process has taken over," he told her. "And then I want to get you into the MRI to track its movement up your arm. We need to carefully monitor how it spreads once it leaves your limb. After we have that information, as requested, we'll work on the trigger. We'll test it while you are still under imaging, so we can collect the data about the rate of spread."

She nodded her consent.

"Your friend at the NIST, Dr. Hughs, will be arriving shortly. Her expertise will increase the efficiency with which we obtain this information. She's been studying the injection a bit longer, and is ahead of our research."

My phone vibrated on the counter, jarring me from the clinically calm manner with which the doctor shared how they would proceed to use Mary's body. Moving in tiny circles along the hard countertop as it continued vibrating, I caught a glimpse of Taden's screen image and lunged for it before I missed her.

"Taden!" Desperation colored my voice.

"I'm sorry I missed your messages." she said, her breathing heavy.

"Is everything all right? I've been worried," I asked her with a reprimanding tone.

"I'm sorry. I'm okay. What's going on with you? I saw all those messages—"

"Are you with Marius?" She didn't answer right away. Her heavy breathing accelerated, and I was sure she was walking somewhere in a hurry.

"I was. He's with Abel. Dakotah got me up to speed about him. They're releasing him soon. Now that they know he's innocent, they have a few more questions to ask him about his contacts with the immunization."

"Speaking of the immunization…" I inserted.

"I'm really sorry. It was confidential. I wasn't at liberty to tell you," she explained.

"She could die, Taden."

"I wish it didn't happen that way. We thought she was colluding. I never expected she'd inject herself with the real thing."

"It sounds like you're going somewhere," I said. "Where?"

"I'm on my way back to the NIST."

"I need you to turn around and get him on the phone. Dakotah said she would tell you. President Moore urgently needs to speak with him."

She clicked her tongue and continued to breathe heavily, but I could tell she was stationary. "Yeah, okay, I'm turning around. Why don't you fill me in while I head back inside to find him."

"Since we've been sitting in this clinic and she's undergoing all these tests, she has been sharing with me everything she knew about how the vaccine was initiated in the first place."

"Okay. I'm listening."

"A while ago, Marius was approached by a medical group who'd engineered a modern immunization, which for the first time ever could be delivered through a microscopic chip."

"A chip?" she asked, her voice thick with worry.

"Yeah, a chip."

"That's what Dakotah saw in Abel's memory."

"Hmm. She said it was supposed to release three strains of antigens within the system once it moved into the bloodstream."

"Aside from the information about the chip, that's what everyone has been told about the vaccine," Taden said.

"Yeah, but no one knows this part—the medical group got Mary's attention when they told Marius that before Berthold disappeared, he released an inactive virus into the population, waiting to use it as population control."

"How would giving everyone a virus benefit Berthold?"

"Mary said that with the threat of activating it, he could operate on a whole new level of a fear-based regime."

"Do we know how it's activated?"

"It's looking like some type of radiation is the trigger."

"That's crazy," Taden replied. "So how did the medical group know about any of this?"

"They engineered the virus for him. But with Berthold gone, they sought out Mary. She was the only presidential candidate at the time. They made an offer to provide the antidote via this immunization."

"And she agreed because she thought one of the antigens would counteract a virus she believed Berthold *already* released into the population?" she asked.

"Yes. She thought she could use the immunization as a trust move with the citizens *and* eradicate the danger of Berthold's legacy at the same time."

"But we know that the vaccines actually contain Berthold's virus. Why would he need to infect people twice?"

"So that's the kicker," I told her. I noticed Mary was about to leave the room with her doctor. "Taden, hold on a second." I moved the phone from my ear. "President Moore, don't leave yet. I'm about to get Marius on the phone."

Bringing the phone back to my ear, I finished updating Taden. "The medical group was a ploy. Berthold never did release a virus into the population."

"How did President Moore learn this?" she queried.

"When all the chaos ensued tonight, this security-type guy who works for Marius whisked Mary and me out of the ball and brought us to this clinic. Apparently he intercepted information between Berthold—who is still alive by the way—and these engineers." I could hear Taden pacing back and forth as she listened.

"We did know about Berthold. That's why Abel was deployed."

"Ahh. Okay," I murmured. "That makes sense. I guess Berthold had received intel that a secret group was attempting to assassinate him, so he staged his own assassination to get them off of his scent. Meanwhile, the virus he really did intend to release through his chip injection never launched. Instead, he devised a plan to trick Mary into delivering it into the population. Once initiated, Berthold will commence the next phase of his plan. We don't know what that is."

"Okay. I can't believe this. I wish I had checked my phone an hour ago," she confessed. "I'm sure Abel would've appreciated all of this sooner." I had to bite my tongue not to add something sassy to Taden, because she really should've answered her flipping phone. "I'm right outside the room, about to go in. Are you ready?"

"Yeah, I was ready like an hour ago, too," I said, unable to resist the dig.

She knocked on the door, then I heard her whisper with Ms. Farkas.

"I have to speak to him."

A pause; I couldn't hear Danika's response. I could picture her face, though. I'm sure she didn't expect Taden to want to talk to Marius.

"Yes, it's urgent."

I'd bet money Danika tried to dissuade Taden from communicating with him. It wouldn't serve her interests if this conversation spiraled out of control. Marius could become belligerent and give them nothing, and an unfocused Taden would impede time travel discoveries.

"No, I'll be okay."

I wondered who asked my sister if she'd be okay. Didn't seem like a Danika thing to do.

"Mmm-hmm."

Her heels clicked on a hard surface as she walked toward him.

"Hey," she whispered to someone. "I apologize for disrupting, but he has a phone call."

There was silence. No one moved about the room or responded to Taden's interruption.

"He has a phone call?" It was Abel. He was in the room with Marius. That must have been awkward for Taden to walk into.

"Yes. It's urgent. Otherwise…"

"Yeah. Sure. No problem." His voice boomed into the phone, like he was speaking directly into it. Abel was typically a soft-spoken person, so I found this to be slightly surprising.

"President Moore would like to talk to you." She handed the phone to Marius. I heard jostling as his hands were released to grasp it.

"Hello?" Marius said into the phone.

"Hold on one second. I'll get her," I said quickly, giving the phone to Mary, who reached for it with anticipation.

"Marius?" His confirmation gave her a sigh of relief. "Tell me you're safe." She nodded her head, thankful. "Things didn't go how we planned." She hung her head. "I'm in a precarious situation. Since I've already received the injection, it's spreading through my body. Turns out it's not the antivirus we intended to give the people. It's actually the opposite."

I could hear his voice roar through the phone, although I couldn't make out what he was telling her. Reading her body language, she shared his outrage and concern.

"I know. I know. It's too late now. Berthold's people must have manipulated the injections. I don't know how they…it doesn't matter. It's multiplying in my body as we speak. They want to amputate my arm to prevent the spread. I've turned it down. I want them to use me for observation and data collection so they can try to get a step ahead of this."

Whatever he told her after made her eyes well up, followed by waves of chin quivering. In an attempt not to further impose on her privacy, I turned my back. Feeling like I shouldn't be involved made me miss her. Even though she was in proximity, talking on *my* phone with the man she seemed to be in love with, I felt the loss of her. With me and Maria, the way we used to be, I would've held her hand through this type of thing. She wouldn't have gone through any of this without knowing I was here for her.

Once she regained her composure, she said, "This is what we have been fighting for. I can't bow out of the fight now. I know you just want me to be safe, but remember what this is about. You have to find him, and you have to stop this before all these people die. He has the trigger—he must. It won't activate until he says so. The fate of this country is within our control." Her voice softened. "I believe in you, and I love you." For levity, she added, "Now don't mess this up," and forced a chuckle for his benefit.

It dawned on me. Why wasn't I showing her I cared about her? She should've known I was emotionally available for her. She hadn't asked for a private moment from me. I'd been the one to impose this on her. She was in visible turmoil, and I chose to look away. No relationship ever worked by looking away. Instead of pretending I couldn't see her fear or empathize with the overwhelming choices she was forced to keep making, I wanted her to know she wasn't alone.

Before I could talk myself out of the instinct to love Mary, I whirled myself back around to face her. The loneliness she felt in the fight of her life trickled down her cheeks, and there she was. I could truly see her, once I listened to myself. Before I knew what I was doing my arms were around her, giving her permission to sob into my shoulder. I brought the phone back to my ear.

"Can you give the phone back to Taden?"

"Is Mary okay?" he asked me.

"At the moment she is. We don't have a lot of time, though. I need to talk to Taden." He cleared his throat, told Taden the phone was for her, and handed it over.

"Ruth?"

"Yeah, it's me again. I have to go. Mary is about to go back into imaging. Dakotah's on her way. Between the two of us, we'll be in contact. Keep your phone near you this time." I hung up and used my free arm to fully envelop Mary.

CHAPTER 39

TADEN

Still waiting for The Patriots to release Marius so he could take leave to be with President Moore, I was granted the once-in-a-lifetime moment of watching him enter the waiting area with Quinn at his side. Seeing them reunited at last brought me an incredible amount of peace.

Quinn mouthed the words *thank you,* and I winked at her. Marius glanced at me and smiled. The first genuine smile Marius Touma had ever given me.

He put his arm around his sister and the two of them walked out of the building. For the first time in as long as I can remember, my breathing felt light and free. I was lost in the image of Quinn and Marius walking to her car when I felt a hand on my arm. I jumped, startled from my reverie.

"I didn't mean to scare you," Abel stated.

I hadn't had time to prepare for the conversation we were undoubtedly about to have.

"It's okay, I was in a daze."

"I need to talk to you." He sounded worried. "There's something no one else can know."

CHAPTER 40

RUTH

"I'm going to call my media contact," I said, releasing her. "That way, when Marius gets here, we'll be ready to go live."

"Thank you, Ruth," she told me. "I'm really glad you're here."

I smiled gently and walked away to make my phone call.

Once Dakotah arrived and got involved, the process felt a little more under control. I trusted her completely, and knew she would do everything she could to keep Mary's safety a priority.

They were able to track the dissemination of replicating DNA before it even fully traveled up her arm, which meant the next step was about to begin. It was a terrifying prospect, because it entailed testing to find the virus' trigger.

"As I was testing the inactive virus, applying various stimuli, I was able to trigger its radioactive decay process," Dakotah explained. "The function of the virus switches from replication to electron-grabbing. It grabs electrons from its surroundings and then becomes absorbed into the nucleus, increasing the density of the electrons within the nucleus. This will trigger the radioactive decay, which in turn damages DNA."

Mary and I both stared blankly at her.

"Essentially," she went on to explain, "it's destroying the proteins in the cells at a faster rate than they can repair themselves, allowing a fast-acting cancer to spread throughout the body."

"Holy shit," I muttered under my breath.

"So, if I don't have my arm removed right now—" She looked to her hand. "—it's possible that a fast-acting cancer will begin spreading?"

"Correct," the doctor next to Dakotah said.

"How long will I have if the cancer begins?"

"It's hard to say, but it looks like anywhere from a few days to a week."

I was relieved when Dakotah stepped away from working on that plan and instead began the process of studying how to stop the cellular damage once it was triggered. If they were going to jumpstart the thing that would kill Mary, it felt somewhat comforting to know at least one of these medical scientists, the one I trusted most, was working on a cure.

Mortified, I watched as they aimed the radiation lens at her finger. She remained brave. I couldn't imagine volunteering to allow something to happen which could cause such desolation in my body.

The thought of self-inflicted destruction flashed through my mind, and I remembered my drug-induced choices from the other timeline. It used to feel so good to know that, even if my world was crumbling around me, I could escape it all with Oxy.

I wanted to escape then, and a quick scan of the medical facility revealed several cabinets certain to provide me a free pass out of this horror. I often avoided situations like this which tempted me to take the easy way out of dealing with life. Even though in this timeline I never chose a path that led me to become addicted, I still had the very real memory. Only, the memory of being high created a nostalgia. This stirred the desire within me to *actually* experience the high even more.

I tried to find an anchor, something to hold me in place. I looked at the bravery Mary faced and remembered how she helped me overcome these feelings in our old timeline. The very least I could do was resist the drugs calling out to me and stay here, in the moment, and help her overcome what she had to face. Resisting the urge I paced the floor, chewing my nails.

From radiation she went right back into the MRI so they could monitor the rate of cell damage and look for any signs of cancer growth. She was released from the imaging just long enough to give samples and undergo another round of radiation—this time focused solely on her arm—before she returned to the imaging process.

I watched through a window, listening to the doctors discuss her results. They weren't aware the door was ajar and I could hear their conversation.

"We are not letting this spread past her arm," the first doctor claimed.

"She ordered us not to remove it," the second reminded him.

"I don't care. If we have to put her under we will, but as soon as the virus reaches her upper arm it comes off. We work for Mr. Touma, and his orders were clear. Nothing is to happen to this woman."

What would a best friend do in this predicament? Mary had made her wishes known, but I couldn't help wanting the same as Marius in this case. I didn't want any harm to come to her, neither a virus invading her body nor her arm getting removed.

However, losing her arm seemed much less daunting.

Mary knew releasing this information would cause mass hysteria, not only for the people who'd already gotten the injection into their system. Everyone everywhere would be in panic. Weighing the outcome, it felt more pertinent to prevent as many people from getting this as she could. It was the only method she could see to avoid additional casualties. I couldn't understand what the delay was with Marius. Mary didn't want to do this without him, and I wasn't going to make her.

As uneasy as his presence made me, I knew it had the opposite effect on her. Plus, between Marius and me, we would surely come up with a good speech for her to record and get out into the world. If not, the number of people infected was going to rapidly increase once the morning started. The urgency of getting this information public was dire.

While she remained in the MRI, I wrote her speech. Marius and Quinn arrived as I finished my draft and I handed it to him. He read it over, pacing back and forth, pausing once to look through the glass window at her in the machine. Quinn sat next to me, wringing her hands in her lap, nervously peering between the two of us. I'm sure it was difficult for her to accept Marius. The awkward silence between us grew, leaving no other option but to watch Marius read through the speech. He tapped in a few new sentences, deleted others, and finally handed the tablet back to me.

"I think this is ready for her to share live. How much longer is she going to be in that thing?" he asked, obviously anxious to see her. "If this is going to have any impact we need to get her on the air, now." I couldn't have agreed with him more.

I rose from my seat and flagged down the doctor tracking her progress. He was still just as annoyed with me as he was to begin with, but they got her out of the machine and gave us the image scans to include in our broadcast. The pressure to get this done quickly was enormous. The people needed to be informed right away, and Mary needed to get back in the MRI.

Mary appeared, resigned to her fate. People would listen to what she said just on account of how she looked, staring death in the eyes. In just one day the constant testing of bloodwork, tissue samples, and scans of her arm had taken its toll on her exhausted body. She needed a break, some solace from this storm, but there wasn't time.

We decided not to adjust anything, not even her hair or makeup. She was going to remain in her hospital gown, and during the recording we encouraged the medical team to take her next set of bloodwork and tissue samples. That way we didn't interfere with their progress, and the world could see the real trauma underway.

Taden updated The Patriot Party of our plan and Danika had been incessantly calling my phone. She never called me directly. While it was odd, I didn't intend on answering. It wasn't a matter of whether or not I would speak with Danika, but when. This moment was too time-sensitive. I intended to call her back as soon as the broadcast aired.

The country was already buzzing with excitement. Multitudes had turned out for immunizations before morning even dawned.

The shortage of the injections from the party planted fear of not having enough to go around, which seeded a supply and demand mentality. The media spin created an elevated status about being one of the lucky people who got to be included in the testing and receive the vaccine for free. It was reminiscent of crowd behavior during an old tradition shoppers used to participate in called Black Friday. Hordes of people collected at immunization sites.

"They've already started giving them," I said aloud. "I thought we had until the morning."

Media aired footage of proud individuals pointing their fingers in the air in satisfaction at having the same experience as their beloved President Moore.

CHAPTER 41

TADEN

"I was just about to leave and head back to the lab, for real this time. You want to come with me?" I asked Abel. The upward quirk of his mouth relayed his acceptance. "Don't get any bright ideas, Dr. Mihal. This is purely professional."

His disappointment was evident, yet he smiled at the humor we still managed to carry. On our way to my car, Abel received a notification on his phone.

"President Moore's briefing is live." He played it so we could both listen while I drove. "She looks terrible. We just saw her yesterday. She looks like she's aged years since then."

I glanced down at his screen. Abel's summation was on target. To add to the seriousness, President Moore's words were frightening. Scans of the virus working its way through her body were shown.

I could only imagine Dakotah was operating under massive doses of adrenaline at this point. If anyone would be able to figure out how to stop this thing, it was Dakotah. Thinking about her reminded me that Abel had something he wanted to talk to me about.

"What did you want to—" My question trailed off when the broadcast of President Moore cut out to be replaced with a hijacked feed, starring none other than Finn Berthold himself. I slammed the brakes upon seeing his face.

"Holy shit," Abel groaned. I pulled over to the side of the road to better watch the broadcast.

Berthold addressed the nation.

"Good morning, great citizens of *my* country. I'm back. I'm sorry if I worried you. I was avoiding a clear and imminent danger. In the wake of my absence, it appears your new president has infected you with a terrible disease through her vaccine. Now it's just sitting in your systems, lying in wait." Taunting the screen, he stuck out his bottom lip.

Suddenly, a high-pitched noise rang outside the car. I could hear the sound in the background of his recording as well. Berthold cleared his throat, "Oh no," he said. "I think she's just triggered them to do their *real* job." He put his hand to his mouth as if mortified. "They aren't exactly going to do what *you* thought they would, but they will certainly do the job she intended for them. But I have great news." He pointed his finger in the air like he had just had an idea. "I have the antidote. For my loyal citizens, of course. Don't you worry. I'll rescue you from President Moore's evil grips."

After he finished his cryptic message, the feed cut and returned to President Moore, who unknowingly launched into what the radioactivity of her virus entailed.

I put my hand on Abel's. "You have to go back."

"What?" He blinked at me.

"We shouldn't waste any time debating this or approving it through the proper channels. We just need to get you back in time."

"That's exactly what I needed to talk to you about. I think we have a leak, or a mole. I was going to tell you I should go back to the night Berthold staged his assassination and make sure the job gets done."

"We're on the same page," I said, aware of our ability to still connect. But then I considered the last few months, during which we'd seriously disconnected. It was Abel who made that happen. I respected his wishes, but it hadn't made me feel anything other than lonely. To break the solitude of my feelings, I glanced into the rearview mirror and snapped on the turn signal to merge back into traffic.

"Taden." He positioned himself to look at me, his full attention on me. My foot pressed heavier on the gas pedal.

"Hmm?" My mouth had gone dry. We didn't need to have this talk. I wouldn't remember it anyway. After he traveled back and got rid of Berthold, it would undo every moment since the night of his fake assassination. The only way I would remember any of this is if I went with him. While it wasn't necessary that I remember all that had occurred, I didn't want to forget anymore.

"I'm going with you," I said the instant it entered my thoughts. I didn't want to offer him any time to refuse. "We are doing this without approval anyway. You're not going alone. I want to remember all of this. I want to remember what it was like losing you. I don't ever want to take you for granted. I need to remember that Marius isn't evil, and know the feeling of justification for saving him. I want to remember that Quinn is his sister and the moment I saw them reunited. This is too personal to wipe from my mind. And Abel…" I paused, almost losing the nerve to say what I had to tell him. "I'm not spending another minute of my life without you."

I took a deep breath and held it, fearing he might still refuse me. I had every reason to believe he wouldn't. Just in case he had any doubts I reached into the bag next to me, pulled out *The Great Gatsby*, and handed it to him. He didn't argue with me. Instead, he placed his hand on my leg and we drove the rest of the way in silence.

CHAPTER 42

RUTH

Mary's last scan showed the cancer had started to grow and the cell replication was making its way toward her shoulder. I watched the medical team eye each other, signaling it was time. President Moore thought she was giving another blood sample, when actually they gave her a sedative.

As soon as she was unconscious, Mary's amputation surgery began. I couldn't believe it had come to this. She would no longer have her left arm. I couldn't imagine any outcome where she woke up and wasn't angry, and I knew she would (rightfully) direct most of her anger at Marius and me. The heaviness of the situation was unbearable, and waiting with Quinn and Marius wasn't making me feel any better.

I hadn't heard anything from Dakotah in a while, so I checked in with her, hoping she had some good news about an antidote.

"Knock-knock," I said in place of actually knocking on her door, not wanting to startle her. She was deeply involved in her work. Sitting on a high-top chair, hunched over a microscope, she was dropping insanely small amounts of liquid with some type of sophisticated dropper onto a slide.

"Hey there, how's the progress?" I asked, knowing I was interrupting her crucial, time-sensitive work.

"I'm making some, but not nearly quickly enough. Do you have an update for me from out there?"

"I do. Unfortunately, she's losing her arm." Dakotah stopped. She turned around on her stool. "I'm too late?"

"Well, I wouldn't say you're too late. There are thousands of people with this in their system who need what you're working on. By tomorrow, everyone who has gotten this injection will have cancer spreading through their bodies. Their only hope is something that can kill it."

She nodded knowingly. "I guess I should get back to work, then."

"Here. I brought you some lunch. You should take a minute to eat. I know how you and Taden get once you're busy working on some save-the-world science shit." She laughed at me. "It's nothing special, just a sandwich and chips from the vending machine." I set it down next to her and patted her back. "Thanks, you know. For always saving the world. I think you're pretty awesome." Her smile filled her face and lit up her beautiful eyes. "I'm gonna get back to Mary. I'll check back in later. Maybe dinner?" I added, so she could mentally prepare herself for another break later.

"You're trying to big sister me, eh?" she said, chuckling. "All right. Thanks for lunch. I promise I'll eat it in a little bit." Before I turned the corner, she'd already swung back around on her stool and resumed her invaluable microscopic task.

The last hope we had that maybe Mary wouldn't lose her arm was gone. A storm of emotion was on the horizon, and it wasn't just about Mary. All these people. They were all going to die.

I returned to the waiting room to find Marius watching a replay of Mary's broadcast. As I walked in, he beckoned me with his index finger and wide eyes. Striding to see what had him so appalled, I caught the image of a very-not-dead President Berthold speaking to the nation. Goosebumps prickled my skin. In the replay, he pointed to the air and an alarm sound rang out.

"We heard that alarm coming from outside the building during her broadcast, remember?"

He nodded, closing his eyes. "It triggered the radiation, didn't it? Dammit. Everyone's going to get sick now, aren't they?"

The tension ramped up. Quinn rose to her feet.

"You guys, I'm not doing any good here. Dr. Barrett could probably really use me at the lab right now." She turned to Marius. "I'll catch up with you this evening. Focus on President Moore right now." She wrapped her arms around him. In return, he held nothing back. "Jeez, Marius. I can't breathe." She giggled, and playfully pushed her brother.

"Give one of those bear hugs to my sister for me, could ya?" I yelled after Quinn as she walked out the door. In perfect timing, the doctor entered the room.

Marius and I rushed the doctor in unison. "How is she?"

"She's doing just fine, all things considered. She's still asleep, and will be coming to shortly. You can wait in her room if you'd like. She will be confused when she wakes up, and it will need to be addressed delicately to keep her as calm as possible. Since we operated under your orders, Mr. Touma, we thought it best to let you handle her questions."

"I can stay here. Let you go alone," I told him.

"Nonsense. We're going to distract Mary by you telling us who you and your sister really are and what you're up to." He smirked, waving me to follow him. My mind was racing. In the midst of all this craziness, I had forgotten Marius recognized Taden and me from the night we rescued him. It made sense he hadn't forgotten though.

Mary had already questioned me about Taden on the way here. I wasn't going to be able to fend them off much longer. What would I even say to them? I'd been clearly directed not to mention a word about time travel to either of them, and with that option off the table it didn't leave a lot of room for clearing the air. We settled into chairs on either side of her bed. She was hooked up to an IV, stirring in restless sleep. I watched it drip into her remaining arm and, once again, found myself aching to feel a painkiller's hold on my own body. Her eyelids flickered, reminding me to stop thinking about myself.

She woke to find both of us on edge, watching her and waiting for her to awaken. Her uncertainty grew in the stillness. I walked to her and placed a hand on her right arm. Marius got to his feet, trudging over to her, and raised his hand to the place where her other arm used to be but rested it on her head instead. She looked to her left, at him, then at her bandages.

"What happened?" Panic washed slowly over her face. "I didn't want this." She was still groggy and apparently found it difficult to talk. Marius stroked her forehead in an attempt to soothe her.

"Shh. You need to rest. We can talk about it later." He leaned in and kissed above her brow. It was tender and vulnerable, and I still couldn't get used to seeing Marius in that light.

"Are you thirsty? Can I get you anything to drink? Maybe some ice chips?"

She nodded once, so weakly I wasn't sure she responded. Regardless, I took the opportunity to have a minute away from Marius and collect my thoughts. As soon as I was in the hallway, I texted Dakotah an update on President Moore's status. When I spoke to her earlier she seemed pretty concerned, and I wanted to keep her in the loop. I called Taden to figure out what the story was going to be for Marius and Mary. She didn't answer, but as I was shoving my phone back into my pocket—fully annoyed with my sister—I felt it vibrate.

She texted me back, "*Sorry I didn't answer. I'm taking care of all this. I love you.*" I shook my head because I knew what she meant. Taden was going back in time.

CHAPTER 43

ABEL

Nothing I could say was going to stop her, and the truth was I didn't want to stop her. The only thing I could think when she told me she was going back with me was, *thank God*. I didn't want to leave the timeline where she loved me, and the only way I was going back to change everything was letting her go with me. I didn't intend to change her mind.

She was nervous. It had been a long time since she'd traveled back, and this trip would be full-on military style. Before we left, we got into tactical gear and I ran her through some refreshers on handling and shooting her gun as well as a few basic self-defense maneuvers.

We had to leave the assassination timeline knowing with certainty we killed Berthold. I shared the plan, making sure she understood I was to do the heavy lifting. She was only there for backup. With our TRBs attached to our arms and preset to send us into our time jump, we headed to our destination. I wanted us to arrive exactly where Berthold was the night of his fake assassination to prevent any travel by foot once we arrived. This meant we had to depart from that location in this timeline. On our way out of the building, we ran into Quinn.

"Oh hey, guys. Where you headed?" she asked, looking us up and down with interest.

Taden sighed and threw her hands up in the air. "Okay. Listen, we're about to jump a timeline but no one can know. Got it?" Quinn vigorously nodded her head, pleased to be included in Taden's secret. "Since you know, do us a favor and monitor our TRBs from Dakotah's desk. We will send any pertinent memories through her server. If something comes in through there that strikes you as an important piece of information to tell Dakotah, tell her. *Only* her."

"Roger that," she said, saluting Taden and stretching tall with importance.

We reached our launching site with about five minutes to spare before the serum sent us back to kill Berthold. It wasn't a lot of time, but it was all I had to tell her how I truly felt those months without her.

"I want you to know," I said, looking deeply into her blue eyes, "every single day, I missed you. I thought about you all the time. There isn't one thing I forgot. I remembered it all. All I saw when I closed my eyes was you. The way you look at me. The smile you save only for me. The feeling of being seen by you. I just didn't know how to do what I was there to do and give in to my need to be with you. I'm sorry about the distance I put between us, I just didn't know what else to do. But I want you to know I missed you, I thought about you every day, and I love you."

She didn't say anything, but she put her hand on my cheek and brushed it with her thumb until we dissolved into time.

CHAPTER 44

TADEN

I didn't miss the overwhelming nausea caused from teleporting into the past. Gaining my equilibrium I leaned forward, putting my hands on my knees, heaving from the momentum. Abel stood with ease, patiently waiting for me to regain my composure. A slow grin played about his lips.

"Well, well, look at Mr. Tough Guy," I said through my gasps. He laughed, poking fun. Before long, I rose to meet his posture. "I'm ready. Let's do it."

"Let's recap one more time."

"I know it. I got it all."

He nodded his head, then urged, "Just one more run-through, for me. He will be arriving at his apartment building in about—" He glanced at his TRB. "—fifteen minutes. Once he's inside a gunshot will go off, and the fake assassination will be staged. You and I will hide out in the locations I showed you on the map." He pointed at the staircase for me, and the post in front of the elevator right past the main entrance for him. "We'll wait for that moment there. After I've taken him out, I'll meet you on the staircase and we'll go to the roof. By the time we reach the top floor, our TRBs should send us back to our timeline."

"I'm ready. If you need backup, I'll be there."

I kissed him hard.

"I love you," I said, then I sprinted up the stairs, assuming position for Berthold. Time seemed to be in fast forward. Sweat beaded along my hairline. We couldn't mess this up. The nation was depending on us. I heard the commotion outside, then the fake assassination attempt, followed by the noisy entrance of Berthold just in front of his bodyguard.

I crouched down with my gun drawn to get a clear view of the chaos in the entryway and to be sure Abel had the situation under control.

Then I couldn't believe my eyes. I did a double take to be sure I saw clearly. I wasn't mistaken.

Danika Farkas was shaking Berthold's hand.

"Sir, we have your room ready, and the body is all set to pass as you." She turned to two men standing behind her, waiting for her command. They were definitely not Mr. Warren and Mr. Richardson. "Fire your weapons, and be sure to hit the angles you were told. This has to look legitimate." As soon as the gunshots were released Abel fired his gun twice in succession, hitting his target in two fatal locations. He wasted no time in racing up the stairs to find me locked on the steps in shock.

"I'm just as surprised as you. Come on. We have to get out of here before anyone looks for us. With the commotion, we have less than a minute before they figure out he's actually been assassinated this time." He grabbed my arm and pulled me upward. We ran two steps at a time, trying like hell to get to the roof. Before we set foot on the blacktop, I felt the familiar swirl of my internal self begin to fade from that timeline. Returning to our present timeline, the image of Ms. Farkas shaking hands with Berthold was inked into my mind. Not only was I sick from the ratcheting time travel wreaked on the body, but I also had no idea how I was to reconcile the image I carried of Danika Farkas my entire career with the woman I'd just witnessed betraying the work she did for our country.

Abel was right. We definitely had a mole. If my life had depended on it, I would have never suspected it was her. I might've even gone so far as to wonder if *I,* somehow, entangled myself with the enemy before I questioned her authenticity. Rocked to my core, I dry heaved until anything available in my stomach made its way out. Abel leaned over me, rubbing my back.

"We have to make sure Quinn didn't tell Danika we left."

"I told her not to tell anyone but Dakotah. I trust her."

As soon as I said the word "trust" aloud, Danika shaking Berthold's hand flashed through my mind again and I vomited more.

"My God, Abel. What are we going to do?"

"We'll figure it out. The only two people who for sure know what happened are you and me."

"And Dakotah's data base," I interjected.

"Shit, you're right. No one will believe what we saw."

"I don't believe what we saw," I muttered robotically, void of feeling.

"It makes sense why Danika wanted me in the past. She needed me out of the way so I didn't make her. She must not have connected with Berthold until after he took office."

"That's why she put you ahead of the power switch with his dad," I said. "She knew you wouldn't discover she was a traitor."

Abel put his hand in mine. "The future is our only option."

 We'd returned to a world where President Berthold had truly been assassinated and Mary Moore had become the first non-natural citizen as president.

With him gone, an endemic was no longer at play.

But Danika Farkas, head of The Patriot Party, still was.

Contact the Author

Follow D.M. Taylor on social media
Facebook: @authordmtaylor
Instagram: @authordmtaylor

Sign Up for D.M. Taylor's mailing list
to receive updates on upcoming books in The Reckoning Series.
https://www.subscribepage.com/dmtaylorthereckoning

A Note From Dr. Pasterski

Dear Reader,

Please support my girls, Taden and Ruth Barrett, by zipping on over to Amazon and leaving a positive review for D.M. Taylor. We really appreciate Ms. Taylor for her dedication to share their story with such care. She is currently collecting the details for the last book in the series, of my Barrett girls. The best way we can encourage Ms. Taylor to continue is to leave a positive review for The Reckoning and Endemic on Amazon.

Much love,
Dr. Pasterski

Coming in 2021
BOOK 3 of The Reckoning

RECOIL

CHAPTER 1

SNEAK PEEK

I stood outside our apartment door, looked through the half-moon window, and knocked. I hadn't seen my mom since the day she died.

So much pain was wrapped up in that day, I was worried facing her in this moment would undo me. She was my mom. She was equipped to handle an emotional breakdown from her daughter. How would she feel about seeing a version of me that had aged twenty years?

She opened the door and a flood of memories with it.

"Oh, Taden!" She put her hand to her mouth. "You are magnificent."

Her face showed recognition and wonder. I couldn't speak, and the sight of her was what home felt like.

"How did you?" She was engulfed with pride as she began to understand that her daughter did become a scientist and had traveled to her from the future.

My mom never doubted my intelligence and she rooted her belief that I could accomplish anything. Still, there in our doorway, I was just realizing the depth of her confidence by the rate she grasped how I was there.

"Come here," she squealed, holding her arms wide open. My mom danced me around the hallway, jumping with excitement. I couldn't see through my burning eyes, but I could smell her and feel the warmth of her skin. There is nothing like being held by the person who is your essence. It was a living dream. A dream that I'd often held on to, and yet never considered to be attainable.

Eventually she settled and pulled herself from me, still holding my hands. "I need to see you. Your beautiful womanly face still sprinkled with freckles. Those blue eyes are just as vibrant as the ones I saw on you this morning, before you went off to school."

I looked into hers as well. Every feature was just as I'd remembered. Only I hadn't allowed myself to see her in my mind for years. The soft glow of her skin, mirroring the myriad of freckles she gave to me. Her brown eyes settling on me with familiar pride. I still hadn't said a word.

"Oh Taden, just this morning I was talking to you, the younger you, and couldn't help but think listening to you ramble about your science project, how amazing your brain is. Now, here you are! Tell me everything! I can't wait to know how you did this." She brought me to the couch where we sat, leaving no space between us. Her every focus poured onto me, waiting to listen to her genius daughter.

"I don't know where to start." I paused, trying to stifle the lump in my throat. I pushed my tongue to the roof of my mouth and took a deep breath through my nose. Once I felt steadied I tried my voice again. "It looks like you've already come to the conclusion that I've come here from the future. I've discovered time travel, Mom."

"I knew it!" She beamed. "Tell me more."

"I'm a physicist. I work at the NIST. Dr. Pasterski got me the job."

She was now the speechless one.

I held up my left hand. "I recently got married."

She grabbed my hand, studying the ring. "It's beautiful and so you. Tell me about him."

"He's kind, and tries really hard to be funny." We both laughed.

"Tell me about the wedding."

"It was small." I looked down, rubbing my knee. "We went to the courthouse. Only a few people."

"What did I wear?" she asked with a tone of jest.

Silence fell upon me. Unable to hold back, my chin quivered and she knew.

"It was my cancer diagnosis, wasn't it?"

I nodded.

"How's your dad? Your sister?"

"They're good. It was hard to lose you. It took the three of us a long time to adjust, but we've learned how to deal with the loss. I mean, in the best way we could."

She reached for me and I fell into her chest.

"I figured out time travel so I could see you again."

"You figured out time travel to see me, and I don't even have anything exciting to tell you," she said, her hand moving in small circles on my back.

"Mom, I'm just happy to be here with you."

"I wish your dad was home to see you."

Altering the timeline in The Reckoning to save Dad prevented his death backward in time, too. I hadn't considered it. She didn't lose him. They were still married and living happily.

I sat up, folding my hands together, preparing to tell her why I'd come. Why I'd gone through my grief, accepted her loss. And then, after all of it, jumped backward in time to see her.

"Mom, I'm here with a request." I bit my lip in hesitation. "I'm not sure how you're going to feel about this.

"Go ahead. Tell me."

I stared at her, considering my words. Finally, I just blurted it out. "I want to bring you into the future." She blinked through squinted eyes. "I've only figured out time travel into the past. I've been working on how to get into the future for a while now, and I've just figured it out. So, I've come to test my theory."

"Honey."

"Mom. I know you think I'm just trying to bypass your death. But I need this to be secret, and I can only bring someone I'm a descendant of."

"Why not your dad?"

She wasn't going to agree to this. I had a feeling.

"Look. It's the beginning stages of your cancer. If you come with me to my present, medically speaking you'd have a much better chance of surviving this."

"Sweetheart, I…" She trailed off. "It's just an overwhelming idea for me to grasp. All of this is. Seeing you, from the future. Learning I died from the cancer growing inside me and then this offer to bypass it by traveling to the future with you to treat it."

"Will you consider it?" She held her smile. "I know it's a lot to think about. I'm gonna go back and let you mull it over."

"I will. I'll think about it."